There was a sudden gleam of light in the middle of the room, in front of Fred Benson. It was a mist, through which a blue light seemed to shine. The mist vanished and a man appeared, wearing a baggy green combat-uniform like the one Fred had worn fifty years before.

The man only moved once, with an automatic pistol in his hand, pointed directly at Fred . . .

THE WORLDS OF H. BEAM PIPER

**EDITED BY
JOHN F.
CARR**

SF
ACE BOOKS, NEW YORK

An Ace Book

Published by arrangement with the Estate of H. Beam Piper

ISBN: 0-441-91052-1

First Ace Printing: February 1983
Published simultaneously in Canada

Manufactured in the United States of America
Ace Books, 200 Madison Avenue, New York, New York 10016

Acknowledgments

"Time and Time Again" © 1947. First appeared in *Astounding Science Fiction*, April 1947

"Operation R.S.V.P." © 1951. First appeared in *Amazing Stories*, January 1951

"Genesis" © 1951. First appeared in *Future*, September 1951

"The Mercenaries" © 1950. First appeared in *Astounding Science Fiction*, March 1950

"Dearest" © 1951. First appeared in *Weird Tales*, March 1951

"Hunter Patrol" by H. Beam Piper and John J. McGuire © 1959. First appeared in *Amazing Stories*, May 1959

"Flight From Tomorrow" © 1950. First appeared in *Future*, September-October 1950

"The Answer" © 1959. First appeared in *Fantastic Universe*, December 1959

"Crossroads of Destiny" © 1959. First appeared in *Fantastic Universe*, July 1959

"Day of the Moron" © 1951. First appeared in *Astounding Science Fiction*, September 1951

Contents

Introduction
by
John F. Carr

With the publication of THE WORLDS OF H. BEAM PIPER, all the *known* short stories of H. Beam Piper will be in print. Until the Piper revival of the mid-1970s (when the legal difficulties surrounding Piper's estate were cleared up and Ace Books, under the editorship of Jim Baen, began publishing his long-out-of-print novels, such as LORD KALVAN OF OTHERWHEN, SPACE VIKING, and LITTLE FUZZY), none of Piper's short fiction was even in print, much less collected together.

Now, Piper's Terro-Human Future History stories have been published in FEDERATION and EMPIRE, while the Paratime Police yarns can be found in PARATIME! THE WORLDS OF H. BEAM PIPER includes all the remaining stories that did not fit into either series or somehow slipped between the cracks. Some of them had been virtually unobtainable ("Flight From Tomorrow," "The Answer," "Genesis"), having appeared in such obscure publications as *Fantastic Universe* and *Future Science Fiction Stories*, available only to collectors. "Dearest," Piper's only true fantasy story, appeared in *Weird Tales*, and was unknown even to many collectors.

As is common to science fiction writers, when Piper coined a new term or invented a new artifact, he tended to reuse it in later stories. This helped fuel the debate about whether Piper's stories constituted one very broad series or several. John Clute, addressing the issue in *The Science Fiction Encyclopedia*, in 1979 wrote: "Many of his (Piper's) novels and stories, including the 'Fuzzy' sequence, are set in a common future history, but are insufficiently connected to be regarded as a coherent series." It is now becoming clear that we have two distinct series, which coexist in the same universe.

Due to Piper's untimely death, there are still a number of large gaps in his Terro-Human Future History series. Jerry Pournelle and I, having rediscovered Piper's overall historical template, intend to write several "linking novels," including the long-awaited sequel to SPACE VIKING—THE RETURN OF SPACE VIKING.

Jerry and I spent several years studying Jerry's correspondence with Piper, a few existing notes, and several of Piper's favorite books before we suddenly discovered the key to bridging the gaps in Piper's chronology—how to explain the disappearance of Merlin, why the League of Civilized Worlds was destined to fail, how and why Odin was to become the capital of the First Galactic Empire, and many other seeming inconsistencies.

There should be a few surprises for everyone interested in Piper's history of the future.

There are five major themes that run through the fiction of H. Beam Piper, and they are more apparent in the stories of this volume than anywhere else.

Piper's concept of *self-reliant* man is probably the most pervasive theme. Piper himself was a good example of the self-reliant man; Jerry Pournelle and others have described him as a courtly gentleman, aloof but friendly, an independent thinker who knew his own mind.

In "Oomphel in the Sky," Piper gives one of the best summations of the self-reliant man: He's the man who "actually knows what has to be done and how to do it, and he's going right ahead and doing it, without holding a dozen conferences and round-table discussions and giving everybody a fair and equal chance to foul things up for him.''

It is true that Piper's self-reliant man greatly resembled John W. Campbell's *Citizen*—the man who knows his rights, as well as his obligations, and acts upon them. As with many of the early *Astounding* writers, it is difficult to appraise the extent of Campbell's influence. The real question is: Did H. Beam Piper write about self-reliant heroes because he knew that Campbell would buy the stories, or did Campbell buy his stories because Piper wrote about the kind of characters Campbell liked to feature in *Astounding*?

Most of Piper's friends would say the latter hypothesis was more true. The prominence of the self-reliant man throughout Piper's fiction (characters such as Allan Hartley and his father in "Time and Time Again," Piper's first published science fiction) would indicate that Piper, certainly influenced by Alfred Korzybski (the Polish-born father of General Semantics) and John W. Campbell, wrote about the kind of men he believed in.

John H. Costello, who wrote a three-part series about H. Beam Piper for *Renaissance* (a highly regarded fanzine published quarterly by John J. Pierce in the 1960s) made the following statement in his introduction:

> Into his stories he (Piper) put a great deal of philosophy—of the Campbellian sort—and, this writer thinks, a great deal of himself. Which is fortunate, as he was in life a most private man, and other than reminiscences from some of the people who knew him there is little to put down on paper that Piper did not state, either explicitly or between the lines, in his published works.

This contention is further bolstered by some autobiographical comments Piper made in his only published mystery novel, MURDER IN THE GUNROOM, in which one of the characters, a science fiction writer named Pierre Jarret, expresses some of Piper's own feelings about the field and his writing when answering the question ''What are you writing?'':

> Science-fiction. I do a lot of stories for the pulps
> . . . *Space Trails*, and *Other Worlds*, *Wonder
> Stories*; mags like that. Most of it's standardized
> formula-stuff; what's known in the trade as space-
> operas. My best stuff goes to *Astonishing*. Parentheti
> cally, you mustn't judge any of these magazines by their
> names. It seems to be a convention to use hyperbolic
> names for science-fiction magazines; a heritage from
> what might be called an earlier and ruder day. What I do
> for *Astonishing* is really hard work, and I enjoy it. I'm
> working now on one of them, based on J.W. Dunne's
> time-theories, if you know what they are.

Certainly, Robert A. Heinlein did not quit writing about his *competent man* when he stopped writing for Campbell in the 1950s, and I doubt that Piper would have changed his viewpoint had he stopped writing for Campbell. More light should be shed upon the subject when Perry Chapdelaine and George Hay finally publish the John W. Campbell letters and we can study the Piper/Campbell correspondence.

Jack Holloway of the ''Fuzzy'' novels, Conn Maxwell of THE COSMIC COMPUTER, Verkan Vall of the Paratime Police, and Lucas Trask of SPACE VIKING were the embodiments of Piper's idealized self-reliant man. Their foils were the fools, the misguided, the incompetent, and the mad King-John figures, such as the psychotic Andray Dunnan and Zaspar Makann of SPACE VIKING.

However, their greatest opponent was not the crazed or the corrupt, but most often society itself. This brings us to another of Piper's most important themes: The fragility of civilization, and its correlate, the threat of barbarism, both from within and without.

Piper was not happy with the course of modern civilization; in a number of letters he admitted a longing for the sanity and simplicity of the Christian Era (Sixteenth Century). Nazism and the nuclear bomb had shaken his faith in the rationality of man. He much preferred a simpler era of universal faith and limited warfare.

Most of Piper's later work is laced with references about the instability of man's political institutions and civilizations. The Terro-Human Future History is the chronicle of the rise and fall of galaxy-spanning civilizations. ''It may just be that there is something fundamentally unworkable about government itself . . . maybe a workable system of government is a political-science impossibility . . .'' comments Lucas Trask, close to the end of SPACE VIKING, one of Piper's last works.

In every society there is always the threat of the Barbarian, from within or without—the un-noble savage. In SPACE VIKING, it is the Space Vikings themselves who are the barbarians, overturning tombstones in the graveyard of the old Terran Federation. Yet, even at their worst, they are engaged in honest butchery compared to the nefarious do-gooders and do-nothings who conspire to bring down the Mardukan Monarchy.

The barbarians are rising . . . Every Society rests on a barbarian base. The people who don't understand civilization, and wouldn't like it if they did. The hitch-hikers. The people who create nothing, and who don't appreciate what others have created for them, and who think civilization is something that just exists and that all they need to do is enjoy what they can understand of it—luxuries, a high living standard, and easy work for high pay . . .

It wasn't the war that put Hitler into power. It was the fact that the ruling class of his nation, the people who kept things running, were discredited. The masses, the homemade barbarians, didn't have anybody to take their responsibilities for them.

While Piper was an advocate of representative government in his early fiction, before his death he appeared to be leaning toward monarchy as the best form of human government. In letters and conversations with Jerry Pournelle, he mentioned a growing disenchantment with representative democracy; he saw it becoming a sinecure for bureaucrats, fat-cat politicians, and welfarers.

But even a self-reliant monarch had to be aware of the barbarians within. "You have to learn, too, that a ruler cannot afford to be guided by his fears of what people will say about him. Not even what history will say about him. A ruler's only judge is himself," says Lucas Trask in SPACE VIKING to Prince Bentrik, the surviving heir of the Mardukan throne after a Hitler-style revolution.

The Cold War and the nuclear arms race played a large part in Piper's growing pessimism. In a 1963 letter to Charles and Marcia Brown he said, "You will undoubtedly see me at the Discon, if we are all alive by then, and Washington hasn't been H-bombed in the meantime."

Nuclear power and its awesome destructive force is another major theme running through most of his novels and short stories. The Terran Federation is born in the nuclear hellfire of the Thirty Days War; ULLER UPRISING is about an alien race of sepoys who secretly build a nuclear bomb to rid themselves of their human overlords; and many of his short stories are concerned with the threat of nuclear war or its aftermath.

FIRST CYCLE, a posthumous novel, edited and expanded by Michael Kurland, is a slightly fleshed-out polemic on the danger of an East-West confrontation and nuclear war. Long after the binary worlds have been devastated by atomic warfare a Terran Federation survey craft arrives. One of the crew gives us Piper's final warning about nuclear warfare: "It's obvious that the rockets must have been launched simultaneously from both planets . . . You know, that wasn't really a war. That was a suicide pact."

His early optimism for nuclear power, and the belief that man could adapt to the effects of radiation quickly dissipated when the Russians developed their own atomic bomb and the Cold War began to heat up. A year before his death he wrote: "It must have been lovely, living in an era when the Clausewitzian 'extension of politics by other means' was accomplished with nothing more lethal or expensive . . . than black powder.''

Piper's love of history and growing disenchantment with the modern world lead him further and further into a romantic vision of the past. In a letter to Jerry Pournelle, where he comments on a Chicago convention speech that Jerry gave on Thermonuclear Grand Strategy, Piper said, ''I live either in the Fifth to Twentieth Centuries, Atomic Era (Piper History of the Future), or in the Fifteenth and Sixteenth Centuries, so-called Christian Era, and as far as possible I boycott the contemporary scene.''

His lifelong interest in firearms (Piper was an expert marksman and a well-known gun collector) and history culminated in his major—and unfortunately lost—historical novel about the Christian Era, ONLY THE ARQUEBUS. As he mentions in a letter to Jerry Pournelle, ''Having just finished a story in the Seventh Century A.E. (FUZZY SAPIENS), I have now dug out the historical novel on which I have been working intermittently, when I have not been pressed by necessity to get something quickly saleable done, for the last couple of years. This is early Sixteenth Century C.E. (Christian Era)—1502–1503, to be exact—and Ferdinand of Spain and Louis XII of France are fighting over the Kingdom of Naples.''

He never lived to complete ONLY THE ARQUEBUS, but he did use his expertise on the early days of black powder and Renaissance military history to good effect in LORD KALVAN OF OTHERWHEN—the story of a Pennsylvania State Trooper who is mistakenly vaulted into a parallel world where gunpowder has recently been invented and its production is kept secret and monopolized by an unsavory religious cult.

Not all of Piper's stories and themes were concerned with nuclear war or the fall of civilization. He was also fascinated by the idea of lost races—especially the Old Martians—a theme that dominated a good part of the science fiction of Piper's youth. H. Rider Haggard, Edgar Rice Burroughs,

Grant Allen, A. Merritt, and many others wrote exciting adventures about lost races, civilizations, and worlds in inaccessible regions of the globe—Africa, the North and South Poles, the Himalayas, or the Amazon Basin.

He incorporates this theme most poignantly in "Omnilingual," (reprinted in FEDERATION) where an archaeological expedition travels to Mars and discovers the ruins of the Old Martians, and in "The Keeper," (reprinted in EMPIRE) where it is man himself—at least on Terra—whose own past has become lost in the heavy mist of history.

A final important theme in Piper's work was life after death. His first published story, "Time and Time Again," is about a soldier killed on the battlefield who *awakens*, as a child back at home again with his parents. Reincarnation is an important element in many of his early Paratime stories, especially "Last Enemy," which takes place on the Second Level Akor-Neb Sector where reincarnation is so important it becomes a political issue: What happens to property and inheritance rights when you can trace your previous incarnations?

Piper, certainly in his early stories, took these ideas very seriously, and on more than one occasion remarked that this was not his first life. If so, I would like to believe that on some alternative time-line—a Fourth Level Europo-American Sector, of course—another H. Beam Piper is hard at work finishing the sequel to LORD KALVAN OF OTHERWHEN or filling in the final centuries of his Terro-Human Future History Chronology.

TIME AND TIME AGAIN

"Time and Time Again," Piper's first published story, is appropriately a time-travel story. Unlike many of his later stories, this is less a cautionary tale, and more a story of hope.

BLINDED BY THE BOMB-FLASH and numbed by the narcotic injection, he could not estimate the extent of his injuries, but he knew that he was dying. Around him, in the darkness, voices sounded as through a thick wall.

"They mighta left mosta these Joes where they was. Half of them won't even last till the truck comes."

"No matter; so long as they're alive, they must be treated," another voice, crisp and cultivated, rebuked. "Better start taking names, while we're waiting."

"Yes, sir." Fingers fumbled at his identity badge. "Hartley, Allan; Captain, G5, Chem. Research AN/73/D. Serial, SO-23869403J."

"Allan Hartley!" The medic officer spoke in shocked surprise. "Why, he's the man who wrote 'Children of the Mist,' 'Rose of Death,' and 'Conqueror's Road'!"

9

He tried to speak, and must have stirred; the corpsman's voice sharpened.

"Major, I think he's part conscious. Mebbe I better give him 'nother shot."

"Yes, yes; by all means, sergeant."

Something jabbed Allan Hartley in the back of the neck. Soft billows of oblivion closed in upon him, and all that remained to him was a tiny spark of awareness, glowing alone and lost in a great darkness.

The Spark grew brighter. He was more than a something that merely knew that it existed. He was a man, and he had a name, and a military rank, and memories. Memories of the searing blue-green flash, and of what he had been doing outside the shelter the moment before, and memories of the month-long siege, and of the retreat from the north, and memories of the days before the War, back to the time when he had been little Allan Hartley, a schoolboy, the son of a successful lawyer, in Williamsport, Pennsylvania.

His mother he could not remember; there was only a vague impression of the house full of people who had tried to comfort him for something he could not understand. But he remembered the old German woman who had kept house for his father, afterward, and he remembered his bedroom, with its chintz-covered chairs, and the warm-colored patch quilt on the old cherry bed, and the tan curtains at the windows, edged with dusky red, and the morning sun shining through them. He could almost see them, now.

He blinked. He *could* see them!

For a long time, he lay staring at them unbelievingly, and then he deliberately closed his eyes and counted ten seconds, and as he counted, terror gripped him. He was afraid to open them again, lest he find himself blind, or gazing at the filth and wreckage of a blasted city, but when he reached ten, he forced himself to look, and gave a sigh of relief. The sunlit curtains and the sun-gilded mist outside were still there.

He reached out to check one sense against another, feeling the rough monk's cloth and the edging of maroon silk thread.

They were tangible as well as visible. Then he saw that the back of his hand was unscarred. There should have been a scar, souvenir of a rough-and-tumble brawl of his cub reporter days. He examined both hands closely. An instant later, he had sat up in bed and thrown off the covers, partially removing his pajamas and inspecting as much of his body as was visible.

It was the smooth body of a little boy.

That was ridiculous. He was a man of forty-three; an army officer, a chemist, once a best-selling novelist. He had been married, and divorced ten years ago. He looked again at his body. It was only twelve years old. Fourteen, at the very oldest. His eyes swept the room, wide with wonder. Every detail was familiar: the flower-splashed chair covers; the table that served as desk and catch-all for his possessions; the dresser, with its mirror stuck full of pictures of aircraft. It was the bedroom of his childhood home. He swung his legs over the edge of the bed. They were six inches too short to reach the floor.

For an instant, the room spun dizzily, and he was in the grip of utter panic, all confidence in the evidence of his senses lost. Was he insane? Or delirious? Or had the bomb really killed him; was this what death was like? What was that thing about "ye become as little children"? He started to laugh, and his juvenile larynx made giggling sounds. They seemed funny, too, and aggravated his mirth. For a little while, he was on the edge of hysteria and then, when he managed to control his laughter, he felt calmer. If he were dead, then he must be a discarnate entity, and would be able to penetrate matter. To his relief, he was unable to push his hand through the bed. So he was alive; he was also fully awake, and, he hoped, rational. He rose to his feet and prowled about the room, taking stock of its contents.

There was no calendar in sight, and he could find no newspapers or dated periodicals, but he knew that it was prior to July 18, 1946. On that day, his fourteenth birthday, his father had given him a light .22 rifle, and it had been hung on a pair of rustic forks on the wall. It was not there now, nor ever had been. On the table, he saw a boys' book of military aircraft, with a clean, new dustjacket; the flyleaf was inscribed: *To Allan Hartley, from his father, on his thirteenth birthday, 7/18 '45*. Glancing out the window at the foliage on the trees, he estimated the date at late July or early August, 1945; that would make him just thirteen.

His clothes were draped on a chair beside the bed. Stripping off his pajamas, he donned shorts, then sat down and picked up a pair of lemon-colored socks, which he regarded with disfavor. As he pulled one on, a church bell began to clang. St. Boniface, up on the hill, ringing for early Mass; so this was Sunday. He paused, the second sock in his hand.

There was no question that his present environment was actual. Yet, on the other hand, he possessed a set of memories completely at variance with it. Now, suppose, since his environment were not an illusion, everything else were? Suppose all these troublesome memories were no more than a dream? Why, he was just little Allan Hartley, safe in his ro_m on a Sunday morning, badly scared by a nightmare! Too much science fiction, Allan; too many comic books!

That was a wonderfully comforting thought, and he hugged it to him contentedly. It lasted all the while he was buttoning up his shirt and pulling on his pants, but when he reached for his shoes, it evaporated. Ever since he had wakened, he realized, he had been occupied with thoughts utterly incomprehensible to any thirteen-year-old; even thinking in words that would have been so much Sanskrit to himself at thirteen. He shook his head regretfully. The just-a-dream hypothesis went by the deep six.

He picked up the second shoe and glared at it as though it were responsible for his predicament. He was going to have to be careful. An unexpected display of adult characteristics might give rise to some questions he would find hard to answer credibly. Fortunately, he was an only child; there would be no brothers or sisters to trip him up. Old Mrs. Stauber, the housekeeper, wouldn't be much of a problem; even in his normal childhood, he had bulked like an intellectual giant in comparison to her. But his father—

Now there the going would be tough. He knew that shrewd attorney's mind, whetted keen on a generation of lying and reluctant witnesses. Sooner or later, he would forget for an instant and betray himself. Then he smiled, remembering the books he had discovered, in his late teens, on his father's shelves and recalling the character of the openminded agnostic lawyer. If he could only avoid the inevitable unmasking until he had a plausible explanatory theory.

Blake Hartley was leaving the bathroom as Allan Hartley opened his door and stepped into the hall. The lawyer was bare-armed and in slippers; at forty-eight, there was only a faint powdering of gray in his dark hair, and not a gray thread in his clipped mustache. The old Merry Widower, himself, Allan thought, grinning as he remembered the white-haired but still vigorous man from whom he'd parted at the outbreak of the War.

" 'Morning, Dad," he greeted.

" 'Morning, son. You're up early. Going to Sunday school?"

Now there was the advantage of a father who'd cut his first intellectual tooth on Tom Paine and Bob Ingersoll; attendance at divine services was on a strictly voluntary basis.

"Why, I don't think so; I want to do some reading, this morning."

"That's always a good thing to do," Blake Hartley approved. "After breakfast, suppose you take a walk down to the station and get me a *Times*." He dug in his trouser pocket and came out with a half dollar. "Get anything you want for yourself, while you're at it."

Allan thanked his father and pocketed the coin.

"Mrs. Stauber'll still be at Mass," he suggested. "Say I get the paper now; breakfast won't be ready till she gets here."

"Good idea." Blake Hartley nodded, pleased. "You'll have three-quarters of an hour, at least."

So far, he congratulated himself, everything had gone smoothly. Finishing his toilet, he went downstairs and onto the street, turning left at Brandon to Campbell, and left again in the direction of the station. Before he reached the under-

pass, a dozen half-forgotten memories had revived. Here was
a house that would, in a few years, be gutted by fire. Here
were four dwellings standing where he had last seen a five-
story apartment building. A gasoline station and a weed-
grown lot would shortly be replaced by a supermarket. The
environs of the station itself were a complete puzzle to him,
until he oriented himself.

He bought a New York *Times*, glancing first of all at the
date line. Sunday, August 5, 1945; he'd estimated pretty
closely. The battle of Okinawa had been won. The Potsdam
Conference had just ended. There were still pictures of the
B-25 crash against the Empire State Building, a week ago
Saturday. And Japan was still being pounded by bombs from
the air and shells from off-shore naval guns. Why, tomorrow,
Hiroshima was due for the Big Job! He was probably the only
person in Williamsport who knew that.

On the way home, a boy, sitting on the top step of a front
porch, hailed him. Allan replied cordially, trying to remember who it was. Of course; Larry Morton! He and Allan had
been buddies. They probably had been swimming, or playing
Commandos and Germans, the afternoon before. Larry had
gone to Cornell the same year that Allan had gone to Penn
State; they had both graduated in 1954. Larry had gotten into
some Government bureau, and then he had married a Pittsburgh girl, and had become twelfth vice-president of her
father's firm. He had been killed, in 1968, in a plane crash.

"You gonna Sunday school?" Larry asked, mercifully
unaware of the fate Allan foresaw for him.

"Why, no. I have some things I want to do at home." He'd
have to watch himself. Larry would spot a difference quicker
than any adult. "Heck with it," he added.

"Golly, I wisht I c'ld stay home from Sunday school
whenever I wanted to," Larry envied. "How about us goin'
swimmin', at the Canoe Club, 'safter?"

Allan thought fast. "Gee, I wisht I c'ld," he replied,
lowering his grammatical sights. "I gotta stay home, 'safter.
We're expectin' comp'ny; coupla aunts of mine. Dad wants
me to stay home when they come."

That went over all right. Anybody knew that there was no

rational accounting for the vagaries of the adult mind, and no appeal from adult demands. The prospect of company at the Hartley home would keep Larry away, that afternoon. He showed his disappointment.

"Aw, jeepers creepers!" he blasphemed euphemistically.

"Mebbe t'morrow," Allan said. "If I c'n make it. I gotta go, now; ain't had breakfast yet." He scuffed his feet boyishly, exchanged so-longs with his friend, and continued homeward.

As he had hoped, the Sunday paper kept his father occupied at breakfast, to the exclusion of any dangerous table talk. Blake Hartley was still deep in the financial section when Allan left the table and went to the library. There should be two books there to which he wanted badly to refer. For a while, he was afraid that his father had not acquired them prior to 1945, but he finally found them, and carried them onto the front porch, along with a pencil and a ruled yellow scratch pad. In his experienced future—or his past-to-come—Allan Hartley had been accustomed to doing his thinking with a pencil. As reporter, as novelist plotting his work, as amateur chemist in his home laboratory, as scientific warfare research officer, his ideas had always been clarified by making notes. He pushed a chair to the table and built up the seat with cushions, wondering how soon he would become used to the proportional disparity between himself and the furniture. As he opened the books and took his pencil in his hand, there was one thing missing. If he could only smoke a pipe, now!

His father came out and stretched in a wicker chair with the *Times* book-review section. The morning hours passed. Allan Hartley leafed through one book and then the other. His pencil moved rapidly at times; at others, he doodled absently. There was no question, any more, in his mind, as to what or who he was. He was Allan Hartley, a man of forty-three, marooned in his own thirteen-year-old body, thirty years back in his own past. That was, of course, against all common sense, but he was easily able to ignore that objection. It had been made before: against the astronomy of Copernicus, and the geography of Columbus, and the biology of Darwin, and the industrial technology of Samuel Colt, and the military doctrines of Charles de Gaulle. Today's common sense had a habit of turning into tomorrow's utter nonsense. What he needed, right now, but bad, was a theory that would explain what had happened to him.

Understanding was beginning to dawn when Mrs. Stauber came out to announce midday dinner.

"I hope you won't mind haffin' it so early," she apologized. "Mein sister, Jennie, offer in Nippenose, she iss sick; I vant to go see her, dis afternoon, yet. I'll be back in blenty time to get supper, Mr. Hartley."

"Hey, Dad!" Allan spoke up. "Why can't we get our own supper, and have a picnic, like? That'd be fun, and Mrs. Stauber could stay as long as she wanted to."

His father looked at him. Such consideration for others was a most gratifying deviation from the juvenile norm; dawn of altruism, or something. He gave hearty assent.

"Why, of course, Mrs. Stauber. Allan and I can shift for ourselves, this evening; can't we, Allan? You needn't come back till tomorrow morning."

"Ach, t'ank you! T'ank you so mooch, Mr. Hartley."

At dinner, Allan got out from under the burden of conversation by questioning his father about the War and luring him into a lengthy dissertation on the difficulties of the forthcoming invasion of Japan. In view of what he remembered of the next twenty-four hours, Allan was secretly amused. His father was sure that the War would run on to mid-1946.

After dinner, they returned to the porch, Hartley *père* smoking a cigar and carrying out several law books. He only glanced at these occasionally; for the most part, he sat and blew smoke rings, and watched them float away. Some thrice-guilty felon was about to be triumphantly acquitted by a weeping jury; Allan could recognize a courtroom masterpiece in the process of incubation.

It was several hours later that the crunch of feet on the walk caused father and son to look up simultaneously. The approaching visitor was a tall man in a rumpled black suit; he had knobby wrists and big, awkward hands; black hair flecked with gray, and a harsh, bigoted face. Allan remembered him. Frank Gutchall. Lived on Campbell Street; a religious fanatic, and some sort of lay preacher. Maybe he needed legal advice; Allan could vaguely remember some incident—

"Ah, good afternoon, Mr. Gutchall. Lovely day, isn't it?" Blake Hartley said.

Gutchall cleared his throat. "Mr. Hartley, I wonder if you could lend me a gun and some bullets," he began, embarrassedly. "My little dog's been hurt, and it's suffering something terrible. I want a gun, to put the poor thing out of its pain."

"Why, yes; of course. How would a twenty-gauge shotgun do?" Blake Hartley asked. "You wouldn't want anything heavy."

Gutchall fidgeted. "Why, er, I was hoping you'd let me have a little gun." He held his hands about six inches apart. "A pistol, that I could put in my pocket. It wouldn't look right, to carry a hunting gun on the Lord's day; people wouldn't understand that it was for a work of mercy."

The lawyer nodded. In view of Gutchall's religious beliefs, the objection made sense.

"Well, I have a Colt .38-special," he said, "but you know, I belong to this Auxiliary Police outfit. If I were called out for duty, this evening, I'd need it. How soon could you bring it back?"

Something clicked in Allan Hartley's mind. He remembered, now, what that incident had been. He knew, too, what he had to do.

"Dad, aren't there some cartridges left for the Luger?" he asked.

Blake Hartley snapped his fingers. "By George, yes! I have a German automatic I can let you have, but I wish you'd bring it back as soon as possible. I'll get it for you."

Before he could rise, Allan was on his feet.

"Sit still, Dad; I'll get it. I know where the cartridges are." With that, he darted into the house and upstairs.

The Luger hung on the wall over his father's bed. Getting it down, he dismounted it, working with rapid precision. He used the blade of his pocketknife to unlock the endpiece of the breechblock, slipping out the firing pin and buttoning it into his shirt pocket. Then he reassembled the harmless pistol, and filled the clip with 9-millimeter cartridges from the bureau drawer.

There was an extension telephone beside the bed. Finding Gutchall's address in the directory, he lifted the telephone, and stretched his handkerchief over the mouthpiece. Then he dialed Police Headquarters.

"This is Blake Hartley," he lied, deepening his voice and copying his father's tone. "Frank Gutchall, who lives at . . . take this down"—he gave Gutchall's address—"has just borrowed a pistol from me, ostensibly to shoot a dog. He has no dog. He intends shooting his wife. Don't argue about how I know; there isn't time. Just take it for granted that I do. I disabled the pistol—took out the firing pin—but if he finds out what I did, he may get some other weapon. He's on his way home, but he's on foot. If you hurry, you may get a man there before he arrives, and grab him before he finds out the pistol won't shoot."

"O.K., Mr. Hartley. We'll take care of it. Thanks."

"And I wish you'd get my pistol back, as soon as you can. It's something I brought home from the other War, and I shouldn't like to lose it."

"We'll take care of that, too. Thank you, Mr. Hartley."

He hung up, and carried the Luger and the loaded clip down to the porch.

"Look, Mr. Gutchall; here's how it works," he said, showing it to the visitor. Then he slapped in the clip and yanked up on the toggle loading the chamber. "It's ready to shoot, now; this is the safety." He pushed it on. "When you're ready to shoot, just shove it forward and up, and then pull the trigger. You have to pull the trigger each time; it's loaded for eight shots. And be sure to put the safety back when you're through shooting."

"Did you load the chamber?" Blake Hartley demanded.

"Sure. It's on safe, now."

"Let me see." His father took the pistol, being careful to keep his finger out of the trigger guard, and looked at it. "Yes, that's all right." He repeated the instructions Allan had given, stressing the importance of putting the safety on after using. "Understand how it works, now?" he asked.

"Yes, I understand how it works. Thank you, Mr. Hartley. Thank you, too, young man."

Gutchall put the Luger in his hip pocket, made sure it wouldn't fall out, and took his departure.

"You shouldn't have loaded it," Hartley *père* reproved, when he was gone.

Allan sighed. This was it; the masquerade was over.

"I had to, to keep you from fooling with it," he said. "I didn't want you finding out that I'd taken out the firing pin."

"You what?"

"Gutchall didn't want that gun to shoot a dog. He has no dog. He means to shoot his wife with it. He's a religious maniac; sees visions, hears voices, receives revelations, talks with the Holy Ghost. The Holy Ghost probably put him up to this. I'll submit that any man who holds long conversations with the Deity isn't to be trusted with a gun, and neither is any man who lies about why he wants one. And while I was at it, I called the police, on the upstairs phone. I had to use your name; I deepened my voice and talked through a handkerchief."

"You—" Blake Hartley jumped as though bee-stung. "Why did you have to do that?"

"You know why. I couldn't have told them, 'This is little Allan Hartley, just thirteen years old; please, Mr. Policeman, go and arrest Frank Gutchall before he goes root-toot-toot at his wife with my papa's Luger.' That would have gone over big, now, wouldn't it?"

"And suppose he really wants to shoot a dog; what sort of a mess will I be in?"

"No mess at all. If I'm wrong—which I'm not—I'll take the thump for it, myself. It'll pass for a dumb kid trick, and nothing'll be done. But if I'm right, you'll have to front for me. They'll keep your name out of it, but they'd give me a lot of cheap boy-hero publicity, which I don't want." He picked up his pencil again. "We should have the complete returns in about twenty minutes."

That was a ten-minute underestimate, and it was another quarter-hour before the detective-sergeant who returned the Luger had finished congratulating Blake Hartley and giving him the thanks of the Department. After he had gone, the lawyer picked up the Luger, withdrew the clip, and ejected the round in the chamber.

"Well," he told his son, "you were right. You saved that woman's life." He looked at the automatic, and then handed it across the table. "Now, let's see you put that firing pin back."

Allan Hartley dismantled the weapon, inserted the missing part, and put it together again, then snapped it experimentally and returned it to his father. Blake Hartley looked at it again, and laid it on the table.

"Now, son, suppose we have a little talk," he said softly.

"But I explained everything," Allan objected innocently.

"You did not," his father retorted. "Yesterday you'd never have thought of a trick like this; why, you wouldn't even have known how to take this pistol apart. And at dinner, I caught you using language and expressing ideas that were entirely outside anything you'd ever known before. Now, I want to know—and I mean this literally."

Allan chuckled. "I hope you're not toying with the rather medieval notion of possession," he said.

Blake Hartley started. Something very like that must have been flitting through his mind. He opened his mouth to say something, then closed it abruptly.

"The trouble is, I'm not sure you aren't right," his son continued. "You say you find me—changed. When did you first notice a difference?"

"Last night, you were still my little boy. This morning—" Blake Hartley was talking more to himself than to Allan. "I don't know. You were unusually silent at breakfast. And come to think of it, there was something . . . something strange . . . about you when I saw you in the hall upstairs. . . . Allan!'' he burst out, vehemently. "What has happened to you?''

Allan Hartley felt a twinge of pain. What his father was going through was almost what he, himself, had endured, in the first few minutes after waking.

"I wish I could be sure, myself, Dad,'' he said. "You see, when I woke, this morning, I hadn't the least recollection of anything I'd done yesterday. August 4, 1945, that is,'' he specified. "I was positively convinced that I was a man of forty-three, and my last memory was of lying on a stretcher, injured by a bomb explosion. And I was equally convinced that this had happened in 1975.''

"Huh?'' His father straightened. "Did you say nineteen *seventy*-five?'' He thought for a moment. "That's right; in 1975, you will be forty-three. A bomb, you say?''

Allan nodded. "During the siege of Buffalo, in the Third World War,'' he said, "I was a captain in G5—Scientific Warfare, General Staff. There'd been a transpolar air invasion of Canada, and I'd been sent to the front to check on service failures of a new lubricating oil for combat equipment. A week after I got there, Ottawa fell, and the retreat started. We made a stand at Buffalo, and that was where I copped it. I remember being picked up, and getting a narcotic injection. The next thing I knew, I was in bed, upstairs, and it was 1945 again, and I was back in my own little thirteen-year-old body.''

"Oh, Allan, you just had a nightmare to end nightmares!'' his father assured him, laughing a trifle too heartily. "That's all!''

"That was one of the first things I thought of. I had to reject it; it just wouldn't fit the facts. Look; a normal dream is part of the dreamer's own physical brain, isn't it? Well, here is a part about two thousand per cent greater than the whole from which it was taken. Which is absurd.''

"You mean all this Battle of Buffalo stuff? That's easy. All the radio commentators have been harping on the horrors of World War III, and you couldn't have avoided hearing some of it. You just have an undigested chunk of H. V.

Kaltenborn raising hell in your subconscious.''

"It wasn't just World War III; it was everything. My four years at high school, and my four years at Penn State, and my seven years as a reporter on the Philadelphia *Record*. And my novels: *Children of the Mist, Rose of Death, Conqueror's Road*. They were no kid stuff. Why, yesterday I'd never even have thought of some of the ideas I used in my detective stories, that I published under a *nom-de-plume*. And my hobby, chemistry; I was pretty good at that. Patented a couple of processes that made me as much money as my writing. You think a thirteen-year-old just dreamed all that up? Or, here; you speak French, don't you?'' He switched languages and spoke at some length in good conversational slang-spiced Parisian. "Too bad you don't speak Spanish, too,'' he added, reverting to English. "Except for a Mexican accent you could cut with a machete, I'm even better there than in French. And I know some German, and a little Russian.''

Blake Hartley was staring at his son, stunned. It was some time before he could make himself speak.

"I could barely keep up with you, in French,'' he admitted. "I can swear that in the last thirteen years of your life, you had absolutely no chance to learn it. All right; you lived till 1975, you say. Then, all of a sudden, you found yourself back here, thirteen years old, in 1945. I suppose you remember everything in between?'' he asked. "Did you ever read James Branch Cabell? Remember Florian de Puysange, in 'The High Place'?''

"Yes. You find the same idea in 'Jurgen' too,'' Allan said. "You know, I'm beginning to wonder if Cabell mightn't have known something he didn't want to write.''

"But it's impossible!'' Blake Hartley hit the table with his hand, so hard that the heavy pistol bounced. The loose round he had ejected from the chamber toppled over and started to roll, falling off the edge. He stooped and picked it up. "How can you go back, against time? And the time you claim you came from doesn't exist, now; it hasn't happened yet.'' He reached for the pistol magazine, to insert the cartridge, and as he did, he saw the books in front of his son. "Dunne's

'Experiment with Time,' '' he commented. ''And J. N. M. Tyrrell's 'Science and Psychical Phenomena.' Are you trying to work out a theory?''

''Yes.'' It encouraged Allan to see that his father had unconsciously adopted an adult-to-adult manner. ''I think I'm getting somewhere, too. You've read these books? Well, look, Dad; what's your attitutde on precognition? The ability of the human mind to exhibit real knowledge, apart from logical inference, of future events? You think Dunne is telling the truth about his experiences? Or that the cases in Tyrrell's book are properly verified, and can't be explained away on the basis of chance?''

Blake Hartley frowned. ''I don't know,'' he confessed. ''The evidence is the sort that any court in the world would accept, if it concerned ordinary, normal events. Especially the cases investigated by the Society for Psychical Research; they *have* been verified. But how can anybody know of something that hasn't happened yet? If it hasn't happened yet, it doesn't exist, and you can't have real knowledge of something that has no real existence.''

''Tyrrell discusses that dilemma, and doesn't dispose of it. I think I can. If somebody has real knowledge of the future, then the future must be available to the present mind. And if any moment other than the bare present exists, then all time must be totally present; every moment must be perpetually coexistent with every other moment,'' Allan said.

''Yes. I think I see what you mean. That was Dunne's idea, wasn't it?''

''No. Dunne postulated an infinite series of time dimensions, the entire extent of each being the bare present moment of the next. What I'm postulating is the perpetual coexistence of every moment of time in this dimension, just as every graduation on a yardstick exists equally with every other graduation, but each at a different point in space.''

''Well, as far as duration and sequence go, that's all right,'' the father agreed. ''But how about the 'Passage of Time'?''

''Well, time *does* appear to pass. So does the landscape you see from a moving car window. I'll suggest that both are illusions of the same kind. We imagine time to be dynamic, because we've never viewed it from a fixed point, but if it is totally present, then it must be static, and in that case, we're moving through time.''

"That seems all right. But what's your car window?''

"If all time is totally present, then you must exist simultaneously at every moment along your individual life span,'' Allan said. "Your physical body, and your mind, and all the thoughts contained in your mind, each at its appropriate moment in sequence. But what is it that exists only at the bare moment we think of as *now*?''

Blake Hartley grinned. Already, he was accepting his small son as an intellectual equal.

"Please, teacher; what?''

"Your consciousness. And don't say, 'What's that?' Teacher doesn't know. But we're only conscious of one moment; the illusory *now*. This is 'now,' and it was 'now' when you asked that question, and it'll be 'now' when I stop talking, but each is a different moment. We imagine that all those nows are rushing past us. Really, they're standing still, and our consciousness is whizzing past them.''

His father thought that over for some time. Then he sat up. "Hey!'' he cried, suddenly. "If some part of our ego is time-free and passes from moment to moment, it must be extraphysical, because the physical body exists at every moment through which the consciousness passes. And if it's extraphysical, there's no reason whatever for assuming that it passes out of existence when it reaches the moment of the death of the body. Why, there's logical evidence for survival, independent of any alleged spirit communication! You can toss out Patience Worth, and Mrs. Osborne Leonard's Feda, and Sir Oliver Lodge's son, and Wilfred Brandon, and all the other spirit-communicators, and you still have evidence.''

"I hadn't thought of that,'' Allan confessed. "I think you're right. Well, let's put that at the bottom of the agenda and get on with this time business. You 'lose consciousness' as in sleep; where does your consciousness go? I think it simply detaches from the moment at which you go to sleep, and moves backward or forward along the line of moment-sequence, to some prior or subsequent moment, attaching there.''

''Well, why don't we know anything about that?'' Blake Hartley asked. ''It never seems to happen. We go to sleep tonight, and it's always tomorrow morning when we wake; never day-before-yesterday, or last month, or next year.''

''It never . . . or almost never . . . *seems* to happen; you're right there. Know why? Because if the consciousness goes forward, it attaches at a moment when the physical brain contains memories of the previous, consciously unexperienced, moment. You wake, remembering the evening before, because that's the memory contained in your mind at that moment, and back of it are memories of all the events in the interim. See?''

''Yes. But how about backward movement, like this experience of yours?''

''This experience of mine may not be unique, but I never heard of another case like it. What usually happens is that the memories carried back by the consciousness are buried in the subconscious mind. You know how thick the wall between the subconscious and the conscious mind is. These dreams of Dunne's, and the cases in Tyrrell's book, are leakage. That's why precognitions are usually incomplete and distorted, and generally trivial. The wonder isn't that good cases are so few; it's surprising that there are any at all.'' Allan looked at the papers in front of him. ''I haven't begun to theorize about how I managed to remember everything. It may have been the radiations from the bomb, or the effect of the narcotic, or both together, or something at this end, or a combination of all three. But the fact remains that my subconscious barrier didn't function, and everything got through. So, you see, I am obsessed—by my own future identity.''

''And I'd been afraid that you'd been, well, taken over by some . . . some outsider.'' Blake Hartley grinned weakly. ''I don't mind admitting, Allan, that what's happened has been a shock. But that other . . . I just couldn't have taken that.''

·   ·   ·

"No. Not and stayed sane. But really, I am your son; the same entity I was yesterday. I've just had what you might call an educational short cut."

"I'll say you have!" His father laughed in real amusement. He discovered that his cigar had gone out, and re-lit it. "Here; if you can remember the next thirty years, suppose you tell me when the War's going to end. This one, I mean."

"The Japanese surrender will be announced at exactly 1901—7:01 P.M. present style—on August 14. A week from Tuesday. Better make sure we have plenty of grub in the house by then. Everything will be closed up tight till Thursday morning; even the restaurants. I remember, we had nothing to eat in the house but some scraps."

"Well! It is handy, having a prophet in the family! I'll see to it Mrs. Stauber gets plenty of groceries in. . . . Tuesday a week? That's pretty sudden, isn't it?"

"The Japs are going to think so," Allan replied. He went on to describe what was going to happen.

His father swore softly. "You know, I've heard talk about atomic energy, but I thought it was just Buck Rogers stuff. Was that the sort of bomb that got you?"

"That was a firecracker to the bomb that got me. That thing exploded a good ten miles away."

Blake Hartley whistled softly. "And that's going to happen in thirty years! You know, son, if I were you, I wouldn't like to have to know about a thing like that." He looked at Allan for a moment. "Please, if you know, don't ever tell me when I'm going to die."

Allan smiled. "I can't. I had a letter from you just before I left for the front. You were seventy-eight, then, and you were still hunting, and fishing, and flying your own plane. But I'm not going to get killed in any Battle of Buffalo, this time, and if I can prevent it, and I think I can, there won't be any World War III."

"But— You say all time exists, perpetually coexistent and totally present," his father said. "Then it's right there in front of you, and you're getting closer to it, every watch tick."

Allan Hartley shook his head. "You know what I remembered, when Frank Gutchall came to borrow a gun?" he asked. "Well, the other time, I hadn't been home. I'd been swimming at the Canoe Club, with Larry Morton. When I got home, about half an hour from now, I found the house full of cops. Gutchall talked the .38 officers' model out of you, and gone home; he'd shot his wife four times through the body, finished her off with another one back of the ear, and then used his sixth shot to blast his brains out. The cops traced the gun; they took a very poor view of your lending it to him. You never got it back."

"Trust that gang to keep a good gun," the lawyer said.

"I didn't want us to lose it, this time, and I didn't want to see you lose face around City Hall," Allan said. "But my main reason for fixing Frank Gutchall up with a padded cell was that I wanted to know whether or not the future could be altered. I have it on experimental authority that it can be. There must be additional dimensions of time; lines of alternate probabilities. Something like William Seabrook's witch-doctor friend's Fan-Shaped Destiny. When I brought memories of the future back to the present, I added certain factors to the causal chain. That set up an entirely new line of probabilities. On no notice at all, I stopped a murder and a suicide. With thirty years to work, I can stop a world war. I'll have the means to do it, too."

"The means?"

"Unlimited wealth and influence. Here." Allan picked up a sheet and handed it to his father. "Used properly, we can make two or three million on that, alone. A list of all the Kentucky Derby, Preakness, and Belmont winners to 1970. That'll furnish us primary capital. Then, remember, I was something of a chemist. I took it up, originally, to get background material for one of my detective stories; it fascinated me, and I made it a hobby, and then a source of income. I'm thirty years ahead of any chemist in the world, now. You remember *I. G. Farbenindustrie?* Ten years from now, we'll make them look like pikers."

His father looked at the yellow sheet. "Assault, at eight to one," he said. "I can scrape up about five thousand for that— Yes; in ten years— Any other little operations you have in mind?" he asked.

"About 1950, we start building a political organization, here in Pennsylvania. In 1960, I think we can elect you President. The world situation will be crucial, then. I think President Hartley can be trusted to take a strong line of policy. In the meantime, you can read Machiavelli."

"That's my little boy, talking!" Blake Hartley said softly. "All right, son; I'll do just what you tell me, and when you grow up, I'll be president. . . . Let's go get supper, now."

THE MERCENARIES

In "The Mercenaries," Piper came up with one of his most intriguing ideas: bands of Free Scientists who sell their work and expertise to various governments, like bands of condottiere. As political neutrals and outsiders, the Free Scientists must never take sides in a national conflict. "The Mercenaries" is the story of what happens when Duncan MacLeod discovers a traitor among the MacLeod Team. Not only is their work threatened, but so is the integrity of the MacLeod Team.

Jerry Pournelle believes "The Mercenaries" is one of Piper's strongest stories and one with great series potential. I agree, and I think you will too.

DUNCAN MACLEOD hung up the suit he had taken off, and sealed his shirt, socks and underwear in a laundry envelope bearing his name and identity-number, tossing this into one of the wire baskets provided for the purpose. Then, naked except for the plastic identity disk around his neck, he went over to the desk, turned in his locker key, and passed into the big room beyond.

Four or five young men, probably soldiers on their way to

town, were coming through from the other side. Like Mac-
Leod, they wore only the plastic disks they had received in
exchange for the metal ones they wore inside the reservation,
and they were being searched by attendants who combed
through their hair, probed into ears and nostrils, peered into
mouths with tiny searchlights, and employed a variety of
magnetic and electronic detectors.

To this search MacLeod submitted wearily. He had become quite a connoisseur of security measures in fifteen
years' research and development work for a dozen different
nations, but the Tonto Basin Research Establishment of the
Philadelphia Project exceeded anything he had seen before.
There were gray-haired veterans of the old Manhattan Project
here, men who had worked with Fermi at Chicago, or with
Oppenheimer at Los Alamos, twenty years before, and they
swore in amused exasperation when they thought of how the
relatively mild regulations of those days had irked them. And
yet, the very existence of the Manhattan Project had been
kept a secret from all but those engaged in it, and its purpose
from most of them. Today, in 1965, there might have been
a few wandering tribesmen in Somaliland or the Kirghiz
Steppes who had never heard of the Western Union's Philadelphia Project, or of the Fourth Komintern's Red Triumph
Five-Year Plan, or of the Islamic Kaliphate's Al-Borak Un-
dertaking, or of the Ibero-American Confederation's Cavor
Project, but every literate person in the world knew that the
four great power-blocs were racing desperately to launch the
first spaceship to reach the Moon and build the Lunar fortress
that would insure world supremacy.

He turned in the nonmagnetic identity disk at the desk on
the other side of the search room, receiving the metal one he
wore inside the reservation, and with it the key to his inside
locker. He put on the clothes he had left behind when he had
passed out, and filled his pockets with the miscellany of small
articles he had not been allowed to carry off the reservation.
He knotted the garish necktie affected by the civilian workers
and in particular by members of the MacLeod Research Team

to advertise their nonmilitary status, lit his pipe, and walked out into the open gallery beyond.

Karen Hilquist was waiting for him there, reclining in one of the metal chairs. She looked cool in the belted white coveralls, with the white turban bound around her yellow hair, and very beautiful, and when he saw her, his heart gave a little bump, like a geiger responding to an ionizing particle. It always did that, although they had been together for twelve years, and married for ten. Then she saw him and smiled, and he came over, fanning himself with his sun helmet, and dropped into a chair beside her.

"Did you call our center for a jeep?" he asked. When she nodded, he continued: "I thought you would, so I didn't bother."

For a while, they sat silent, looking with bored distaste at the swarm of steel-helmeted Army riflemen and tommy-gunners guarding the transfer platforms and the vehicles gate. A string of trucks had been passed under heavy guard into the clearance compound; they were now unloading supplies onto a platform, at the other side of which other trucks were backed waiting to receive the shipment. A hundred feet of bare concrete and fifty armed soldiers separated these men and trucks from the outside, preventing contact.

"And still they can't stop leaks," Karen said softly. "And we get blamed for it."

MacLeod nodded and started to say something, when his attention was drawn by a commotion on the driveway. A big Tucker limousine with an O.D. paint job and the single-starred flag of a brigadier general was approaching, horning impatiently. In the back seat MacLeod could see a heavy-shouldered figure with the face of a bad-tempered Great Dane—General Daniel Nayland, the military commander of Tonto Basin. The inside guards jumped to attention and saluted; the barrier shot up as though rocket-propelled, and the car slid through; the barrier slammed down behind it. On the other side, the guards were hurling themselves into a frenzy of saluting. Karen made a face after the receding car and muttered something in Hindustani. She probably didn't know the literal meaning of what she had called General Nayland, but she understood that it was a term of extreme opprobrium.

Her husband contributed: "His idea of Heaven would be a huge research establishment, where he'd be a five-star general, and Galileo, Newton, Priestley, Dalton, Maxwell, Planck and Einstein would be tech sergeants."

"And Marie Curie and Lise Meitner would be WAC corporals," Karen added. "He really hates all of us, doesn't he?"

"He hates our Team," MacLeod replied. "In the first place, we're a lot of civilians, who aren't subject to his regulations and don't have to salute him. We're working under contract with the Western Union, not with the United States Government, and as the United States participates in the Western Union on a treaty basis, our contract has the force of a treaty obligation. It gives us what amounts to extraterritoriality, like Europeans in China during the Nineteenth Century. So we have our own transport, for which he must furnish petrol, and our own armed guard, and we fly our own flag over Team Center, and that gripes him as much as anything else. That and the fact that we're foreigners. So wouldn't he love to make this espionage rap stick on us!"

"And our contract specifically gives the United States the right to take action against us in case we endanger the national security," Karen added. She stuffed her cigarette into the not-too-recently-emptied receiver beside her chair, her blue eyes troubled. "You know, some of us could get shot over this, if we're not careful. Dunc, does it really have to be one of our own people who—?"

"I don't see how it could be anybody else," MacLeod said. "I don't like the idea any more than you do, but there it is."

"Well, what are we going to do? Is there nobody whom we can trust?"

"Among the technicians and guards, yes. I could think of a

score who are absolutely loyal. But among the Team itself—the top researchers—there's nobody I'd take a chance on but Kato Sugihara.''

"Can you even be sure of him? I'd hate to think of him as a traitor, but—''

"I have a couple of reasons for eliminating Kato,'' MacLeod said. "In the first place, outside nucleonic and binding-force physics, there are only three things he's interested in. Jitterbugging, hand-painted neckties, and Southern-style cooking. If he went over to the Komintern, he wouldn't be able to get any of those. Then, he only spends about half his share of the Team's profits, and turns the rest back into the Team Fund. He has a credit of about a hundred thousand dollars, which he'd lose by leaving us. And then, there's another thing. Kato's father was killed on Guadalcanal, in 1942, when he was only five. After that he was brought up in the teachings of Bushido by his grandfather, an old-time samurai. Bushido is open to some criticism, but nobody can show where double-crossing your own gang is good Bushido. And today, Japan is allied with the Western Union, and in any case, he wouldn't help the Komintern. The Japs'll forgive Russia for that Mussolini backstab in 1945 after the Irish start building monuments to Cromwell.''

A light-blue jeep, lettered *MacLeod Research Team* in cherry-red, was approaching across the wide concrete apron. MacLeod grinned.

"Here it comes. Fasten your safety belt when you get in; that's Ahmed driving.''

Karen looked at her watch. "And it's almost time for dinner. You know, I dread the thought of sitting at the table with the others, and wondering which of them is betraying us.''

"Only nine of us, instead of thirteen, and still one is a Judas,'' MacLeod said. "I suppose there's always a place for Judas, at any table.''

The MacLeod Team dined together, apart from their assistants and technicians and students. This was no snobbish attempt at class-distinction; matters of Team policy were often discussed at the big round table, and the more confidential details of their work. People who have only their knowledge and their ideas to sell are wary about bandying either loosely, and the six men and three women who faced each other across the twelve-foot diameter of the teakwood table had no other stock-in-trade.

They were nine people of nine different nationalities, or they were nine people of the common extra-nationality of science. That Duncan MacLeod, their leader, had grown up in the Transvaal and his wife had been born in the Swedish university town of Upsala was typical not only of their own group but of the hundreds of independent research-teams that had sprung up after the Second World War. The scientist-adventurer may have been born of the relentless struggle for scientific armament supremacy among nations and the competition for improved techniques among industrial corporations during the late 1950s and early '60s, but he had been begotten when two masses of uranium came together at the top of a steel tower in New Mexico in 1945. And, because scientific research is pre-eminently a matter of pooling brains and efforts, the independent scientists had banded together into teams whose leaders acquired power greater than that of any *condottiere* captain of Renaissance Italy.

Duncan MacLeod, sitting outwardly relaxed and merry, and secretly watchful and bitterly sad, was such a free-captain of science. One by one, the others had rallied around him, not because he was a greater physicist than they, but because he was a bolder, more clever, less scrupulous adventurer, better able to guide them through the maze of international power-politics and the no less ruthless, if less nakedly violent, world of Big Industry.

There was his wife, Karen Hilquist, the young metallurgist who, before she was twenty-five, had perfected a new hardening process for SKF and an incredibly tough gun-steel for the Bofors works. In the few minutes since they had returned to Team Center, she had managed to change her coveralls for a skirt and blouse, and do something intriguing with her hair.

And there was Kato Sugihara, looking younger than his twenty-eight years, who had begun to demonstrate the existence of whole orders of structure below the level of nuclear particles.

There was Suzanne Maillard, her gray hair upswept from a face that had never been beautiful but which was alive with something rarer than mere beauty; she possessed, at the brink of fifty, a charm and smartness that many women half her age might have envied, and she knew more about cosmic rays than any other person living.

And Adam Lowiewski, his black mustache contrasting so oddly with his silver hair, frantically scribbling equations on his doodling-pad, as though his racing fingers could never keep pace with his brain, and explaining them, with obvious condescension, to the boyish-looking Japanese beside him. He was one of the greatest of living mathematicians by anybody's reckoning—*the* greatest, by his own.

And Sir Neville Lawton, the electronics expert, with thinning red-gray hair and meticulously-clipped mustache, who always gave the impression of being in evening clothes, even when, as now, he was dressed in faded khaki.

And Heym ben-Hillel, the Israeli quantum and wave-mechanics man, his heaping dinner plate an affront to the Laws of Moses, his white hair a fluffy, tangled chaos, laughing at an impassively-delivered joke the English knight had made.

And Rudolf von Heldenfeld, with a thin-lipped killer's mouth and a frozen face that never betrayed its owner's thoughts—he was the specialist in magnetic currents and electromagnetic fields.

And Farida Khouroglu, the Turkish girl whom MacLeod and Karen had found begging in the streets of Istanbul ten years ago, and who had grown up following the fortunes of the MacLeod Team on every continent and in a score of nations. It was doubtful if she had ever had a day's formal schooling in her life, but now she was secretary of the Team, with a grasp of physics that would have shamed many a professor. She had grown up a beauty, too, with the large dark eyes and jet-black hair and paper-white skin of her race. She and Kato Sugihara were very much in love.

A good team; the best physics-research team in a power-mad, knowledge-hungry world. MacLeod thought, toying with the stem of his wineglass, of some of their triumphs: The West Australia Atomic Power Plant. The Segovia Plutonium Works, which had got them all titled as Grandees of the restored Spanish Monarchy. The sea-water chemical extraction plant in Puerto Rico, where they had worked for Associated Enterprises, whose president, Blake Hartley, had later become President of the United States. The hard-won victory over a seemingly insoluble problem in the Belgian Congo uranium mines— He thought, too, of the dangers they had faced together, in a world where soldiers must use the weapons of science and scientists must learn the arts of violence. Of the treachery of the Islamic Kaliphate, for whom they had once worked; of the intrigues and plots which had surrounded them in Spain; of the many attempted kidnapings and assassinations; of the time in Basra when they had fought with pistols and tommy guns and snatched-up clubs and flasks of acid to defend their laboratories.

A good team—before the rot of treason had touched it. He could almost smell the putrid stench of it, and yet, as he glanced from face to face, he could not guess the traitor. And he had so little time—

Kato Sugihara's voice rose to dominate the murmur of conversation around the table.

"I think I am getting somewhere on my photon-neutrino-electron interchange-cycle," he announced. "And I think it can be correlated to the collapsed-matter research."

"So?" von Heldenfeld looked up in interest. "And not with the problem of what goes on in the 'hot layer' surrounding the Earth?"

"No, Suzanne talked me out of that idea," the Japanese replied. "That's just a secondary effect of the effect of cosmic rays and solar radiations on the order of particles existing at that level. But I think that I have the key to the problem of collapsing matter to plate the hull of the spaceship.''

''That's interesting,'' Sir Neville Lawton commented. ''How so?''

''Well, you know what happens when a photon comes in contact with the atomic structure of matter,'' Kato said. ''There may be an elastic collision, in which the photon merely bounces off. Macroscopically, that's the effect we call reflection of light. Or there may be an inelastic collision, when the photon hits an atom and knocks out an electron—the old photoelectric effect. Or, the photon may be retained for a while and emitted again relatively unchanged—the effect observed in luminous paint. Or, the photon may penetrate, undergo a change to a neutrino, and either remain in the nucleus of the atom or pass through it, depending upon a number of factors. All this, of course, is old stuff; even the photo-neutrino interchange has been known since the mid-'50s, when the Gamow neutrino-counter was developed. But now we come to what you have been so good as to christen the Sugihara Effect—the neutrino picking up a negative charge and, in effect, turning into an electron, and then losing its charge, turning back into a neutrino, and then, as in the case of metal heated to incandescence, being emitted again as a photon.

''At first, we thought this had no connection with the spaceship insulation problem we are under contract to work out, and we agreed to keep this effect a Team secret until we could find out if it had commercial possibilities. But now, I find that it has a direct connection with the collapsed-matter problem. When the electron loses its negative charge and reverts to a neutrino, there is a definite accretion of inter-atomic binding-force, and the molecule, or the crystalline lattice or whatever tends to contract, and when the neutrino becomes a photon, the nucleus of the atom contracts.''

Heym ben-Hillel was sitting oblivious to everything but his young colleague's words, a slice of the flesh of the unclean beast impaled on his fork and halfway to his mouth.

"Yes! Certainly!" he exclaimed. "That would explain so many things I have wondered about. And of course, there are other forces at work which, in the course of nature, balance that effect—"

"But can the process be controlled?" Suzanne Maillard wanted to know. "Can you convert electrons to neutrinos and then to photons in sufficient numbers, and eliminate other effects that would cause compensating atomic and molecular expansion?"

Kato grinned, like a tomcat contemplating the bones of a fish he has just eaten.

"Yes, I can. I have." He turned to MacLeod. "Remember those bullets I got from you?" he asked.

MacLeod nodded. He handloaded for his .38-special, and like all advanced cases of handloading-fever, he was religiously fanatical about uniformity of bullet weights and dimensions. Unlike most handloaders, he had available the instruments to secure such uniformity.

"Those bullets are as nearly alike as different objects can be," Kato said. "They weigh 158 grains, and that means one-five-eight-point-zero-zero-practically-nothing. The diameter is .35903 inches. All right; I've been subjecting those bullets to different radiation-bombardments, and the best results have given me a bullet with a diameter of .35892 inches, and the weight is unchanged. In other words, there's been no loss of mass, but the mass has contracted. And that's only been the first test."

"Well, write up everything you have on it, and we'll lay out further experimental work," MacLeod said. He glanced around the table. "So far, we can't be entirely sure. The shrinkage may be all in the crystalline lattice; the atomic structure may be unchanged. What we need is matter that is really collapsed."

"I'll do that," Kato said. "Farida, I'll have all my data available for you before noon tomorrow; you can make up copies for all Team members."

"Make mine on microfilm, for projection," von Heldenfeld said.

"Mine, too," Sir Neville Lawton added.

"Better make microfilm copies for everybody," Heym ben-Hillel suggested. "They're handier than typescript."

MacLeod rose silently and tiptoed around behind his wife and Rudolf von Heldenfeld, to touch Kato Sugihara on the shoulder.

"Come on outside, Kato," he whispered. "I want to talk to you."

The Japanese nodded and rose, following him outside onto the roof above the laboratories. They walked over to the edge and stopped at the balustrade.

"Kato, when you write up your stuff, I want you to falsify everything you can. Put it in such form that the data will be absolutely worthless, but also in such form that nobody, not even Team members, will know it has been falsified. Can you do that?"

Kato's almond-shaped eyes widened. "Of course I can, Dunc," he replied. "But why—?"

"I hate to say this, but we have a traitor in the Team. One of those people back in the dining room is selling us out to the Fourth Komintern. I know it's not Karen, and I know it's not you, and that's as much as I do know, now."

The Japanese sucked in his breath in a sharp hiss. "You wouldn't say that unless you were sure, Dunc," he said.

"No. At about 1000 this morning, Dr. Weissberg, the civilian director, called me to his office. I found him very much upset. He told me that General Nayland is accusing us—by which he meant this Team—of furnishing secret information on our subproject to Komintern agents. He said that British Intelligence agents at Smolensk had learned that the Red Triumph laboratories there were working along lines of research originated at MacLeod Team Center here. They relayed the information to Western Union Intelligence, and WU passed it on to United States Central Intelligence, and now Counter Espionage is riding Nayland about it, and he's trying to make us the goat."

"He would love to get some of us shot," Kato said. "And

that could happen. They took a long time getting tough about espionage in this country, but when Americans get tough about something, they get tough right. But look here; we handed in our progress-reports to Felix Weissberg, and he passed them on to Nayland. Couldn't the leak be right in Nayland's own HQ?''

''That's what I thought, at first,'' MacLeod replied. ''Just wish-thinking, though. Fact is, I went up to Nayland's HQ and had it out with him; accused him of just that. I think I threw enough of a scare into him for a couple of days. I wanted to know just what it was the Komintern was supposed to have got from us, but he wouldn't tell me. That, of course, was classified stuff.''

''Well?''

''Well then, Karen and I got our digestive tracts emptied and went into town, where I could use a phone that didn't go through a military switchboard, and I put through a call to Allan Hartley, President Hartley's son. He owes us a break, after the work we did in Puerto Rico. I told him all I wanted was some information to help clear ourselves, and he told me to wait a half an hour and then call Counter Espionage Office in Washington and talk to General Hammond.''

''Ha! If Allan Hartley's for us, what are we worried about?'' Kato asked. ''I always knew he was the power back of Associated Enterprises and his father was the front-man; I'll bet it's the same with the Government.''

''Allan Hartley's for us as long as our nose is clean. If we let it get dirty, we get it bloodied, too. We have to clean it ourselves,'' MacLeod told him. ''But here's what Hammond gave me: The Komintern knows all about our collapsed-matter experiments with zinc, titanium and nickel. They know about our theoretical work on cosmic rays, including Suzanne's work up to about a month ago. They know about that effect Sir Neville and Heym discovered two months ago.'' He paused. ''And they know about the photo-neutrino-electron interchange.''

Kato responded to this with a gruesome double-take that gave his face the fleeting appearance of an ancient samurai war mask.

"That wasn't included in any report we ever made," he said. "You're right: the leak comes from inside the Team. It must be Sir Neville, or Suzanne, or Heym ben-Hillel, or Adam Lowiewski, or Rudolf von Heldenfeld, or— No! No, I can't believe it could be Farida!" He looked at MacLeod pleadingly. "You don't think she could have—?"

"No, Kato. The Team's her whole life, even more than it is mine. She came with us when she was only twelve, and grew up with us. She doesn't know any other life than this, and wouldn't want any other. It has to be one of the other five."

"Well, there's Suzanne," Kato began. "She had to clear out of France because of political activities, after the collapse of the Fourth Republic and the establishment of the Rightist Directoire in '57. And she worked with Joliot-Curie, and she was at the University of Louvain in the early '50s, when that place was crawling with Commies."

"And that brings us to Sir Neville," MacLeod added. "He dabbles in spiritualism; he and Suzanne do planchette-seances. A planchette can be manipulated. Maybe Suzanne produced a communication advising Sir Neville to help the Komintern."

"Could be. Then, how about Lowiewski? He's a Pole who can't go back to Poland, and Poland's a Komintern country," Kato pointed out. "Maybe he'd sell us out for amnesty, though why he'd want to go back there, the way things are now—?"

"His vanity. You know, missionary-school native going back to the village wearing real pants, to show off to the savages. Used to be a standing joke, down where I came from." MacLeod thought for a moment. "And Rudolf; he's always had a poor view of the democratic system of government. He might feel more at home with the Komintern. Of course, the Ruskis killed his parents in 1945—"

"So what?" Kato retorted. "The Americans killed my father in 1942, but I'm not making an issue out of it. That was another war; Japan's a Western Union country, now. So's Germany— How about Heym, by the way? Remember when the Komintern wanted us to come to Russia and do the same work we're doing here?''

"I remember that after we turned them down, somebody tried to kidnap Karen,'' MacLeod said grimly. ''I remember a couple of Russians got rather suddenly dead trying it, too.''

"I wasn't thinking of that. I was thinking of our round-table argument when the proposition was considered. Heym was in favor of accepting. Now that, I would say, indicates either Communist sympathies or an overtrusting nature,'' Kato submitted. ''And a lot of grade-A traitors have been made out of people with trusting natures.''

MacLeod got out his pipe and lit it. For a long time, he stared out across the mountain-ringed vista of sagebrush, dotted at wide intervals with the bulks of research-centers and the red roofs of the villages.

"Kato, I think I know how we're going to find out which one it is,'' he said. ''First of all, you write up your data, and falsify it so that it won't do any damage if it gets into Komintern hands. And then—''

The next day started in an atmosphere of suppressed excitement and anxiety which, beginning with MacLeod and Karen and Kato Sugihara, seemed to communicate itself by contagion to everybody in the MacLeod Team's laboratories. The top researchers and their immediate assistants and students were the first to catch it; they ascribed the tension under which their leader and his wife and the Japanese labored to the recent developments in the collapsed-matter problem. Then, there were about a dozen implicitly-trusted technicians and guards, who had been secretly gathered in MacLeod's office the night before and informed of the crisis that had arisen. Their associates could not miss the fact that they were preoccupied with something unusual.

They were a variegated crew; men who had been added to the Team in every corner of the world. There was Ahmed Abd-el-Rahman, the Arab jeep-driver who had joined them in Basra. There was the wiry little Greek whom everybody called Alex Unpronounceable. There was an Italian, and two Chinese, and a cashiered French Air Force officer, and a

Malay, and the son of an English earl who insisted that his name was Bertie Wooster. They had sworn themselves to secrecy, had heard MacLeod's story with a polylingual burst of pious or blasphemous exclamations, and then they had scattered, each to the work assigned him.

MacLeod had risen early and submitted to the ordeal of the search to leave the reservation and go to town again, this time for a conference at the shabby back-street cigar store that concealed a Counter Espionage center. He had returned just as Farida Khouroglu was finishing the microfilm copies of Kato's ingeniously-concocted pseudo-data. These copies were distributed at noon, while the Team was lunching, along with carbons of the original typescript.

He was the first to leave the table, going directly to the basement, where Alex Unpronounceable and the man who had got his alias from the works of P. G. Wodehouse, were listening in on the telephone calls going in and out through the Team-center switchboard, and making recordings. For two hours, MacLeod remained with them. He heard Suzanne Maillard and some woman who was talking from a number in the Army married-officers' settlement making arrangements about a party. He heard Rudolf von Heldenfeld make a date with some girl. He listened to a violent altercation between the Team chef and somebody at Army Quartermaster's HQ about the quality of a lot of dressed chicken. He listened to a call that came in for Adam Lowiewski, the mathematician.

"This is Joe," the caller said. "I've got to go to town late this afternoon, but I was wondering if you'd have time to meet me at the Recreation House at Oppenheimer Village for a game of chess. I'm calling from there, now."

"Fine; I can make it," Lowiewski's voice replied. "I'm in the middle of a devil's own mathematical problem; maybe a game of chess would clear my head. I have a new queen's-knight gambit I want to try on you, anyhow."

Bertie Wooster looked up sharply. "Now there; that may be what we're—"

The telephone beside MacLeod rang. He scooped it up; named himself into it.

It was Ahmed Abd-el-Rahman. "Look, chief; I tail this guy to Oppenheimer Village," the Arab, who had learned English from American movies, answered. "He goes into the rec-joint. I slide in after him, an' he ain't in sight. I'm lookin' around for him, see, when he comes bargin' outa the Don Ameche box. Then he grabs a table an' a beer. What next?"

"Stay there; keep an eye on him," MacLeod told him. "If I want you, I'll call."

MacLeod hung up and straightened, feeling under his jacket for his .38-special.

"That's it, boys," he said. "Lowiewski. Come on."

"Hah!" Alex Unpronounceable had his gun out and was checking the cylinder. He spoke briefly in description of the Polish mathematician's ancestry, physical characteristics, and probable post-mortem destination. Then he put the gun away, and the three men left the basement.

For minutes that seemed like hours, MacLeod and the Greek waited on the main floor, where they could watch both the elevators and the stairway. Bertie Wooster had gone up to alert Kato Sugihara and Karen. Then the door of one of the elevators opened and Adam Lowiewski emerged, with Kato behind him, apparently lost in a bulky scientific journal he was reading. The Greek moved in from one side, and MacLeod stepped in front of the Pole.

"Hi, Adam," he greeted. "Have you looked into that batch of data yet?"

"Oh, yes. Yes." Lowiewski seemed barely able to keep his impatience within the bounds of politeness. "Of course, it's out of my line, but the mathematics seems sound." He started to move away.

"You're not going anywhere," MacLeod told him. "The chess game is over. The red pawns are taken—the one at Oppenheimer Village, and the one here."

There was a split second in which Lowiewski struggled—almost successfully—to erase the consternation from his face.

"I don't know what you're talking about," he began. His right hand started to slide under his left coat lapel.

MacLeod's Colt was covering him before he could complete the movement. At the same time, Kato Sugihara dropped the paper-bound periodical, revealing the thin-bladed knife he had concealed under it. He stepped forward, pressing the point of the weapon against the Pole's side. With the other hand, he reached across Lowiewski's chest and jerked the pistol from his shoulder-holster. It was one of the elegant little .32 Beretta 1954 Model automatics.

"Into the elevator," MacLeod ordered. An increasing pressure of Kato's knife emphasized the order. "And watch him; don't let him get rid of anything," he added to the Greek.

"If you would explain this outrage—" Lowiewski began. "I assume it is your idea of a joke—"

Without even replying, MacLeod slammed the doors and started the elevator upward, letting it rise six floors to the living quarters. Karen Hilquist and the aristocratic black-sheep who called himself Bertie Wooster were waiting when he opened the door. The Englishman took one of Lowiewski's arms; MacLeod took the other. The rest fell in behind as they hustled the captive down the hall and into the big sound-proofed dining room. They kept Lowiewski standing, well away from any movable object in the room; Alex Unpronounceable took his left arm as MacLeod released it and went to the communicator and punched the all-outlets button.

"Dr. Maillard; Dr. Sir Neville Lawton; Dr. ben-Hillel; Dr. von Heldenfeld; Mlle. Khouroglu," he called. "Dr. MacLeod speaking. Come at once, repeat at once, to the round table— Dr. Maillard; Dr. Sir Neville Lawton—"

Karen said something to the Japanese and went outside. For a while, nobody spoke. Kato came over and lit a cigarette in the bowl of MacLeod's pipe. Then the other Team members entered in a body. Evidently Karen had intercepted them in the hallway and warned them that they would find some unusual situation inside; even so, there was a burst of surprised exclamations when they found Adam Lowiewski under detention.

"Ladies and gentlemen," MacLeod said, "I reget to tell you that I have placed our colleague, Dr. Lowiewski, under arrest. He is suspected of betraying confidential data to agents of the Fourth Komintern. Yesterday, I learned that data on all our work here, including Team-secret data on the Sugihara Effect, had got into the hands of the Komintern and was being used in research at the Smolensk laboratories. I also learned that General Nayland blames this Team as a whole with double-dealing and selling this data to the Komintern. I don't need to go into any lengthy exposition of General Nayland's attitude toward this Team, or toward Free Scientists as a class, or toward the research-contract system. Nor do I need to point out that if he pressed these charges against us, some of us could easily suffer death or imprisonment."

"So he had to have a victim in a hurry, and pulled my name out of the hat," Lowiewski sneered.

"I appreciate the gravity of the situation," Sir Neville Lawton said. "And if the Sugihara Effect was among the data betrayed, I can understand that nobody but one of us could have betrayed it. But why, necessarily, should it be Adam? We all have unlimited access to all records and theoretical data."

"Exactly. But collecting information is the smallest and easiest part of espionage. Almost anybody can collect information. Where the spy really earns his pay is in transmitting information. Now, think of the almost fantastic security measures in force here, and consider how you would get such information, including masses of mathematical data beyond any human power of memorization, out of this reservation."

"Ha, nobody can take anything out," Suzanne Maillard said. "Not even one's breakfast. Is Adam accused of sorcery, too?"

"The only material things that are allowed to leave this reservation are sealed cases of models and data shipped to the different development plants. And the Sugihara Effect never was reported, and wouldn't go out that way," Heym ben-Hillel objected.

"But the data on the Sugihara Effect reached Smolensk,"

MacLeod replied. "And don't talk about Darwin and Wallace; it wasn't a coincidence. This stuff was taken out of the Tonto Basin Reservation by the only person who could have done so, in the only way that anything could leave the reservation without search. So I had that person shadowed, and at the same time I had our telephone lines tapped, and eavesdropped on all calls entering or leaving this center. And the person who had to be the spy-courier called Adam Lowiewski, and Lowiewski made an appointment to meet him at the Oppenheimer Village Recreation House to play chess."

"Very suspicious, very suspicious," Lowiewski derided. "I receive a call from a friend at the same time that some anonymous suspect is using the phone. There are only five hundred telephone conversations a minute on this reservation."

"Immediately, Dr. Lowiewski attempted to leave this building," MacLeod went on. "When I intercepted him, he tried to draw a pistol. This one." He exhibited the Beretta. "I am now going to have Dr. Lowiewski searched, in the presence of all of you." He nodded to Alex and the Englishman.

They did their work thoroughly. A pile of Lowiewski's pocket effects was made on the table; as each item was added to it, the Pole made some sarcastic comment.

"And that pack of cigarettes; unopened," he jeered. "I suppose I communicated the data to the manufacturers by telepathy, and they printed it on the cigarette papers in invisible ink."

"Maybe not. Maybe you opened the pack, and then resealed it," Kato suggested. "A heated spatula under the cellophane; like this."

He used the point of his knife, to illustrate. The cellophane came unsealed with surprising ease: so did the revenue stamp. He dumped out the contents of the pack: sixteen cigarettes, four cigarette tip-ends, four bits snipped from the other ends—and a small aluminum microfilm capsule.

Lowiewski's face twitched. For an instant, he tried vainly

to break loose from the men who held him. Then he slumped into a chair. Heym ben-Hillel gasped in shocked surprise. Suzanne Maillard gave a short, felinelike cry. Sir Neville Lawton looked at the capsule curiously and said: "Well, my sainted Aunt Agatha!"

"That's the capsule I gave him, at noon," Farida Khouroglu exclaimed, picking it up. She opened it and pulled out a roll of colloidex projection film. There was also a bit of cigarette paper in the capsule, upon which a notation had been made in Kyrilic characters.

Rudolf von Heldenfeld could read Russian. " 'Data on new development of photon-neutrino-electron interchange. 22 July, '65. Vladmir.' Vladmir, I suppose, is this *schweinhund's* code name," he added.

The film and the paper passed from hand to hand. The other members of the Team sat down; there was a tendency to move away from the chair occupied by Adam Lowiewski. He noticed this and sneered.

"Afraid of contamination from the moral leper?" he asked. "You were glad enough to have me correct your stupid mathematical errors."

Kato Sugihara picked up the capsule, took a final glance at the cigarette pack, and said to MacLeod: "I'll be back as soon as this is done." With that, he left the room, followed by Bertie Wooster and the Greek.

Heym ben-Hillel turned to the others; his eyes had the hurt and puzzled look of a dog that has been kicked for no reason. "But why did he do this?" he asked.

"He just told you," MacLeod replied. "He's the great Adam Lowiewski. Checking math for a physics-research team is beneath his dignity. I suppose the Komintern offered him a professorship at Stalin University." He was watching Lowiewski's face keenly. "No," he continued. "It was probably the mathematics chair of the Soviet Academy of Sciences."

"But who was this person who could smuggle microfilm out of the reservation?" Suzanne Maillard wanted to know.

"Somebody has invented teleportation, then?"

MacLeod shook his head. "It was General Nayland's chauffeur. It had to be. General Nayland's car is the only thing that gets out of here without being searched. The car itself is serviced at Army vehicle's pool; nobody could hide anything in it for a confederate to pick up outside. Nayland is a stuffed shirt of the first stuffing, and a tinpot Hitler to boot, but he is fanatically and incorruptibly patriotic. That leaves the chauffeur. When Nayland's in the car, nobody even sees him; he might as well be a robot steering-device. Old case of Father Brown's Invisible Man. So, since he had to be the courier, all I did was have Ahmed Abd-el-Rahman shadow him, and at the same time tap our phones. When he contacted Lowiewski, I knew Lowiewski was our traitor."

Sir Neville Lawton gave a strangling laugh. "Oh, my dear Aunt Fanny! And Nayland goes positively crackers on security. He gets goose pimples every time he hears somebody saying '$E=mc^2$,' for fear a Komintern spy might hear him. It's a wonder he hasn't put the value of Planck's Constant on the classified list. He sets up all these fantastic search rooms and barriers, and then he drives through the gate, honking his bloody horn, with his chauffeur's pockets full of top secrets. Now I've seen everything!"

"Not quite everything," MacLeod said. "Kato's going to put that capsule in another cigarette pack, and he'll send one of his lab girls to Oppenheimer Village with it, with a message from Lowiewski to the effect that he couldn't get away. And when this chauffeur takes it out, he'll run into a Counter Espionage roadblock on the way to town. They'll shoot him, of course, and they'll probably transfer Nayland to the Mississippi Valley Flood Control Project, where he can't do any more damage. At least, we'll have him out of our hair."

"If we have any hair left," Heym ben-Hillel gloomed. "You've got Nayland into trouble, but you haven't got us out of it."

"What do you mean?" Suzanne Maillard demanded. "He's found the traitor and stopped the leak."

"Yes, but we're still responsible, as a team, for this

betrayal," the Israeli pointed out. "This Nayland is only a symptom of the enmity which politicians and militarists feel toward the Free Scientists, and of their opposition to the research-contract system. Now they have scandal to use. Our part in stopping the leak will be ignored; the publicity will be about the treason of a Free Scientist."

"That's right," Sir Neville Lawton agreed. "And that brings up another point. We simply can't hand this fellow over to the authorities. If we do, we establish a precedent that may wreck the whole system under which we operate."

"Yes; it would be a fine thing if governments start putting Free Scientists on trial and shooting them," Farida Khouroglu supported him. "In a few years, none of us would be safe."

"But," Suzanne cried, "you are not arguing that this species of an animal be allowed to betray us unpunished?"

"Look," Rudolf von Heldenfeld said. "Let us give him his pistol, and one cartridge, and let him remove himself like a gentleman. He will spare himself the humiliation of trial and execution, and us all the embarrassment of having a fellow scientist pilloried as a traitor."

"Now there's a typical Prussian suggestion," Lowiewski said.

Kato Sugihara, returning alone, looked around the table. "Did I miss something interesting?" he asked.

"Oh, very," Lowiewski told him. "Your Junker friend thinks I should perform *seppuku*."

Kato nodded quickly. "Excellent idea!" he congratulated von Heldenfeld. "If he does, he'll save everybody a lot of trouble. Himself included." He nodded again. "If he does that, we can protect his reputation, after he's dead."

"I don't really see how," Sir Neville objected. "When the Counter Espionage people were brought into this, the thing went out of our control."

"Why, this chauffeur was the spy, as well as the spy-courier," MacLeod said. "The information he transmitted was picked up piecemeal from different indiscreet lab-workers and students attached to our team. Of course, we are investigating, mumble-mumble. Naturally, no one will admit, mumble-mumble. No stone will be left unturned, mumble-mumble. Disciplinary action, mumble-mumble.''

"And I suppose he got that microfilm piecemeal, too?" Lowiewski asked.

"Oh, that?" MacLeod shrugged. "That was planted on him. One of our girls arranged an opportunity for him to steal it from her, after we began to suspect him. Of course, Kato falsified everything he put into that report. As information, it's worthless.''

"Worthless? It's better than that," Kato grinned. "I'm really sorry the Komintern won't get it. They'd try some of that stuff out with the big betatron at Smolensk, and a microsecond after they'd throw the switch, Smolensk would look worse than Hiroshima did.''

"Well, why would our esteemed colleague commit suicide, just at this time?" Karen Hilquist asked.

"Maybe plutonium poisoning," Farida suggested. "He was doing something in the radiation-lab and got some Pu in him, and of course, shooting's not as painful as that. So—"

"Oh, my dear!" Suzanne protested. "That but stinks! The great Adam Lowiewski, descending from his pinnacle of pure mathematics, to perform a vulgar experiment? With actual *things?*" The Frenchwoman gave an exaggerated shudder. "Horrors!"

"Besides, if our people began getting radioactive, somebody would be sure to claim we were endangering the safety of the whole establishment, and the national-security clause would be invoked, and some nosy person would put a geiger on the dear departed," Sir Neville added.

"Nervous collapse," Karen said. "According to the laity, all scientists are crazy. Crazy people kill themselves. Adam Lowiewski was a scientist. Ergo Adam Lowiewski killed himself. Besides, a nervous collapse isn't instrumentally detectable.''

Heym ben-Hillel looked at MacLeod, his eyes troubled.

"But, Dunc; have we the right to put him to death, either

by his own hand or by an Army firing squad?" he asked. "Remember he is not only a traitor; he is one of the world's greatest mathematical minds. Have we a right to destroy that mind?"

Von Heldenfeld shouted, banging his fist on the table: "I don't care if he's Gauss and Riemann and Lorenz and Poincare and Minkowski and Whitehead and Einstein, all collapsed into one! The man is a stinking traitor, not only to us, but to all scientists and all sciences! If he doesn't shoot himself, hand him over to the United States, and let them shoot him! Why do we go on arguing?"

Lowiewski was smiling, now. The panic that had seized him in the hallway below, and the desperation when the cigarette pack had been opened, had left him.

"Now I have a modest proposal, which will solve your difficulties," he said. "I have money, papers, clothing, everything I will need, outside the reservation. Suppose you just let me leave here. Then, if there is any trouble, you can use this fiction about the indiscreet underlings, without the unnecessary embellishment of my suicide—"

Rudolf von Heldenfeld let out an inarticulate roar of fury. For an instant, he was beyond words. Then he sprang to his feet.

"Look at him!" he cried. "Look at him, laughing in our faces, for the dupes and fools he thinks we are!" He thrust out his hand toward MacLeod. "Give me the pistol! He won't shoot himself; I'll do it for him!"

"It would work, Dunc. Really, it would," Heym ben-Hillel urged.

"No," Karen Hilquist contradicted. "If he left here, everybody would know what had happened, and we'd be accused of protecting him. If he kills himself, we can get things hushed up; dead traitors are good traitors. But if he remains alive, we must disassociate ourselves from him by handing him over."

"And wreck the prestige of the Team?" Lowiewski asked.

"At least you will not live to see that!" Suzanne retorted.

Heym ben-Hillel put his elbows on the table and his head in his hands. "Is there no solution to this?" he almost wailed.

"Certainly; an obvious solution," MacLeod said, rising. "Rudolf has just stated it. Only I'm leader of this Team, and there are, of course, jobs a team-leader simply doesn't delegate." The safety catch of the Beretta clicked a period to his words.

"No!" The word was wrenched almost physically out of Lowiewski. He, too, was on his feet, a sudden desperate fear in his face. "No! You wouldn't murder me!"

"The term is 'execute,' " MacLeod corrected. Then his arm swung up, and he shot Adam Lowiewski through the forehead.

For an instant, the Pole remained on his feet. Then his knees buckled, and he fell forward against the table, sliding to the floor.

MacLeod went around the table, behind Kato Sugihara and Farida Khouroglu and Heym ben-Hillel, and stood looking down at the man he had killed. He dropped the automatic within a few inches of the dead renegade's outstretched hand, then turned to face the others.

"I regret," he addressed them, his voice and face blank of expression, "to announce that our distinguished colleague, Dr. Adam Lowiewski, has committed suicide by shooting, after a nervous collapse resulting from overwork."

Sir Neville Lawton looked critically at the motionless figure on the floor.

"I'm afraid we'll have trouble making that stick, Dunc," he said. "You shot him at about five yards; there isn't a powder mark on him."

"Oh, sorry; I forgot." MacLeod's voice was mockingly contrite. "It was Dr. Lowiewski's expressed wish that his remains be cremated as soon after death as possible, and that funeral services be held over his ashes. The big electric furnace in the metallurgical lab will do, I think."

"But . . . but there'll be all sorts of formalities—" the Englishman protested.

"Now you forget. Our contract," MacLeod reminded him. "We stand upon our contractual immunity; we certainly won't allow any stupid bureaucratic interference with our deceased colleague's wishes. We have a regular M.D. on our payroll, in case anybody has to have a death certificate to keep him happy, but beyond that—" He shrugged.

"It burns me up, though!" Suzanne Maillard cried. "After the spaceship is built, and the Moon is annexed to the Western Union, there will be publicity, and people will eulogize this species of an Iscariot!"

Heym ben-Hillel, who had been staring at MacLeod in shocked disbelief, roused himself.

"Well, why not? Isn't the creator of the Lowiewski function transformations and the rules of inverse probabilities worthy of eulogy?" He turned to MacLeod. "I couldn't have done what you did, but maybe it was for the best. The traitor is dead; the mathematician will live forever."

"You miss the whole point," MacLeod said. "Both of you. It wasn't a question of revenge, like gangsters bumping off a double-crosser. And it wasn't a question of whitewashing Lowiewski for posterity. We are the MacLeod Research Team. We owe no permanent allegiance to, nor acknowledge the authority of, any national sovereignty or any combination of nations. We deal with national governments as with equals. In consequence, we must make and enforce our own laws.

"You must understand that we enjoy this status only on sufferance. The nations of the world tolerate the Free Scientists only because they need us, and because they know they can trust us. Now, no responsible government official is going to be deceived for a moment by this suicide story we've confected. It will be fully understood that Lowiewski was a traitor, and that we found him out and put him to death. And, as a corollary, it will be understood that this Team, as a Team, is fully trustworthy, and that when any individual Team member is found to be untrustworthy, he will be dealt with promptly and without public scandal. In other words, it will be understood, from this time on, that the MacLeod Team is worthy of the status it enjoys and the responsibilities concomitant with it.''

DEAREST

Although he was a lifelong agnostic, there is a great deal of evidence that Piper believed in reincarnation. He certainly wrote a number of stories about life after death. In "Dearest," which appeared in Weird Tales, *he takes this speculation into another realm.*

COLONEL ASHLEY HAMPTON chewed his cigar and forced himself to relax, his glance slowly traveling the room, lingering on the mosaic of book-spines in the tall cases, the sunlight splashed on the faded pastel colors of the carpet, the soft-tinted autumn landscape outside the French windows, the trophies of Indian and Filipino and German weapons on the walls. He could easily feign relaxation here in the library of Greyrock, as long as he looked only at these familiar inanimate things and avoided the five people gathered in the room with him, for all of them were enemies.

There was his nephew, Stephen Hampton, greying at the temples but youthfully dressed in sports-clothes, leaning with obvious if slightly premature proprietorship against the fireplace, a whiskey-and-soda in his hand. There was Myra,

57

Stephen's smart, sophisticated-looking blonde wife, reclining in a chair beside the desk. For these two, he felt an implacable hatred. The others were no less enemies, perhaps more dangerous enemies, but they were only the tools of Stephen and Myra. For instance, T. Barnwell Powell, prim and self-satisfied, sitting on the edge of his chair and clutching the briefcase on his lap as though it were a restless pet which might attempt to escape. He was an honest man, as lawyers went; even ethical. No doubt he had convinced himself that his clients were acting from the noblest and most disinterested motives. And Doctor Alexis Vehrner, with his Vandyke beard and his Viennese accent as phony as a Soviet election, who had preempted the chair at Colonel Hampton's desk. That rankled the old soldier, but Doctor Vehrner would want to assume the position which would give him the appearance of commanding the situation, and he probably felt that Colonel Hampton was no longer the master of Greyrock. The fifth, a Neanderthal type in a white jacket, was Doctor Vehrner's attendant and bodyguard; he could be ignored, an enlisted man who would unthinkingly obey the orders of a superior.

"But you are not cooperating, Colonel Hampton," the psychiatrist complained. "How can I help you if you do not cooperate?"

Colonel Hampton took the cigar from his mouth. His white mustache, tinged a faint nicotine-yellow, twitched angrily.

"Oh; you call it helping me, do you?" he asked acidly.

"But why else am I here?" the doctor parried.

"You're here because my loving nephew and his charming wife can't wait to see me buried in the family cemetery; they want to bury me alive in that private Bedlam of yours," Colonel Hampton replied.

"See!" Myra Hampton turned to the psychiatrist. "We are *persecuting* him! We are all *envious* of him! We are *plotting against* him!"

"Of course; this sullen and suspicious silence is a common paranoid sympton; one often finds such symptoms in cases of senile dementia," Doctor Vehrner agreed.

•   •   •

Colonel Hampton snorted contemptuously. Senile dementia! Well, he must have been senile and demented, to bring this pair of snakes into his home, because he felt an obligation to his dead brother's memory. And he'd willed Greyrock, and his money, and everything, to Stephen. Only Myra couldn't wait till he died; she'd Lady-Macbethed her husband into this insanity accusation.

". . . . however, I must fully satisfy myself, before I can sign the commitment," the psychiatrist was saying. "After all, the patient is a man of advanced age."

Almost eighty, seventy-eight, to be exact. Colonel Hampton could hardly realize that he had been around so long. He had been a little boy, playing soldiers. He had been a young man, breaking the family tradition of Harvard by wangling an appointment to West Point. He had been a new second lieutenant at a little post in Wyoming, in the last dying flicker of the Indian Wars. He had been a first lieutenant, trying to make soldiers of militiamen and hoping for orders to Cuba before the Spaniards gave up. He had been the hard-bitten captain of a hard-bitten company, fighting Moros in the jungles of Mindanao. Then, through the early years of the Twentieth Century, after his father's death, he had been that *rara avis* in the American service, a really wealthy professional officer. He had played polo, and served a turn as military attache at the Paris embassy. He had commanded a regiment in France in 1918, and in the post-war years had rounded out his service in command of a regiment of cavalry, before retiring to Greyrock. Too old for active service, or even a desk at the Pentagon, he had drilled a Home Guard company of 4-F's and boys and paunchy middle-agers through the Second World War. Then he had been an old man, sitting alone in the sunlight . . . until a wonderful thing had happened.

"Get him to tell you about this invisible playmate of his," Stephen suggested. "If that won't satisfy you, I don't know what will."

It had begun a year ago last June. He had been sitting on a bench on the east lawn, watching a kitten playing with a crumpled bit of paper on the walk, circling warily around it as though it were some living prey, stalking cautiously, pouncing and striking the paper ball with a paw and then pursuing it madly. The kitten, whose name was Smokeball, was a friend of his; soon she would tire of her game and jump up beside him to be petted.

Then suddenly, he seemed to hear a girl's voice beside him:

"Oh, what a darling little cat! What's it's name?"

"Smokeball," he said, without thinking. "She's about the color of a shrapnel-burst. . . ." Then he stopped short, looking about. There was nobody in sight, and he realized that the voice had been inside his head rather than in his ear.

"What the devil?" he asked himself. "Am I going nuts?"

There was a happy little laugh inside of him, like bubbles rising in a glass of champagne.

"Oh, no; I'm really here," the voice, inaudible but mentally present, assured him. "You can't see me, or touch me, or even really hear me, but I'm not something you just imagined. I'm just as real as . . . as Smokeball, there. Only I'm a different kind of reality. Watch."

The voice stopped, and something that had seemed to be close to him left him. Immediately, the kitten stopped playing with the crumpled paper and cocked her head to one side, staring fixedly as at something above her. He'd seen cats do that before—stare wide-eyed and entranced, as though at something wonderful which was hidden from human eyes. Then, still looking up and to the side, Smokeball trotted over and jumped onto his lap, but even as he stroked her, she was looking at an invisible something beside him. At the same time, he had a warm and pleasant feeling, as of a happy and affectionate presence near him.

"No," he said, slowly and judicially. "That's not just my imagination. But who—or what—are you?"

"I'm. . . . Oh, I don't know how to think it so that you'll understand." The voice inside his head seemed baffled, like a physicist trying to explain atomic energy to a Hottentot. "I'm not material. If you can imagine a mind that doesn't need a brain to think with. . . . Oh, I can't explain it now! But when I'm talking to you, like this, I'm really thinking inside your brain, along with your own mind, and you hear the words without there being any sound. And you just don't know any words that would express it.''

He had never thought much, one way or another, about spiritualism. There had been old people, when he had been a boy, who had told stories of ghosts and apparitions, with the firmest conviction that they were true. And there had been an Irishman, in his old company in the Philippines, who swore that the ghost of a dead comrade walked post with him when he was on guard.

''Are you a spirit?'' he asked. ''I mean, somebody who once lived in a body, like me?''

''N-no.'' The voice inside him seemed doubtful. ''That is, I don't think so. I know about spirits; they're all around, everywhere. But I don't think I'm one. At least, I've always been like I am now, as long as I can remember. Most spirits don't seem to sense me. I can't reach most living people, either; their minds are closed to me, or they have such disgusting minds I can't bear to touch them. Children are open to me, but when they tell their parents about me, they are laughed at, or punished for lying, and then they close up against me. You're the first grown-up person I've been able to reach for a long time.''

''Probably getting into my second childhood,'' Colonel Hampton grunted.

''Oh, but you mustn't be ashamed of that!'' the invisible entity told him. ''That's the beginning of real wisdom— becoming childlike again. One of your religious teachers said something like that, long ago, and a long time before that, there was a Chinaman whom people called Venerable Child, because his wisdom had turned back again to a child's simplicity.''

''That was Lao Tze,'' Colonel Hampton said, a little surprised. ''Don't tell me you've been around that long.''

''Oh, but I have! Longer than that; oh, for very long.'' And yet the voice he seemed to be hearing was the voice of a young girl. "You don't mind my coming to talk to you?" it continued. "I get so lonely, so dreadfully lonely, you see."

"Urmh! So do I," Colonel Hampton admitted. "I'm probably going bats, but what the hell? It's a nice way to go bats, I'll say that. . . . Stick around, whoever you are, and let's get acquainted. I sort of like you."

A feeling of warmth suffused him, as though he had been hugged by someone young and happy and loving.

"Oh, I'm glad. I like you, too; you're nice!"

"Yes, of course." Doctor Vehrner nodded sagely. "That is a schizoid tendency; the flight from reality into a dream-world peopled by creatures of the imagination. You understand, there is usually a mixture of psychotic conditions, in cases like this. We will say that this case begins with simple senile dementia—physical brain degeneration, a result of advanced age. Then the paranoid symptoms appear; he imagines himself surrounded by envious enemies, who are conspiring against him. The patient then withdraws into himself, and in his self-imposed isolation, he conjures up imaginary companionship. I have no doubt. . . ."

In the beginning, he had suspected that this unseen visitor was no more than a figment of his own lonely imagination, but as the days passed, this suspicion vanished. Whatever this entity might be, an entity it was, entirely distinct from his own conscious or subconscious mind.

At first she—he had early come to think of the being as feminine—had seemed timid, fearful lest her intrusions into his mind prove a nuisance. It took some time for him to assure her that she was always welcome. With time, too, his impression of her grew stronger and more concrete. He found that he was able to visualize her, as he might visualize something remembered, or conceived of in imagination—a lovely young girl, slender and clothed in something loose and filmy, with flowers in her honey-colored hair, and clear blue eyes, a pert, cheerful face, a wide, smiling mouth and an impudently up-tilted nose. He realized that this image was merely a sort of allegorical representation, his own private object-abstraction from a reality which his senses could never picture as it existed.

It was about this time that he had begun to call her Dearest. She had given him no name, and seemed quite satisfied with that one.

"I've been thinking," she said, "I ought to have a name for you, too. Do you mind if I call you Popsy?"

"Huh?" He had been really startled at that. If he needed any further proof of Dearest's independent existence, that was it. Never, in the uttermost depths of his subconscious, would he have been likely to label himself Popsy. "Know what they used to call me in the Army?" he asked. "Slaughterhouse Hampton. They claimed I needed a truck-load of sawdust to follow me around and cover up the blood." He chuckled. "Nobody but you would think of calling me Popsy."

There was a price, he found, that he must pay for Dearest's companionship—the price of eternal vigilance. He found that he was acquiring the habit of opening doors and then need-lessly standing aside to allow her to precede him. And, although she insisted that he need not speak aloud to her, that she could understand any thought which he directed to her, he could not help actually pronouncing the words, if only in a faint whisper. He was glad that he had learned, before the end of his plebe year at West Point, to speak without moving his lips.

Besides himself and the kitten, Smokeball, there was one other at Greyrock who was aware, if only faintly, of Dear-est's presence. That was old Sergeant Williamson, the Col-onel's servant, a retired first sergeant from the regiment he had last commanded. With increasing frequency, he would notice the old man pause in his work, as though trying to identify something too subtle for his senses, and then shake his head in bewilderment.

One afternoon in early October—just about a year ago—he had been reclining in a chair on the west veranda, smoking a cigar and trying to re-create, for his companion, a mental picture of an Indian camp as he had seen it in Wyoming in the middle '90's, when Sergeant Williamson came out from the house, carrying a pair of the Colonel's field-boots and a polishing kit. Unaware of the Colonel's presence, he set down his burden, squatted on the floor and began polishing the boots, humming softly to himself. Then he must have caught a whiff of the Colonel's cigar. Raising his head, he saw the Colonel, and made as though to pick up the boots and polishing equipment.

"Oh, that's all right, Sergeant," the Colonel told him. "Carry on with what you're doing. There's room enough for both of us here."

The old ex-sergeant resumed his soft humming, keeping time with the brush in his hand.

"You know, Popsy, I think he knows I'm here," Dearest said. "Nothing definite, of course; he just feels there's something here that he can't see."

"I wonder. I've noticed something like that. He doesn't seem to mind, either. I'm going to ask him." He raised his voice. "Sergeant, do you seem to notice anything peculiar around here, lately?"

The repetitious little two-tone melody broke off short. The soldier-servant lifted his face and looked into the Colonel's. His brow wrinkled, as though he were trying to express a thought for which he had no words.

"You noticed it too, sir?" he asked. "Why, yessuh, Cunnel; Ah don't know how to say it, but it's like . . . like a kinda . . . a *blessedness*." He chuckled. "That's it, Cunnel; a blessedness. I'm getting r'lígion, *now?*"

"Well, all this is very interesting, I'm sure, Doctor," T. Barnwell Powell was saying, polishing his glasses on a piece of tissue and keeping one elbow on his briefcase at the same time. "But really, it's not getting us anywhere, so to say. You know, we must have that commitment signed by you. Now, is it or is it not your opinion that this man is of unsound mind?"

"Have patience, Mr. Powell. You must admit that as long as this gentleman refuses to talk, I cannot be said to have interviewed him."

"What if he won't talk?" Stephen Hampton burst out. "We've told you about his behavior; how he sits for hours mumbling to this imaginary person he thinks is with him, and how he always steps aside when he opens a door, to let somebody who isn't there go through ahead of him, and how . . . Oh, hell, what's the use? If he were in his right mind, he'd speak up and try to prove it, wouldn't he? What do you say, Myra?''

Myra was silent, and Colonel Hampton found himself watching her with interest. Her mouth had twisted into a wry grimace, and she was clutching the arms of her chair until her knuckles whitened. She seemed to be in some intense pain. Colonel Hampton hoped she were; preferably with something slightly fatal.

Sergeant Williamson's suspicion that he might be getting religion became a reality, for a time, that winter, after The Miracle.

It had been a blustery day in mid-January, with a high wind driving swirls of snow across the fields, and Colonel Hampton, fretting indoors for several days, decided to go out and fill his lungs with fresh air. Bundled warmly, swinging his black-thorn cane, he had set out, accompanied by Dearest, to tramp cross-country to the village, three miles from Grey-rock. They had enjoyed the walk through the white, wind-swept desolation, the old man and his invisible companion, until the accident had happened.

A sheet of glassy ice had lain treacherously hidden under a drift of snow; when he stepped upon it, his feet shot from under him, the stick flew from his hand, and he went down. When he tried to rise, he found that he could not. Dearest had been almost frantic.

''Oh, Popsy, you must get up!'' she cried. ''You'll freeze if you don't. Come on, Popsy; try again!''

He tried, in vain. His old body would not obey his will.

''It's no use, Dearest; I can't. Maybe it's just as well,'' he said. ''Freezing's an easy death, and you say people live on as spirits, after they die. Maybe we can always be together, now.''

''I don't know. I don't want you to die yet, Popsy. I never

was able to get through to a spirit, and I'm afraid. . . .
Wait! Can you crawl a little? Enough to get over there under
those young pines?''

''I think so.'' His left leg was numb, and he believed that it
was broken. ''I can try.''

He managed to roll onto his back, with his head toward the
clump of pine seedlings. Using both hands and his right heel,
he was able to propel himself slowly through the snow until
he was out of the worst of the wind.

''That's good; now try to cover yourself,'' Dearest advised. ''Put your hands in your coat pockets. And wait here;
I'll try to get help.''

Then she left him. For what seemed a long time, he lay
motionless in the scant protection of the young pines, suffering miserably. He began to grow drowsy. As soon as he
realized what was happening, he was frightened, and the
fright pulled him awake again. Soon he felt himself drowsing
again. By shifting his position, he caused a jab of pain from
his broken leg, which brought him back to wakefulness.
Then the deadly drowsiness returned.

This time, he was wakened by a sharp voice, mingled with a
throbbing sound that seemed part of a dream of the cannonad-
ing in the Argonne.

It was, he realized, Sergeant Williamson's voice. ''Gittin'
soft in de haid, am I?''

He turned his face, to see the battered jeep from Greyrock,
driven by Arthur, the stableman and gardener, with Sergeant
Williamson beside him. The old man jumped to the ground
and ran toward him. At the same time, he felt Dearest with
him again.

''We made it, Popsy! We made it!'' she was exulting. ''I
was afraid I'd never make him understand, but I did. And you
should have seen him bully that other man into driving the
jeep. Are you all right, Popsy?''

''You all right, Cunnel?'' Sergeant Williamson was asking.

''My leg's broken, I think, but outside of that I'm all

right,'' he answered both of them. "How did you happen to find me, Sergeant?"

The old soldier rolled his eyes upward. He replied, solemnly, "An angel appeared unto me." He shook his head slowly. "I'm a sinful man, Cunnel; I couldn't see the angel face to face, but the glory was before me, and guided me.''

They used his cane and a broken-off bough to splint the leg; they wrapped him in a horse-blanket and hauled him back to Greyrock and put him to bed, with Dearest clinging solicitously to him. The fractured leg knit slowly, though the physician was amazed at the speed with which, considering his age, he made recovery, and with his unfailing cheerfulness. He did not know, of course, that he was being assisted by an invisible nurse. For all that, however, the leaves on the oaks around Greyrock were green again before Colonel Hampton could leave his bed and hobble about the house on a cane.

Arthur, the young man who had driven the jeep, had become one of the most solid pillars of the little church beyond the village, as a result. Sergeant Williamson had also become an attendant at church for a while, and then stopped. Without being able to define, or spell, or even pronounce the term, Sergeant Williamson was a strict pragmatist. And Sergeant Williamson could not find the blessedness at the church. Instead, it seemed to center about the room where his employer and former regiment commander lay. Be that as it may, he could always find the blessedness in Colonel Hampton's room, and sometimes, when the Colonel was asleep, the blessedness would follow him out and linger with him for a while.

Colonel Hampton wondered, anxiously, where Dearest was, now. He had not felt her presence since his nephew had brought his lawyer and the psychiatrist into the house. He wondered if she had voluntarily separated herself from him for fear he might give her some sign of recognition that these harpies would fasten upon as an evidence of unsound mind. He could not believe that she had deserted him entirely, now when he needed her most. . . .

"Well, what can I do?" Doctor Vehrner was complaining. "You bring me here to interview him, and he just sits there and does nothing. . . . Will you consent to my giving him an injection of sodium pentathol?"

"Well, I don't know, now," T. Barnwell Powell objected. "I've heard of that drug—one of the so-called 'truth-serum' drugs. I doubt if testimony taken under its influence would be admissible in a court. . . ."

"This is not a court, Mr. Powell," the doctor explained patiently. "And I am not taking testimony; I am making a diagnosis. Pentathol is a recognized diagnostic agent."

"Go ahead," Stephen Hampton said. "Anything to get this over with. . . . You agree, Myra?"

Myra said nothing. She simply sat, with staring eyes, and clutched the arms of her chair as though to keep from slipping into some dreadful abyss. Once a low moan escaped from her lips.

"My wife is naturally overwrought by this painful business," Stephen said. "I trust that you gentlemen will excuse her. . . . Hadn't you better go and lie down somewhere, Myra?"

She shook her head violently, moaning again. Both the doctor and the attorney were looking at her curiously.

"Well, I object to being drugged," Colonel Hampton said, rising. "And what's more, I won't submit to it."

"Albert!" Doctor Vehrner said sharply, nodding toward the Colonel. The pithecanthropoid attendant in the white jacket hastened forward, pinned his arms behind him and dragged him down into the chair. For an instant, the old man tried to resist; then, realizing the futility and undignity of struggling, subsided. The psychiatrist had taken a leather case from his pocket and was selecting a hypodermic needle.

Then Myra Hampton leaped to her feet, her face working hideously.

"No! Stop! Stop!" she cried.

Everybody looked at her in surprise, Colonel Hampton no less than the others. Stephen Hampton called out her name sharply.

"No! You shan't do this to me! You shan't! You're torturing me! You are all devils!" she screamed. "Devils! *Devils!*"

"Myra!" her husband barked, stepping forward.

With a twist, she eluded him, dashing around the desk and pulling open a drawer. For an instant, she fumbled inside it, and when she brought her hand up, she had Colonel Hampton's .45 automatic in it. She drew back the slide and released it, loading the chamber.

Doctor Vehrner, the hypodermic in his hand, turned. Stephen Hampton sprang at her, dropping his drink. And Albert, the prognathous attendant, released Colonel Hampton and leaped at the woman with the pistol, with the unthinking promptness of a dog whose master is in danger.

Stephen Hampton was the closest to her; she shot him first, point-blank in the chest. The heavy bullet knocked him backward against a small table; he and it fell over together. While he was falling, the woman turned, dipped the muzzle of her pistol slightly and fired again; Doctor Vehrner's leg gave way under him and he went down, the hypodermic flying from his hand and landing at Colonel Hampton's feet. At the same time, Albert was almost upon her. Quickly, she reversed the heavy Colt, pressed the muzzle against her heart, and fired a third shot.

T. Barnwell Powell had let the briefcase slip to the floor; he was staring, slack-jawed, at the tableau of violence which had been enacted before him. The attendant, having reached Myra, was looking down at her stupidly. Then he stooped, and straightened.

"She's dead!" he said, unbelievingly.

Colonel Hampton rose, putting his heel on the hypodermic and crushing it.

"Of course she's dead!" he barked. "You have any first-aid training? Then look after these other people. Doctor Vehrner first; the other man's unconscious; he'll wait."

"No; look after the other man first," Doctor Vehrner said.

Albert gaped back and forth between them.

"Goddammit, you heard me!" Colonel Hampton roared. It was Slaughterhouse Hampton, whose service-ribbons started with the Indian campaigns, speaking; an officer who never for an instant imagined that his orders would not be obeyed. "Get a tourniquet on that man's leg, you!" He moderated his voice and manner about half a degree and spoke to Vehrner. "You are not the doctor, you're the patient, now. You'll do as you're told. Don't you know that a man shot in the leg with a .45 can bleed to death without half trying?"

"Do like the Cunnel says," Williamson said, entering the room. "Git a move on."

He stood just inside the doorway, holding a silver-banded malacca walking-stick that he had taken from the hall-stand. He was grasping it in his left hand, below the band, with the crook out, holding it at his side as though it were a sword in a scabbard, which was exactly what that walking-stick was. Albert looked at him, and then back at Colonel Hampton. Then, whipping off his necktie, he went down on his knees beside Doctor Vehrner, skillfully applying the improvised tourniquet, twisting it tight with an eighteen-inch ruler the Colonel took from the desk and handed to him.

"Go get the first-aid kit, Sergeant," the Colonel said. "And hurry. Mr. Stephen's been shot, too."

"Yessir!" Sergeant Williamson executed an automatic salute and about-face and raced from the room. The Colonel picked up the telephone on the desk.

The County Hospital was three miles from Greyrock; the State Police substation a good five. He dialed the State Police number first.

"Sergeant Mallard? Colonel Hampton, at Greyrock. We've had a little trouble here. My nephew's wife just went *juramentado* with one of my pistols, shot and wounded her husband and another man, and then shot and killed herself. . . . Yes, indeed it is, Sergeant. I wish you'd send somebody over here, as soon as possible, to take charge. . . . Oh, you will? That's good . . . No, it's all over, and nobody to arrest; just the formalities. . . . Well, thank you, Sergeant."

The old cavalryman re-entered the room, without the sword-cane and carrying a heavy leather box on a strap over his shoulder. He set this on the floor and opened it, then knelt beside Stephen Hampton. The Colonel was calling the hospital.

". . . gunshot wounds," he was saying. "One man in the chest and the other in the leg, both with a .45 pistol. And you'd better send a doctor who's qualified to write a death certificate; there was a woman killed, too. . . . Yes, certainly; the State Police have been notified."

"This isn't so bad, Cunnel," Sergeant Williamson raised his head to say. "I've seen men worse off marked 'Duty' inside a month."

Colonel Hampton nodded. "Well, get him fixed up as best you can, till the ambulance gets here. And there's whiskey and glasses on that table, over there. Better give Doctor Vehrner a drink." He looked at T. Barnwell Powell, still frozen to his chair, aghast at the carnage around him. "Give Mr. Powell a drink, too."

Colonel Hampton could have used a drink, too; the library looked like beef-day at an Indian agency. But he was still Slaughterhouse Hampton, and consequently could not afford to exhibit queasiness.

It was then, for the first time since the business had started that he felt the presence of Dearest.

"Oh, Popsy, are you all right?" the voice inside his head was asking. "It's all over, now; you won't have anything to worry about, anymore. But, oh, I was afraid I wouldn't be able to do it!"

"My God, Dearest!" He almost spoke aloud. "Did you make her do that?"

"Popsy!" The voice in his mind was grief-stricken. "You. . . . You're afraid of me! Never be afraid of Dearest, Popsy! And don't hate me for this. It was the only thing I could do. If he'd given you that injection, he could have made you tell him all about us, and then he'd have been sure you were crazy, and they'd have taken you away. And they treat people dreadfully at that place of his. You'd have been driven really crazy before long, and then your mind would have been closed to me, so that I wouldn't have been able to get through to you, any more. What I did was the only thing I could do.''

''I don't hate you, Dearest,'' he replied, mentally. ''And I don't blame you. It was a little disconcerting, though, to discover the extent of your capabilities. . . . How did you manage it?''

''You remember how I made the Sergeant see an angel, the time you were down in the snow?'' Colonel Hampton nodded. ''Well, I made her see . . . things that weren't angels,'' Dearest continued. ''After I'd driven her almost to distraction, I was able to get into her mind and take control of her.'' Colonel Hampton felt a shudder inside of him. ''That was horrible; that woman had a mind like a sewer; I still feel dirty from it! But I made her get the pistol—I knew where you kept it—and I knew how to use it, even if she didn't. Remember when we went shooting that time, along the river?''

''Uhuh. I wondered how she knew enough to unlock the action and load the chamber.'' He turned and faced the others.

Doctor Vehrner was sitting on the floor, with his back to the chair Colonel Hampton had occupied, his injured leg stretched out in front of him. Albert was hovering over him with mother-hen solicitude. T. Barnwell Powell was finishing his whiskey and recovering a fraction of his normal poise.

''Well, I suppose you gentlemen see, now, who was really crazy around here?'' Colonel Hampton addressed them bitingly. ''That woman has been dangerously close to the borderline of sanity for as long as she's been here. I think my precious nephew trumped up this ridiculous insanity complaint against me as much to discredit any testimony I might ever give about his wife's mental condition as to get control of my estate. I also suppose that the tension she was under here, this afternoon, was too much for her, and the scheme

boomeranged on its originators. Curious case of poetic jus-
tice, but I'm sorry you had to be included in it, Doctor.''

"Attaboy, Popsy!" Dearest enthused. "Now you have
them on the run; don't give them a chance to re-form. You
know what Patton always said—Grab 'em by the nose and
kick 'em in the pants.''

Colonel Hampton re-lighted his cigar. "Patton only said
'pants' when he was talking for publication," he told her,
sotto voce. Then he noticed the unsigned commitment paper
lying on the desk. He picked it up, crumpled it, and threw it
into the fire.

"I don't think you'll be needing that," he said. "You
know, this isn't the first time my loving nephew has expressed doubts as to my sanity.'' He sat down in the chair at
the desk, motioning to his servant to bring him a drink. "And
see to the other gentlemen's glasses, Sergeant," he directed.
"Back in 1929, Stephen thought I was crazy as a bedbug to
sell all my securities and take a paper loss, around the first of
September. After October 24th, I bought them back at about
twenty per cent of what I'd sold them for, after he'd lost his
shirt.'' That, he knew, would have an effect on T. Barnwell
Powell. "And in December, 1944, I was just plain nuts,
selling all my munition shares and investing in a company
that manufactured baby food. Stephen thought that
Rundstedt's Ardennes counter-offensive would put off the
end of the war for another year and a half!''

"Baby food, eh?" Doctor Vehrner chuckled.

Colonel Hampton sipped his whiskey slowly, then puffed
on his cigar. "No, this pair were competent liars," he replied. "A good workmanlike liar never makes up a story out
of the whole cloth; he always takes a fabric of truth and
embroiders it to suit the situation.'' He smiled grimly; that
was an accurate description of his own tactical procedure at
the moment. "I hadn't intended this to come out, Doctor, but
it happens that I am a convinced believer in spiritualism. I
suppose you'll think that's a delusional belief, too?''

"Well. . . ." Doctor Vehrner pursed his lips. "I reject

the idea of survival after death, myself, but I think that people who believe in such a theory are merely misevaluating evidence. It is definitely not, in itself, a symptom of a psychotic condition.''

''Thank you, Doctor.'' The Colonel gestured with his cigar. ''Now, I'll admit their statements about my appearing to be in conversation with some invisible or imaginary being. That's all quite true. I'm convinced that I'm in direct-voice communication with the spirit of a young girl who was killed by Indians in this section about a hundred and seventy-five years ago. At first, she communicated by automatic writing; later we established direct-voice communication. Well, naturally, a man in my position would dislike the label of spirit-medium; there are too many invidious associations connected with the term. But there it is. I trust both of you gentlemen will remember the ethics of your respective professions and keep this confidential.''

''Oh, brother!'' Dearest was fairly hugging him with delight. ''When bigger and better lies are told, we tell them, don't we, Popsy?''

''Yes, and try and prove otherwise,'' Colonel Hampton replied, around his cigar. Then he blew a jet of smoke and spoke to the men in front of him.

''I intend paying for my nephew's hospitalization, and for his wife's funeral,'' he said. ''And then, I'm going to pack up all his personal belongings, and all of hers; when he's discharged from the hospital, I'll ship them wherever he wants them. But he won't be allowed to come back here. After this business, I'm through with him.''

T. Barnwell Powell nodded primly. ''I don't blame you, in the least, Colonel,'' he said. ''I think you have been abominably treated, and your attitude is most generous.'' He was about to say something else, when the doorbell tinkled and Sergeant Williamson went out into the hall. ''Oh, dear; I suppose that's the police, now,'' the lawyer said. He grimaced like a small boy in a dentist's chair.

Colonel Hampton felt Dearest leave him for a moment. Then she was back.

"The ambulance." Then he caught a sparkle of mischief in her mood. "Let's have some fun, Popsy! The doctor is a young man, with brown hair and a mustache, horn-rimmed glasses, a blue tie and a tan-leather bag. One of the ambulance men has red hair, and the other has a Mercurochrome stain on his left sleeve. Tell them your spirit-guide told you."

The old soldier's tobacco-yellowed mustache twitched with amusement.

"No, gentlemen, it is the ambulance," he corrected.. "My spirit-control says. . . ." He relayed Dearest's descriptions to them.

T. Barnwell Powell blinked. A speculative look came into the psychiatrist's eyes; he was probably wishing the commitment paper hadn't been destroyed.

Then the doctor came bustling in, brown-mustached, blue-tied, spectacled, carrying a tan bag, and behind him followed the two ambulance men, one with a thatch of flaming red hair and the other with a stain of Mercurochrome on his jacket-sleeve.

For an instant, the lawyer and the psychiatrist gaped at them. Then T. Barnwell Powell put one hand to his mouth and made a small gibbering sound, and Doctor Vehrner gave a faint squawk, and then both men grabbed, simultaneously, for the whiskey bottle.

The laughter of Dearest tinkled inaudibly through the rumbling mirth of Colonel Hampton.

HUNTER PATROL

By H. BEAM PIPER and JOHN J. McGUIRE

*From his works and letters we know that H. Beam Piper
was no utopian and had little faith in the permanence of any
form of human government. If he had any preference, it was
for monarchies in which the rulers had some investment in
the future (the continuance of their line, if nothing else) and
were able to diminish the influence of fools and bunglers, but
he always realized that nothing guaranteed that any single
monarch might not turn out to be a fool!*

*Yet, in "Hunter Patrol," written with John J. McGuire,
Piper does set forth his own version of the utopia that might
be created by one of his self-reliant men. But, as you might
expect, all is not well in this future-world of peace and
tranquility. As the Principle of Perversity would lead one to
predict, this utopia harbors a group of revolutionaries who
go fishing in the past for a needed ingredient in their scheme,
and come up with a fish much bigger than they had bargained
on . . .*

At the crest of the ridge, Benson stopped for an instant,
glancing first at his wristwatch and then back over his shoulder. It was 0539; the barrage was due in eleven minutes, at

the spot where he was now standing. Behind, on the long northeast slope, he could see the columns of black oil smoke rising from what had been the Pan-Soviet advance supply dump. There was a great deal of firing going on, back there; he wondered if the Commies had managed to corner a few of his men, after the patrol had accomplished its mission and scattered, or if a couple of Communist units were shooting each other up in mutual mistaken identity. The result would be about the same in either case—reserve units would be disorganized, and some men would have been pulled back from the front line. His dozen-odd UN regulars and Turkish partisans had done their best to simulate a paratroop attack in force. At least, his job was done; now to execute that classic infantry maneuver described as, "Let's get the hell outa here." This was his last patrol before rotation home. He didn't want anything unfortunate to happen.

There was a little ravine to the left; the stream which had cut it in the steep southern slope of the ridge would be dry at this time of year, and he could make better time, and find protection in it from any chance shots when the interdictory barrage started. He hurried toward it and followed it down to the valley that would lead toward the front—the thinly-held section of the Communist lines, and the UN lines beyond, where fresh troops were waiting to jump from their holes and begin the attack.

There was something wrong about this ravine, though. At first, it was only a vague presentiment, growing stronger as he followed the dry gully down to the valley below. Something he had smelled, or heard, or seen, without conscious recognition. Then, in the dry sand where the ravine debouched into the valley, he saw faint tank-tracks—only one pair. There was something wrong about the vines that mantled one side of the ravine, too . . .

An instant later, he was diving to the right, breaking his fall with the butt of his auto-carbine, rolling rapidly toward the cover of a rock, and as he did so, the thinking part of his mind recognized what was wrong. The tank-tracks had ended against the vine-grown side of the ravine, what he had smelled had been lubricating oil and petrol, and the leaves on some of the vines hung upside down.

Almost at once, from behind the vines, a tank's machine guns snarled at him, clipping the place where he had been standing, then shifting to rage against the sheltering rock. With a sudden motor-roar, the muzzle of a long tank-gun pushed out through the vines, and then the low body of a tank with a red star on the turret came rumbling out of the camouflaged bay. The machine guns kept him pinned behind the rock; the tank swerved ever so slightly so that its wide left tread was aimed directly at him, then picked up speed. Aren't even going to waste a shell on me, he thought.

Futilely, he let go a clip from his carbine, trying to hit one of the vision-slits; then rolled to one side, dropped out the clip, slapped in another. There was a shimmering blue mist around him. If he only hadn't used his last grenade, back there at the supply-dump . . .

The strange blue mist became a flickering radiance that ran through all the colors of the spectrum and became an utter, impenetrable blackness . . .

There were voices in the blackness, and a softness under him, but under his back, when he had been lying on his stomach, as though he were now on a comfortable bed. They got me alive, he thought; now comes the brainwashing!

He cracked one eye open imperceptibly. Lights, white and glaring, from a ceiling far above; walls as white as the lights. Without moving his head, he opened both eyes and shifted them from right to left. Vaguely, he could see people and, behind them, machines so simply designed that their functions were unguessable. He sat up and looked around groggily. The people, their costumes—definitely not Pan-Soviet uniforms—and the room and its machines, told him nothing. The hardness under his right hip was a welcome surprise; they hadn't taken his pistol from him! Feigning even more puzzlement and weakness, he clutched his knees with his elbows and leaned his head forward on them, trying to collect his thoughts.

"We shall have to give up, Gregory," a voice trembled with disappointment.

"Why, Anthony?" The new voice was deeper, more aggressive.

"Look. Another typical reaction; retreat to the foetus."

Footsteps approached. Another voice, discouragement heavily weighting each syllable: "You're right. He's like all the others. We'll have to send him back."

"And look for no more?" The voice he recognized as Anthony faltered between question and statement.

A babel of voices, in dispute; then, clearly, the voice Benson had come to label as Gregory cut in:

"I will never give up!"

He raised his head; there was something in the timbre of that voice reminding him of his own feelings in the dark days when the allies had everywhere been reeling back under the Pan-Soviet hammer-blows.

"Anthony!" Gregory's voice again; Benson saw the speaker; short, stocky, gray-haired, stubborn lines about the mouth. The face of a man chasing an illusive but not uncapturable dream.

"That means nothing." A tall thin man, too lean for the tunic-like garment he wore, was shaking his head.

Deliberately, trying to remember his college courses in psychology, he forced himself to accept, and to assess, what he saw as reality. He was on a small table, like an operating table; the whole place looked like a medical lab or a clinic. He was still in uniform; his boots had soiled the white sheets with the dust of Armenia. He had all his equipment, including his pistol and combat-knife; his carbine was gone, however. He could feel the weight of his helmet on his head. The room still rocked and swayed a little, but the faces of the people were coming into focus.

He counted them, saying each number to himself: one, two, three, four, five men; one woman. He swung his feet over the edge of the table, being careful that it would be between him and the others when he rose, and began inching his right hand toward his right hip, using his left hand, on his brow, to misdirect attention.

"I would classify his actions as arising from conscious effort at cortico-thalamic integration," the woman said, like an archaeologist who has just found a K-ration tin at the bottom of a neolithic kitchen-midden. She had the peculiarly young-old look of the spinster teachers with whom Benson had worked before going to the war.

"I want to believe it, but I'm afraid to," another man for whom Benson had no name-association said. He was portly, gray-haired, arrogant-faced; he wore a short black jacket with a jewelled zipper-pull, and striped trousers.

Benson cleared his throat. "Just who are you people?" he inquired. "And just where am I?"

Anthony grabbed Gregory's hand and pumped it frantically.

"I've dreamed of the day when I could say this!" he cried. "Congratulations, Gregory!"

That touched off another bedlam, of joy, this time, instead of despair. Benson hid his amusement at the facility with which all of them were discovering in one another the courage, vision and stamina of true patriots and pioneers. He let it go on for a few moments, hoping to glean some clue. Finally, he interrupted.

"I believe I asked a couple of questions," he said, using the voice he reserved for sergeants and second lieutenants. "I hate to break up this mutual admiration session, but I would appreciate some answers. This isn't anything like the situation I last remember . . ."

"He remembers!" Gregory exclaimed. "That confirms your first derivation by symbolic logic, and it strengthens the validity of the second . . ."

The schoolteacherish woman began jabbering excitedly; she ran through about a paragraph of what was pure gobbledegook to Benson, before the man with the arrogant face and the jewelled zipper-pull broke in on her.

"Save that for later, Paula," he barked. "I'd be very much

interested in your theories about why memories are unimpaired when you time-jump forward and lost when you reverse the process, but let's stick to business. We have what we wanted; now let's use what we have."

"I never liked the way you made your money," a dark-faced, cadaverous man said, "but when you talk, it makes sense. Let's get on with it."

Benson used the brief silence which followed to study the six. With the exception of the two who had just spoken, there was the indefinable mark of the fanatic upon all of them—people fanatical about different things, united for different reasons in a single purpose. It reminded him sharply of some teachers' committee about to beard a school-board with an unpopular and expensive recommendation.

Anthony—the oldest of the lot, in a knee-length tunic—turned to Gregory.

"I believe you had better . . ." he began.

"As to who we are, we'll explain that, partially, later. As for your question, 'Where am I?' that will have to be rephrased. If you ask, 'When and where am I?' I can furnish a rational answer. In the temporal dimension, you are fifty years futureward of the day of your death; spatially, you are about eight thousand miles from the place of your death, in what is now the World Capital, St. Louis."

Nothing in the answer made sense but the name of the city. Benson chuckled.

"What happened; the Cardinals conquer the world? I knew they had a good team, but I didn't think it was that good."

"No, no," Gregory told him earnestly. "The government isn't a theocracy. At least not yet. But if The Guide keeps on insisting that only beautiful things are good and that he is uniquely qualified to define beauty, watch his rule change into just that."

"I've been detecting symptoms of religious paranoia, messianic delusions, about his public statements . . ." the woman began.

"Idolatry!" another member of the group, who wore a

black coat fastened to the neck, and white neck-bands, rasped. "Idolatry in deed, as well as in spirit!"

The sense of unreality, partially dispelled, began to return. Benson dropped to the floor and stood beside the table, getting a cigarette out of his pocket and lighting it.

"I made a joke," he said, putting his lighter away. "The fact that none of you got it has done more to prove that I am fifty years in the future than anything any of you could say." He went on to explain who the St. Louis Cardinals were.

"Yes; I remember! Baseball!" Anthony exclaimed. "There is no baseball, now. The Guide will not allow competitive sports; he says that they foster the spirit of violence . . ."

The cadaverous man in the blue jacket turned to the man in the black garment of similar cut.

"You probably know more history than any of us," he said, getting a cigar out of his pocket and lighting it. He lighted it by rubbing the end on the sole of his shoe. "Suppose you tell him what the score is." He turned to Benson. "You can rely on his dates and happenings; his interpretation's strictly capitalist, of course," he said.

Black-jacket shook his head. "You first, Gregory," he said. "Tell him how he got here, and then I'll tell him why."

"I believe," Gregory began, "that in your period, fiction writers made some use of the subject of time-travel. It was not, however, given serious consideration, largely because of certain alleged paradoxes involved, and because of an elementalistic and objectifying attitude toward the whole subject of time. I won't go into the mathematics and symbolic logic involved, but we have disposed of the objections; more, we have succeeded in constructing a time-machine, if you want to call it that. We prefer to call it a temporal-spatial displacement field generator."

"It's really very simple," the woman called Paula interrupted. "If the universe is expanding, time is a widening spiral; if contracting, a diminishing spiral; if static, a uniform spiral. The possibility of pulsation was our only worry . . .''

"That's no worry," Gregory reproved her. "I showed you that the rate was too slow to have an effect on . . .''

"Oh, nonsense; you can measure something which exists within a microsecond, but where is the instrument to measure a temporal pulsation that may require years . . . ? You haven't come to that yet.''

"Be quiet, both of you!'' the man with the black coat and the white bands commanded. "While you argue about vanities, thousands are being converted to the godlessness of The Guide, and other thousands of his dupes are dying, unprepared to face their Maker!''

"All right, you invented a time-machine," Benson said. "In civvies, I was only a high school chemistry teacher. I can tell a class of juniors the difference between H_2O and H_2SO_4, but the theory of time-travel is wasted on me . . . Suppose you just let me ask the questions; then I'll be sure of finding out what I don't know. For instance, who won the war I was fighting in, before you grabbed me and brought me here? The Commies?''

"No, the United Nations," Anthony told him. "At least, they were the least exhausted when both sides decided to quit.''

"Then what's this dictatorship . . . The Guide? Extreme Rightist?''

"Walter, you'd better tell him," Gregory said.

"We damn near lost the war," the man in the black jacket and striped trousers said, "but for once, we won the peace. The Soviet Bloc was broken up—all the Satellite States. Most of them turned into little dictatorships, like the Latin American countries after the liberation from Spain, but they were personal, non-ideological, generally benevolent, dictatorships, the kind that can grow into democracies, if they're given time.''

"Capitalistic dictatorships, he means," the cadaverous man in the blue jacket explained.

"Be quiet, Carl," Anthony told him. "Let's not confuse

this with any class-struggle stuff.''

"Actually, the United Nations rules the world," Walter continued. "What goes on in the Ukraine or Latvia or Manchuria is about analogous to what went on under the old United States government in, let's say, Tammany-ruled New York. But here's the catch. The UN is ruled absolutely by one man.''

"How could that happen? In my time, the UN had its functions so subdivided and compartmented that it couldn't even run a war properly. Our army commanders were making war by systematic disobedience.''

"The character was changed shortly after . . . er, that is, after . . .'' Walter was fumbling for words.

"After my death," Benson finished politely. "Go on. Even with a changed character, how did one man get all the powers into his hands?''

"By sorcery!" black-coat-and-white-bands fairly shouted. "By the help of his master, Satan!''

"You know, there are times when some such theory tempts me," Paula said.

"He was a big moneybags," Carl said. "He bribed his way in. See, New York was bombed flat. Where the old UN buildings were, it's still hot. So The Guide donated a big tract of land outside St. Louis, built these buildings—we're in the basement of one of them, right now, if you want a good laugh—and before long, he had the whole organization eating out of his hand. They just voted him into power, and the world into slavery.''

Benson looked around at the others, who were nodding in varying degrees of agreement.

"Substantially, that's it. He managed to convince everybody of his altruism, integrity and wisdom," Walter said. "It was almost blasphemous to say anything against him. I really don't understand how it happened . . .''

"Well, what's he been doing with his power?" Benson asked. "Wise things, or stupid ones?''

"I could be general, and say that he has deprived all of us of our political and other liberties. It is best to be specific,''

Anthony said. "Gregory?"

"My own field—dimensional physics—hasn't been interfered with much, yet. It's different in other fields. For instance, all research in sonics has been arbitrarily stopped. So has a great deal of work in organic and synthetic chemistry. Psychology is a madhouse of . . . what was the old word, licentiousness? No, Lysenkoism. Medicine and surgery—well, there's a huge program of compulsory sterilization, and another one of eugenic marriage-control. And infants who don't conform to certain physical standards don't survive. Neither do people who have disfiguring accidents beyond the power of plastic surgery."

Paula spoke next. "My field is child welfare. Well, I'm going to show you an audio-visual of an interesting ceremony in a Hindu village, derived from the ancient custom of the suttee. It is the Hindu method of conforming to The Guide's demand that only beautiful children be allowed to grow to maturity."

The film was mercifully brief. Even in spite of the drums and gongs, and the chanting of the crowd, Benson found out how loudly a newborn infant can scream in a fire. The others looked as though they were going to be sick; he doubted if he looked much better.

"Of course, we are a more practical and mechanical-minded people, here and in Europe," Paula added, clearly holding down her gorge by main strength. "We have lethal-gas chambers that Hitler would have envied."

"I am a musician," Anthony said. "A composer. If Gregory thinks that the sciences are controlled, he should try to write even the simplest piece of music. The extent of censorship and control over all the arts, and especially music, is incredible." He coughed slightly. "And I have another motive, a more selfish one. I am approaching the compulsory retirement age; I will soon be invited to go to one of the Havens. Even though these Havens are located in the most barren places, they are beauty-spots, verdant beyond belief. It is of only passing interest that, while large numbers of the aged go there yearly, their populations remain constant, and, to judge from the qualities of supplies shipped to them, extremely small.''

"They call me Samuel, in this organization," the man in the long black coat said. "Whoever gave me that alias must have chosen it because I am here in an effort to live up to it. Although I am ordained by no church, I fight for all of them. The plain fact is that this man we call The Guide is really the Antichrist!''

"Well, I haven't quite so lofty a motive, but it's good enough to make me willing to finance this project," Walter said. "It's very simple. The Guide won't let people make money, and if they do, he taxes it away from them. And he has laws to prohibit inheritance; what little you can accumulate, you can't pass on to your children.''

"I put up a lot of money, too, don't forget," Carl told him. "Or the Union did; I'm a poor man, myself." He was smoking an excellent cigar, for a poor man, and his clothes could have come from the same tailor as Walter's. "Look, we got a real Union—the Union of all unions. Every working man in North America, Europe, Australia and South Africa belongs to it. And The Guide has us all hog-tied.''

"He won't let you strike," Benson chuckled.

"That's right. And what can we do? As far as getting anything like a pay-raise . . .''

"Good thing. Another pay-raise in some of my companies would bankrupt them, the way The Guide has us under his thumb . . ." Walter began, but he was cut off.

"Well! It seems as though this Guide has done some good, if he's made you two realize that you're both on the same side, and that what hurts one hurts both," Benson said. "When I shipped out for Turkey in '77, neither Labor nor Management had learned that." He looked from one to another of them. "The Guide must have a really good body-guard, with all the enemies he's made.''

Gregory shook his head. "He lives virtually alone, in a very small house on the UN Capitol grounds. In fact, except for a small police-force, armed only with non-lethal stun-guns, your profession of arms is non-existent.''

''I've been guessing what you want me to do,'' Benson said. ''You want this Guide bumped off. But why can't any of you do it? Or, if it's too risky, at least somebody from your own time? Why me?''

''We can't. Everybody in the world today is conditioned against violence, especially the taking of human life,'' Anthony told him.

''Now, wait a moment!'' This time, he was using the voice he would have employed in chiding a couple of Anatolian peasant partisans who were field-stripping a machine gun the wrong way. ''Those babies in that film you showed me weren't dying of old age . . .''

''This is not violence,'' Paula said bitterly. ''That is humane beneficence. Ugly people would be unhappy, and would make others unhappy, in a world where everybody else is beautiful.''

''And all these oppressive and tryannical laws,'' Benson continued. ''How does he enforce them, without violence, actual or threatened?''

Samuel started to say something about the Power of the Evil One; Paula, ignoring him, said:

''I really don't know; he just does it. Mass hypnotism of some sort. I know music has something to do with it, because there is always music, everywhere. This laboratory, for instance, was secretly soundproofed; we couldn't have worked here, otherwise.''

''All right. I can see that you'd need somebody from the past, preferably a soldier, whose conditioning has been in favor rather than against violence. I'm not the only one you snatched, I take it?''

''No. We've been using that machine to pick up men from battlefields all over the world and all over history,'' Gregory said. ''Until now, none of them could adjust . . . Uggh!'' He shuddered, looking even sicker than when the film was being shown.

"He's thinking," Walter said, "about a French officer from Waterloo who blew out his brains with a pocket-pistol on that table, and an English archer from Agincourt who ran amok with a dagger in here, and a trooper of the Seventh Cavalry from the Custer Massacre."

Gregory managed to overcome his revulsion. "You see, we were forced to take our subjects largely at random with regard to individual characteristics, mental attitudes, adaptability, et cetera." As long as he stuck to high order abstractions, he could control himself. "Aside from their professional lack of repugnance for violence, we took soldiers from battlefields because we could select men facing immediate death, whose removal from the past would not have any effect upon the causal chain of events affecting the present."

A warning buzzer rasped in Benson's brain. He nodded, poker-faced.

"I can see that," he agreed. "You wouldn't dare do anything to change the past. That was always one of the favorite paradoxes in time-travel fiction . . . Well, I think I have the general picture. You have a dictator who is tyrannizing you; you want to get rid of him; you can't kill him yourselves. I'm opposed to dictators, myself; that—and the Selective Service law, of course—was why I was a soldier. I have no moral or psychological taboos against killing dictators, or anybody else. Suppose I cooperate with you; what's in it for me?"

There was a long silence. Walter and Carl looked at one another inquiringly; the others dithered helplessly. It was Carl who answered.

"Your return to your own time and place."

"And if I don't cooperate with you?"

"Guess when and where else we could send you," Walter said.

Benson dropped his cigarette and trampled it.

"Exactly the same time and place?" he asked.

"Well, the structure of space-time demands . . ." Paula began.

"The spatio-temporal displacement field is capable of

identifying that spot—'' Gregory pointed to a ten-foot circle in front of a bank of sleek-cabineted, dial-studded machine ''—with any set of space-time coordinates in the universe. However, to avoid disruption of the structure of space-time, we must return you to approximately the same point in space-time.''

Benson nodded again, this time at the confirmation of his earlier suspicion. Well, while he was alive, he still had a chance.

''All right; tell me exactly what you want me to do.''

A third outbreak of bedlam, this time of relief and frantic explanation.

''Shut up, all of you!'' For so thin a man, Carl had an astonishing voice. ''I worked this out, so let me tell it.'' He turned to Benson. ''Maybe I'm tougher than the rest of them, or maybe I'm not as deeply conditioned. For one thing, I'm tone-deaf. Well, here's the way it is. Gregory can set the machine to function automatically. You stand where he shows you, press the button he shows you, and fifteen seconds later it'll take you forward in time five seconds and about a kilometer in space, to The Guide's office. He'll be at his desk now. You'll have forty-five seconds to do the job, from the time the field collapses around you till it rebuilds. Then you'll be taken back to your own time again. The whole thing's automatic.''

''Can do,'' Benson agreed. ''How do I kill him?''

''I'm getting sick!'' Paula murmured weakly. Her face was whiter than her gown.

''Take care of her, Samuel. Both of you'd better get out of here,'' Gregory said.

''The Lord of Hosts is my strength, He will . . . Uggggh!'' Samuel gasped.

''Conditioning's getting him, too; we gotta be quick,'' Carl said. ''Here. This is what you'll use.'' He handed Benson a two-inch globe of black plastic. ''Take the damn thing, quick! Little button on the side; press it, and get it out of your hand fast . . ." He retched. "Limited-effect bomb; everything within two-meter circle burned to nothing; outside that, great but not unendurable heat. Shut your eyes when you throw it. Flash almost blinding." He dropped his cigar and turned almost green in the face. Walter had a drink poured and handed it to him. "Uggh! Thanks, Walter." He downed it.

"Peculiar sort of thing for a non-violent people to manufacture," Benson said, looking at the bomb and then putting it in his jacket pocket.

"It isn't a weapon. Industrial; we use it in mining. I used plenty of them, in Walter's iron mines."

He nodded again. "Where do I stand, now?" he asked.

"Right over here." Gregory placed him in front of a small panel with three buttons. "Press the middle one, and step back into the small red circle and stand perfectly still while the field builds up and collapses. Face that way."

Benson drew his pistol and checked it; magazine full, a round in the chamber, safety on.

"Put that horrid thing out of sight!" Anthony gasped. "The . . . the other thing . . . is what you want to use."

"The bomb won't be any good if some of his guards come in before the field rebuilds," Benson said.

"He has no guards. He lives absolutely alone. We told you . . ."

"I know you did. You probably believed it, too. I don't. And by the way, you're sending me forward. What do you do about the fact that a time-jump seems to make me pass out?"

"Here. Before you press the button, swallow it." Gregory gave him a small blue pill.

"Well, I guess that's all there is," Gregory continued. "I hope . . ." His face twitched, and he dropped to the floor with a thud. Carl and Walter came forward, and dragged him away from the machine.

"Conditioning got him. Getting me, too," Walter said. "Hurry up, man!"

Benson swallowed the pill, pressed the button and stepped back into the red circle, drawing his pistol and snapping off the safety. The blue mist closed in on him.

This time, however, it did not thicken into blackness. It became luminous, brightening to a dazzle and dimming again to a colored mist, and then it cleared, while Benson stood at raise pistol, as though on a target range. He was facing a big desk at twenty feet, across a thick-piled blue rug. There was a man seated at the desk, a white-haired man with a mustache and a small beard, who wore a loose coat of some glossy plum-brown fabric, and a vividly blue neck-scarf.

The pistol centered on the v-shaped blue under his chin. Deliberately, Benson squeezed, recovered from the recoil, aimed, fired, recovered, aimed, fired. Five seconds gone. The old man slumped across the desk, his arms extended. Better make a good job of it, six, seven, eight seconds; he stepped forward to the edge of the desk, call that fifteen seconds, and put the muzzle to the top of the man's head, firing again and snapping on the safety. There had been something familiar about The Guide's face, but it was too late to check on that, now. There wasn't any face left; not even much head.

A box, on the desk, caught Benson's eyes, a cardboard box with an envelope, stamped *Top Secret! For the Guide Only!* taped to it. He holstered his pistol and caught that up, stuffing it into his pocket, in obedience to an instinct to grab anything that looked like intelligence matter while in the enemy's country. Then he stepped back to the spot where the field had deposited him. He had ten seconds to spare; somebody was banging on a door when the blue mist began to gather around him.

He was crouching, the spherical plastic object in his right hand, his thumb over the button, when the field collapsed. Sure enough, right in front of him, so close that he could smell the very heat of it, was the big tank with the red star on its turret. He cursed the sextet of sanctimonious double-crossers eight thousand miles and fifty years away in space-time. The machine guns had stopped—probably because they couldn't be depressed far enough to aim at him, now; that was a notorious fault of some of the newer Pan-Soviet tanks—and he rocked back on his heels, pressed the button, and heaved, closing his eyes. As the thing left his fingers, he knew that he had thrown too hard. His muscles, accustomed to the heavier cast-iron grenades of his experience, had betrayed him. For a moment, he was closer to despair than at any other time in the whole phantasmagoric adventure. Then he was hit, with physical violence, by a wave of almost solid heat. It didn't smell like the heat of the tank's engines; it smelled like molten metal, with undertones of burned flesh. Immediately, there was a multiple explosion that threw him flat, as the tank's ammunition went up. There were no screams. It was too fast for that. He opened his eyes.

The turret and top armor of the tank had vanished. The two massive treads had been toppled over, one to either side. The body had collapsed between them, and it was running sticky trickles of molten metal. He blinked, rubbed his eyes on the back of his hand, and looked again. Of all the many blasted and burned-out tanks, Soviet and UN, that he had seen, this was the most completely wrecked thing in his experience. And he'd done that with one grenade . . .

At that moment, there was a sudden rushing overhead, and an instant later the barrage began falling beyond the crest of the ridge. He looked at his watch, blinked, and looked again. That barrage was due at 0550; according to the watch, it was 0726. He was sure that, ten minutes ago, when he had looked at it, up there at the head of the ravine, it had been twenty minutes to six. He puzzled about that for a moment, and decided that he must have caught the stem on something and pulled it out, and then twisted it a little, setting the watch ahead. Then, somehow, the stem had gotten pushed back in, starting it at the new setting. That was a pretty far-fetched explanation, but it was the only one he could think of.

But about this tank, now. He was positive that he could remember throwing a grenade . . . Yet he'd used his last grenade back there at the supply dump. He saw his carbine, and picked it up. That silly blackout he'd had, for a second, there; he must have dropped it. Action was open, empty magazine on the ground where he'd dropped it. He wondered, stupidly, if one of his bullets couldn't have gone down the muzzle of the tank's gun and exploded the shell in the chamber . . . Oh, the hell with it! The tank might have been hit by a premature shot from the barrage which was raging against the far slope of the ridge. He reset his watch by guess and looked down the valley. The big attack would be starting any minute, now, and there would be fleeing Commies coming up the valley ahead of the UN advance. He'd better get himself placed before they started coming in on him.

He stopped thinking about the mystery of the blown-up tank, a solution to which seemed to dance maddeningly just out of his mental reach, and found himself a place among the rocks to wait. Down the valley he could hear everything from pistols to mortars going off, and shouting in three or four racial intonations. After a while, fugitive Communists began coming, many of them without their equipment, stumbling in their haste and looking back over their shoulders. Most of them avoided the mouth of the ravine and hurried by to the left or right, but one little clump, eight or ten, came up the dry stream-bed, and stopped a hundred and fifty yards from his hiding-place to make a stand. They were Hindus, with outsize helmets over their turbans. Two of them came ahead, carrying a machine gun, followed by a third with a flame-thrower; the others retreated more slowly, firing their rifles to delay pursuit.

Cuddling the stock of his carbine to his cheek, he divided a ten-shot burst between the two machine-gunners, then, as a matter of principle, he shot the man with the flame-thrower. He had a dislike for flame-throwers; he killed every enemy he found with one. The others dropped their rifles and raised their hands, screaming: ''Hey, Joe! Hey, Joe! You no shoot, me no shoot!''

A dozen men in UN battledress came up and took them prisoner. Benson shouted to them, and then rose and came down to join them. They were British—Argyle and Sutherland Highlanders, advertising the fact by inconspicuous bits of tartan on their uniforms. The subaltern in command looked at him and nodded.

"Captain Benson? We were warned to be on watch for your patrol," he said. "Any of the rest of you lads get out?"

Benson shrugged. "We split up after the attack. You may run into a couple of them. Some are locals and don't speak very good English. I've got to get back to Division, myself; what's the best way?"

"Down that way. You'll overtake a couple of our walking wounded. If you don't mind going slowly, they'll show you the way to advance dressing station, and you can hitch a ride on an ambulance from there."

Benson nodded. Off on the left, there was a flurry of small-arms fire, ending in yells of "Hey, Joe! Hey, Joe!"— the World War III version of "Kamarad"!

His company was a non-T/O outfit; he came directly under Division command and didn't have to bother reporting to any regimental or brigade commanders. He walked for an hour with half a dozen lightly wounded Scots, rode for another hour on a big cat-truck loaded with casualties of six regiments and four races, and finally reached Division Rear, where both the Division and Corps commanders took time to compliment him on the part his last hunter patrol had played in the now complete breakthrough. His replacement, an equine-faced Spaniard with an imposing display of fruit-salad, was there, too; he solemnly took off the bracelet a refugee Caucasian goldsmith had made for his predecessor's predecessor and gave it to the new commander of what had formerly been Benson's Butchers. As he had expected, there was also another medal waiting for him.

A medical check at Task Force Center got him a warning; his last patrol had brought him dangerously close to the edge of combat fatigue. Remembering the incidents of the tank and the unaccountably fast watch, and the mysterious box and envelope which he had found in his coat pocket, he agreed, saying nothing about the questions that were puzzling him. The Psychological Department was never too busy to refuse another case; they hunted patients gleefully, each psych-shark seeking in everyone proof of his own particular theories. It was with relief that he watched them fill out the red tag which gave him a priority on jet transports for home.

Ankara to Alexandria, Alexandria to Dakar, Dakar to Belém, Belém to the shattered skyline of New York, the "hurry-and-wait" procedures at Fort Carlisle, and, after the usual separation promotion, Major Fred Benson, late of Benson's Butchers, was back teaching high school juniors the difference between H_2O and H_2SO_4.

There were two high schools in the city: McKinley High, on the east side, and Dwight Eisenhower High, on the west. A few blocks from McKinley was the Tulip Tavern, where the Eisenhower teachers came in the late afternoons; the McKinley faculty crossed town to do their after-school drinking on the west side. When Benson entered the Tulip Tavern, on a warm September afternoon, he found Bill Myers, the school psychologist, at one of the tables, smoking his pipe, checking over a stack of aptitude test forms, and drinking beer. He got a highball at the bar and carried it over to Bill's table.

"Oh, hi, Fred." The psychologist separated the finished from the unfinished work with a sheet of yellow paper and crammed the whole business into his brief case. "I was hoping somebody'd show up . . ."

Benson lit a cigarette, sipped his highball. They talked at random—school-talk; the progress of the war; personal reminiscences, of the Turkish Theater where Benson had served; and the Madras Beachhead, where Myers had been.

"Bring home any souvenirs?" Myers asked.

"Not much. Couple of pistols, couple of knives, some pictures. I don't remember what all; haven't gotten around to unpacking them, yet . . . I have a sixth of rye and some beer, at my rooms. Let's go around and see what I did bring home."

They finished their drinks and went out.

"What the devil's that?" Myers said, pointing to the

cardboard box with the envelope taped to it, when Benson lifted it out of the gray-green locker.

"Bill, I don't know," Benson said. "I found it in the pocket of my coat, on my way back from my last hunter patrol . . . I've never told anybody about this, before."

"That's the damnedest story I've ever heard, and in my racket you hear some honeys," Myers said, when he had finished. "You couldn't have picked that thing up in some other way, deliberately forgotten the circumstances, and fabricated this story about the tank and the grenade and the discrepancy in your watch subconsciously as an explanation?"

"My subconscious is a better liar than that," Benson replied. "It would have cobbled up some kind of a story that would stand up. This business . . ."

"Top Secret! For the Guide Only!" Myers frowned. "That isn't one of our marks, and if it were Soviet, it'd be tri-lingual, Russian, Hindi and Chinese."

"Well, let's see what's in it. I want this thing cleared up. I've been having some of the nastiest dreams, lately . . ."

"Well, be careful; it may be booby-trapped," Myers said urgently.

"Don't worry; I will."

He used a knife to slice the envelope open without untaping it from the box, and exposed five sheets of typewritten onionskin paper. There was no letterhead, no salutation or address-line. Just a mass of chemical formulae, and a concise report on tests. It seemed to be a report on an improved syrup for a carbonated soft-drink. There were a few cryptic cautionary references to heightened physio-psychological effects.

The box was opened with the same caution, but it proved as innocent of dangers as the envelope. It contained only a half-liter bottle, wax-sealed, containing a dark reddish-brown syrup.

"There's a lot of this stuff I don't dig," Benson said, tapping the sheets of onionskin. "I don't even scratch the surface of this rigamarole about The Guide. I'm going to get to work on this sample in the lab, at school, though. Maybe we have something here.''

At eight-thirty the next evening, after four and a half hours' work, he stopped to check what he had found out.

The school's X ray, an excellent one, had given him a complete picture of the molecular structure of the syrup. There were a couple of long-chain molecules that he could only believe after two re-examinations and a careful check of the machine, but with the help of the notes he could deduce how they had been put together. They would be the Ingredient Alpha and Ingredient Beta referred to in the notes.

The components of the syrup were all simple and easily procurable with these two exceptions, as were the basic components from which these were made.

The mechanical guinea pig demonstrated that the syrup contained nothing harmful to human tissue.

Of course, there were the warnings about heightened psycho-physiological effects . . .

He struck a poison-label on the bottle, locked it up, and went home. The next day, he and Bill Myers got a bottle of carbonated water and mixed themselves a couple of drinks of it. It was delicious—sweet, dry, tart, sour, all of these in alternating waves of pleasure.

''We do have something, Bill,'' he said. ''We have something that's going to give our income-tax experts headaches.''

''You have,'' Myers corrected. ''Where do you start fitting me into it?''

''We're a good team, Bill. I'm a chemist, but I don't know a thing about people. You're a psychologist. A real one; not one of these night-school boys. A juvenile psychologist, too. And what age-group spends the most money in this country for soft-drinks?''

Knowing the names of the syrup's ingredients, and what their molecular structure was like, was only the beginning. Gallon after gallon of the School Board's chemicals went down the laboratory sink; Fred Benson and Bill Myers almost lived in the fourth floor lab. Once or twice there were head-shaking warnings from the principal about the dangers of over-work. The watchmen, at all hours, would hear the occasional twanging of Benson's guitar in the laboratory, and knew that he had come to a dead end on something and was trying to think. Football season came and went; basketball season; the inevitable riot between McKinley and Eisenhower rooters; the Spring concerts. The term-end exams were only a month away when Benson and Myers finally did it, and stood solemnly, each with a beaker in either hand, and took alternate sips of the original and the drink mixed from the syrup they had made.

"Not a bit of difference, Fred," Myers said. "We have it!"

Benson picked up the guitar and began plunking on it.

"Hey!" Myers exclaimed. "Have you been finding time to take lessons on that thing? I never heard you play as well as that!"

They decided to go into business in St. Louis. It was centrally located, and, being behind more concentric circles of radar and counter-rocket defenses, it was in better shape than any other city in the country and most likely to stay that way. Getting started wasn't hard; the first banker who tasted the new drink—named Evri-Flave, at Myers' suggestion—couldn't dig up the necessary money fast enough. Evri-Flave hit the market with a bang and became an instant success; soon the rainbow-tinted vending machines were everywhere, dispensing the slender, slightly-flattened bottles and devouring quarters voraciously. In spite of high taxes and the difficulties of doing business in a consumers' economy upon which a war-time economy had been superimposed, both Myers and Benson were rapidly becoming wealthy. The gregarious Myers installed himself in a luxurious apartment in the city; Benson bought a large tract of land down the river toward Carondelet and started building a home and landscaping the grounds.

The dreams began bothering him again, now that the urgency of getting Evri-Flave, Inc., started had eased. They were not dreams of the men he had killed in battle, or, except for one about a huge, hot-smelling tank with a red star on the turret, about the war. Generally, they were about a strange, beautiful, office-room, in which a young man in uniform killed an older man in a plum-brown coat and a vivid blue neck-scarf. Sometimes Benson identified himself with the killer; sometimes with the old man who was killed.

He talked to Myers about these dreams, but beyond generalities about delayed effects of combat fatigue and vague advice to relax, the psychologist, now head of Sales and Promotion of Evri-Flave, Inc., could give him no help.

The war ended three years after the new company was launched. There was a momentary faltering of the economy, and then the work of reconstruction was crying hungrily for all the labor and capital that had been idled by the end of destruction. There was a new flood-tide of prosperity, and Evri-Flave rode the crest. The estate at Carondelet was finished—a beautiful place, surrounded with gardens, fragrant with flowers, full of the songs of birds and soft music from concealed record-players. It made him forget the ugliness of the war, and kept the dreams from returning so frequently. All the world ought to be like that, he thought; beautiful and quiet and peaceful. People surrounded with such beauty couldn't think about war.

All the world could be like that, if only . . .

The UN chose St. Louis for its new headquarters—many of its offices had been moved there after the bombing of New York—and when the city by the Mississippi began growing into a real World Capital, the flow of money into it almost squared overnight. Benson began to take an active part in politics in the new World Sovereignty party. He did not, however, allow his political activities to distract him from the work of expanding the company to which he owed his wealth and position. There were always things to worry about.

"I don't know," Myers said to him one evening, as they sat over a bottle of rye in the psychologist's apartment. "I could make almost as much money practicing as a psychiatrist, these days. The whole world seems to be going pure, unadulterated nuts! That affair in Munich, for instance."

"Yes." Benson grimaced as he thought of the affair in Munich—a Wagnerian concert which had terminated in an insane orgy of mass suicide. "Just a week after we started our free-sample campaign in South Germany, too . . ."

He stopped short, downing his drink and coughing over it.

"Bill! You remember those sheets of onionskin in that envelope?"

"The foundation of our fortunes; I wonder where you really did get that . . . Fred!" His eyes widened in horror. "That caution about 'heightened psycho-physiological effects,' that we were never able to understand!"

Benson nodded grimly. "And think of all the crazy cases of mass-hysteria—that baseball-game riot in Baltimore; the time everybody started tearing off each others' clothes in Milwaukee; the sex-orgy in New Orleans. And the sharp uptrend in individual psycho-neurotic and psychotic behavior. All in connection with music, too, and all after Evri-Flave got on the market."

"We'll have to stop it; pull Evri-Flave off the market," Myers said. "We can't be responsible for letting this go on."

"We can't stop, either. There's at least a two months' supply out in the hands of jobbers and distributors over whom we have no control. And we have all these contractual obligations, to buy the entire output of the companies that make the syrup for us; if we stop buying, they can sell it in competition with us, as long as they don't infringe our trade-name. And we can't prevent pirating. You know how easily we were able to duplicate that sample I brought back from Turkey. Why, our legal department's kept busy all the time prosecuting unlicensed manufacturers as it is."

"We've got to do something, Fred!" There was almost a whiff of hysteria in Myers' voice.

"We will. We'll start, first thing tomorrow, on a series of tests—just you and I, like the old times at Eisenhower High. First, we want to be sure that Evri-Flave really is responsible, It'd be a hell of a thing if we started a public panic against our own product for nothing. And then . . ."

It took just two weeks, in a soundproofed and guarded

laboratory on Benson's Carondelet estate, to convict their delicious drink of responsibility for that Munich State Opera House Horror and everything else. Reports from confidential investigators in Munich confirmed this. It had, of course, been impossible to interview the two thousand men and women who had turned the Opera House into a pyre for their own immolation, but none of the tiny minority who had kept their sanity and saved their lives had tasted Evri-Flave.

It took another month to find out exactly how the stuff affected the human nervous system, and they almost wrecked their own nervous systems in the process. The real villain, they discovered, was the incredible-looking long-chain compound alluded to in the original notes as Ingredient Beta; its principal physiological effect was to greatly increase the sensitivity of the aural nerves. Not only was the hearing range widened—after consuming thirty cc of Beta, they could hear the sound of an ultrasonic dog-whistle quite plainly—but the very quality of all audible sounds was curiously enhanced and altered. Myers, the psychologist, who was also well grounded in neurology, explained how the chemical produced this effect; it meant about as much to Benson as some of his chemistry did to Bill Myers. There was also a secondary purely psychological effect. Certain musical chords had definite effects on the emotions of the hearer, and the subject, beside being directly influenced by the music, was rendered extremely open to verbal suggestions accompanied by a suitable musical background.

Benson transferred the final results of this stage of the research to the black notebook and burned the scratch-sheets.

"That's how it happened, then," he said. "The Munich thing was the result of all that Götterdämmerung music. There was a band at the baseball park in Baltimore. The New Orleans Orgy started while a local radio station was broadcasting some of this new dance-music. Look, these tone-clusters, here, have a definite sex-excitation effect. This series of six chords, which occur in some of the Wagnerian stuff, effects a combined feeling of godlike isolation and despair. And these consecutive fifths—a sense of danger,

anger, combativeness. You know, we could work out a whole range of emotional stimuli to fit the effects of Ingredient Beta . . .''

"We don't want to," Myers said. "We want to work out a substitute for Beta that will keep the flavor of the drink without the psycho-physiological effects."

"Yes, sure. I have some of the boys at the plant lab working on that. Gave them a lot of syrup without Beta, and told them to work out cheap additives to restore the regular Evri-Flave taste; told them it was an effort to find a cheap substitute for an expensive ingredient. But look, Bill. You and I both see, for instance, that a powerful world-wide supra-national sovereignty is the only guarantee of world peace. If we could use something like this to help overcome antiquated verbal prejudices and nationalistic emotional attachments . . .''

"No!" Myers said. "I won't ever consent to anything like that, Fred! Not even in a cause like world peace; use a thing like this for a good, almost holy, cause now, and tomorrow we, or those who would come after us, would be using it to create a tyranny. You know what year this is, Bill?"

"Why, 1984," Benson said.

"Yes. You remember that old political novel of Orwell's, written about forty years ago? Well, that's a picture of the kind of world you'd have, eventually, no matter what kind of a world you started out to make. Fred, don't ever think of using this stuff for a purpose like that. If you try it, I'll fight you with every resource I have."

There was a fanatical, almost murderous, look in Bill Myers' eyes. Benson put the notebook in his pocket, then laughed and threw up his hands.

"Hey, Joe! Hey, Joe!" he cried. "You're right, of course, Bill. We can't even trust the UN with a thing like this. It makes the H-bomb look like a stone hatchet . . . Well, I'll call Grant, at the plant lab, and see how his boys are coming along with the substitute; as soon as we get it, we can put out a confidential letter to all our distributors and syrup-manufacturers . . .''

· · ·

He walked alone in the garden at Carondelet, watching the color fade out of the sky and the twilight seep in among the clipped yews. All the world could be like this garden, a place of peace and beauty and quiet, if only . . . All the world *would* be a beautiful and peaceful garden, in his own lifetime! He had the means of making it so!

Three weeks later, he murdered his friend and partner, Bill Myers. It was a suicide; nobody but Fred Benson knew that he had taken fifty cc of pure Ingredient Beta in a couple of cocktails while listening to the queer phonograph record that he had played half an hour before blowing his brains out.

The decisions had cost Benson a battle with his conscience from which he had emerged the sole survivor. The conscience was buried along with Bill Myers, and all that remained was a purpose.

Evri-Flave stayed on the market unaltered. The night before the national election, the World Sovereignty party distributed thousands of gallons of Evri-Flave; their speakers, on every radio and television network, were backgrounded by soft music. The next day, when the vote was counted, it was found that the American Nationalists had carried a few backwoods precincts in the Rockies and the Southern Appalachians and one county in Alaska, where there had been no distribution of Evri-Flave.

The dreams came back more often, now that Bill Myers was gone. Benson was only beginning to realize what a large fact in his life the companionship of the young psychologist had been. Well, a world of peace and beauty was an omelet worth the breaking of many eggs . . .

He purchased another great tract of land near the city, and donated it to the UN for their new headquarters buildings; the same architects and landscapists who had created the estate at Carondelet were put to work on it. In the middle of what was to become World City, they erected a small home for Fred Benson. Benson was often invited to address the delegates to the UN; always, there was soft piped-in music behind his words. He saw to it that Evri-Flave was available free to all UN personnel. The Senate of the United States elected him as perpetual U.S. delegate-in-chief to the UN; not long after, the Security Council elected him their perpetual chairman.

In keeping with his new dignities, and to ameliorate his youthful appearance, he grew a mustache and, eventually, a small beard. The black notebook in which he kept the records of his experiments was always with him; page after page was filled with notes. Experiments in sonics, like the one which had produced the ultrasonic stun-gun which rendered lethal weapons unnecessary for police and defense purposes, or the new musical combinations with which he was able to play upon every emotion and instinct.

But he still dreamed, the same recurring dream of the young soldier and the old man in the office. By now, he was consistently identifying himself with the latter. He took to carrying one of the thick-barrelled stun-pistols, always. Alone, he practiced constantly with it, drawing, breaking soap-bubbles with the concentrated sound-waves it projected. It was silly, perhaps, but it helped him in his dreams. Now, the old man with whom he identified himself would draw a stun-pistol, occasionally, to defend himself.

The years drained one by one through the hour-glass of Time. Year after year, the world grew more peaceful, more beautiful. There were no more incidents like the mass-suicide of Munich or the mass-perversions of New Orleans; the playing and even the composing of music was strictly controlled—no dangerous notes or chords could be played in a world drenched with Ingredient Beta. Steadily the idea grew that peace and beauty were supremely good, that violence and ugliness were supremely evil. Even competitive sports which simulated violence; even children born ugly and misshapen . . .

He finished the breakfast which he had prepared for himself—he trusted no food that another had touched—and knotted the vivid blue scarf about his neck before slipping into the loose coat of glossy plum-brown, then checked the stun-pistol and pocketed the black notebook, its plastileather cover glossy from long use. He stood in front of the mirror, brushing his beard, now snow-white. Two years, now, and he would be eighty—had he been anyone but The Guide, he would have long ago retired to the absolute peace and repose of one of the Elders' Havens. Peace and repose, however, were not for The Guide; it would take another twenty years to finish his task of remaking the world, and he would need every day of it that his medical staff could borrow or steal for him. He made an eye-baffling practice draw with the stun-pistol, then holstered it and started down the spiral stairway to the office below.

There was the usual mass of papers on his desk. A corps of secretaries had screened out everything but that which required his own personal and immediate attention, but the business of guiding a world could only be reduced to a certain point. On top was the digest of the world's news for the past twenty-four hours, and below that was the agenda for the afternoon's meeting of the Council. He laid both in front of him, reading over the former and occasionally making a note on the latter. Once his glance strayed to the cardboard box in front of him, with the envelope taped to it—the latest improvement on the Evri-Flave syrup, with the report from his own chemists, all conditioned to obedience, loyalty and secrecy. If they thought he was going to try that damned stuff on himself . . .

There was a sudden gleam of light in the middle of the room, in front of his desk. No, a mist, through which a blue light seemed to shine. The stun-pistol was in his hand—his instinctive reaction to anything unusual—and pointed into the shining mist when it vanished and a man appeared in front of him; a man in the baggy green combat-uniform that he himself had worn fifty years before; a man with a heavy automatic pistol in his hand. The gun was pointed directly at him.

The Guide aimed quickly and pressed the trigger of the ultrasonic stunner. The pistol dropped soundlessly on the thick-piled rug; the man in uniform slumped in an inert heap. The Guide sprang to his feet and rounded the desk, crossing to and bending over the intruder. Why, this was the dream that had plagued him through the years. But it was ending differently. The young man—his face was startlingly familiar, somehow—was not killing the old man. Those years of practice with the stun-pistol . . .

He stooped and picked the automatic up. The young man was unconscious, and The Guide had his pistol, now. He slipped the automatic into his pocket and straightened beside his inert would-be slayer.

A shimmering globe of blue mist appeared around them, brightened to a dazzle, and dimmed again to a colored mist before it vanished, and when it cleared away, he was standing beside the man in uniform, in the sandy bed of a dry stream at the mouth of a little ravine, and directly in front of him, looming above him, was a thing that had not been seen in the world for close to half a century—a big, hot-smelling tank with a red star on its turret.

He might have screamed—the din of its treads and engines deafened him—and, in panic, he turned and ran, his old legs racing, his old heart pumping madly. The noise of the tank increased as machine guns joined the uproar. He felt the first bullet strike him, just above the hips—no pain; just a tremendous impact. He might have felt the second bullet, too, as the ground tilted and rushed up at his face. Then he was diving into a tunnel of blackness that had no end . . .

Captain Fred Benson, of Benson's Butchers, had been jerked back into consciousness when the field began to build around him. He was struggling to rise, fumbling the grenade out of his pocket, when it collapsed. Sure enough, right in front of him, so close that he could smell the very heat of it, was the big tank with the red star on its turret. He cursed the sextet of sanctimonious double-crossers eight thousand miles and fifty years away in space-time. The machine guns had stopped— probably because they couldn't be depressed far enough to aim at him, now; that was a notorious fault of some of the newer Pan-Soviet tanks. He had the bomb out of his pocket, when the machine guns began firing again, this time at something on his left. Wondering what had created the diversion, he rocked back on his heels, pressed the button, and heaved, closing his eyes. As the thing left his fingers, he knew that he had thrown too hard. His muscles, accustomed to the heavier cast-iron grenades, had betrayed him. For a moment, he was closer to despair than at any other time in the whole phantasmagoric adventure. Then he was hit, with physical force, by a wave of almost solid heat. It didn't smell like the heat of the tank's engines; it smelled like molten metal, with undertones of burned flesh. Immediately, there was a multiple explosion that threw him flat, as the tank's ammunition went up. There were no screams. It was too fast for that. He opened his eyes.

The turret and top armor of the tank had vanished. The two massive treads had been toppled over, one to either side. The body had collapsed between them, and it was running sticky trickles of molten metal. He blinked, rubbed his eyes on the back of his hand, and looked again. Of all the many blasted and burned-out tanks, Soviet and UN, that he had seen, this was the most completely wrecked thing in his experience. And he'd done that with one grenade . . .

Remembering the curious manner in which, at the last, the tank had begun firing at something to the side, he looked around, to see the crumpled body in the pale violet-gray trousers and the plum-brown coat. Finding his carbine and reloading it, he went over to the dead man, turning the body over. He was an old man, with a white mustache and a small white beard—why, if the mustache were smaller and there were no beard, he would pass for Benson's own father, who had died in 1962. The clothes weren't Turkish or Armenian or Persian or anything one would expect in this country.

The old man had a pistol in his coat pocket, and Benson pulled it out and looked at it, then did a double-take and grabbed for his own holster, to find it empty. The pistol was his own 9.5 Colt automatic. He looked at the dead man, with the white beard and the vivid blue neck-scarf, and he was sure that he had never seen him before. He'd had that pistol when he'd come down the ravine . . .

There was another pistol under the dead man's coat, in a shoulder-holster; a queer thing with a thick round barrel, like an old percussion paper-box, and a diaphragm instead of a muzzle. Probably projected ultrasonic waves. He holstered his own Colt and pocketed the unknown weapon. There was a black plastileather-bound notebook. It was full of notes. Chemical formulae, yes, and some stuff on sonics; that tied in with the queer pistol. He pocketed that. He'd look both over, when he had time and privacy, two scarce commodities in the Army . . .

At that moment, there was a sudden rushing overhead, and an instant later, the barrage began falling beyond the crest of the ridge. He looked at his watch, blinked, and looked again. That barrage was due at 0550; according to his watch, it was 0726. That was another mystery, to go with the question of who the dead man was, where he had come from, and how he'd gotten hold of Benson's pistol. Yes, and how that tank had gotten blown up. Benson was sure he had used his last grenade back at the supply-dump.

The hell with it; he'd worry about all that later. The attack was due any minute, now, and there would be fleeing Commies coming up the valley ahead of the UN advance. He'd better get himself placed before they started coming in on him.

He stopped thinking about the multiple mystery, a solution to which seemed to dance maddeningly just out of his mental reach, and found himself a place among the rocks to wait, and while he waited, he looked over the plastileather-bound notebook. In civil life, he had been a high school chemistry teacher, but the stuff in this book was utterly new to him. Some of it he could understand readily enough; the rest of it he could dig out for himself. Stuff about some kind of a carbonated soft-drink, and about a couple of unbelievable-looking long-chain molecules . . .

After a while, fugitive Communists began coming up the valley to make their stand.

Benson put away the notebook, picked up his carbine, and cuddled the stock to his cheek . . .

FLIGHT FROM TOMORROW

———

Piper, throughout his body of work, created a number of lasting images: the Old Martian ruins of "Omnilingual"; Merlin, the big brain, in COSMIC COMPUTER; the frozen earth of "The Keeper"; and the fuzzies. One of the most distinctive images is The Ancient Spaceport—*a concrete-filled valley, set between mountains, in "Flight From Tomorrow."*

In a number of ways, "Flight From Tomorrow" is also the precursor of Piper's Terro-Human Future History. Here we find the first mention of Atomic Era dating—a system based upon the date the first uranium pile went into operation and used extensively in his future history until the First Galactic Empire. The story is also notable for including a panoramic sweep of history, the hallmark of Piper's later fiction.

The theme is nuclear destruction. His view of Terra as an atomic graveyard appears throughout his future history, as well as in other stories, such as "The Return." The scientific premise—that man could, in time, adapt to radiation—seems quaint today; in the late 1940s, when this story was written, it was more plausible. However, the grasping ambition and treachery that form the basis of the plot are as contemporary as today's newspaper.

1

But yesterday, a whole planet had shouted: *Hail Hradzka! Hail the Leader!* Today they were screaming: *Death to Hradzka! Kill the tyrant!*

The Palace, where Hradzka, surrounded by his sycophants and guards, had lorded it over a solar system, was now an inferno. Those who had been too closely identified with the dictator's rule to hope for forgiveness were fighting to the last, seeking only a quick death in combat; one by one, their isolated points of resistance were being wiped out. The corridors and chambers of the huge palace were thronged with rebels, loud with their shouts, and with the rasping hiss of heat-beams and the crash of blasters, reeking with the stench of scorched plastic and burned flesh, of hot metal and charred fabric. The living quarters were overrun; the mob smashed down walls and tore up floors in search of secret hiding-places. They found strange things—the space-ship that had been built under one of the domes, in readiness for flight to the still-loyal colonies on Mars or the Asteroid Belt, for instance—but Hradzka himself they could not find.

At last, the search reached the New Tower which reared its head five thousand feet above the palace, the highest thing in the city. They blasted down the huge steel doors, cut the power from the energy-screens. They landed from antigrav-cars on the upper levels. But except for barriers of metal and concrete and energy, they met with no opposition. Finally, they came to the spiral stairway which led up to the great metal sphere which capped the whole structure.

General Zarvas, the Army Commander who had placed himself at the head of the revolt, stood with his foot on the lowest step, his followers behind him. There was Prince Burvanny, the leader of the old nobility, and Ghorzesko Orhm, the merchant, and between them stood Tobbh, the chieftain of the mutinous slaves. There were clerks; laborers; poor but haughty nobles; and wealthy merchants who had long been forced to hide their riches from the dictator's tax-gatherers, and soldiers, and spacemen.

"You'd better let some of us go first sir," General Zarvas'

orderly, a blood-stained bandage about his head, his uniform in rags, suggested. "You don't know what might be up there."

The General shook his head. "I'll go first." Zarvas Pol was not the man to send subordinates into danger ahead of himself. "To tell the truth, I'm afraid we won't find anything at all up there."

"You mean . . . ?" Ghorzesko Orhm began.

"The time-machine," Zarvas Pol replied. "If he's managed to get it finished, the Great Mind only knows where he may be, now. Or when."

He loosened the blaster in his holster and started up the long spiral. His followers spread out, below; sharp-shooters took position to cover his ascent. Prince Burvanny and Tobbh the Slave started to follow him. They hesitated as each motioned the other to precede him; then the nobleman followed the general, his blaster drawn, and the brawny slave behind him.

The door at the top was open, and Zarvas Pol stepped through but there was nothing in the great spherical room except a raised dais some fifty feet in diameter, its polished metal top strangely clean and empty. And a crumpled heap of burned cloth and charred flesh that had, not long ago, been a man. An old man with a white beard, and the seven-pointed star of the Learned Brothers on his breast, advanced to meet the armed intruders.

"So he is gone, Kradzy Zago?" Zarvas Pol said, holstering his weapon. "Gone in the time-machine, to hide in yesterday or tomorrow. And you let him go?"

The old one nodded. "He had a blaster, and I had none," He indicated the body on the floor. "Zoldy Jarv had no blaster, either, but he tried to stop Hradzka. See, he squandered his life as a fool squanders his money, getting nothing for it. And a man's life is not money, Zarvas Pol."

"I do not blame you, Kradzy Zago," General Zarvas said. "But now you must get to work, and build us another time-machine, so that we can hunt him down."

"Does revenge mean so much to you, then?"

The soldier made an impatient gesture. "Revenge is for

fools, like that pack of screaming beasts below. I do not kill for revenge; I kill because dead men do no harm.''

"Hradzka will do us no more harm,'' the old scientist replied. "He is a thing of yesterday; of a time long past and half-lost in the mists of legend.''

"No matter. As long as he exists, at any point in space-time, Hradzka is still a threat. Revenge means much to Hradzka; he will return for it, when we least expect him.''

The old man shook his head. "No, Zarvas Pol. Hradzka will not return.''

Hradzka holstered his blaster, threw the switch that sealed the time-machine, put on the antigrav-unit and started the time-shift unit. He reached out and set the destination-dial for the mid-Fifty-Second Century of the Atomic Era. That would land him in the Ninth Age of Chaos, following the Two-Century War and the collapse of the World Theocracy. A good time for his purpose; the world would be slipping back into barbarism, and yet possess the technologies of former civilizations. A hundred little national states would be trying to regain social stability, competing and warring with one another. Hradzka glanced back over his shoulder at the cases of books, record-spools, tri-dimensional pictures, and scale-models. These people of the past would welcome him and his science of the future, would make him their leader.

He would start in a small way, by taking over the local feudal or tribal government, would arm his followers with weapons of the future. Then he would impose his rule upon neighboring tribes, or princedoms, or communes, or whatever, and build a strong sovereignty; from that he envisioned a world empire, a Solar System empire.

Then, he would build time-machines, many time-machines. He would recruit an army such as the universe had never seen, a swarm of men from every age in the past. At that point, he would return to the Hundredth Century of the Atomic Era, to wreak vengeance upon those who had risen against him. A slow smile grew on Hradzka's thin lips as he thought of the tortures with which he would put Zarvas Pol to death.

He glanced up at the great disc of the indicator and frowned. Already he was back to the year 7500, A.E., and the temporal-displacement had not begun to slow. The disc was turning even more rapidly—7000, 6000, 5500; he gasped slightly. Then he had passed his destination; he was now in the Fortieth Century, but the indicator was slowing. The hairline crossed the Thirtieth Century, the Twentieth, the Fifteenth, the Tenth. He wondered what had gone wrong, but he had recovered from his fright by this time. When this insane machine stopped, as it must around the First Century of the Atomic Era, he would investigate, make repairs, then shift forward to his target-point. Hradzka was determined upon the Fifty-Second Century; he had made a special study of the history of that period, and learned the language spoken then, and he understood the methods necessary to gain power over the natives of that time.

The indicator-disc came to a stop, in the First Century. He switched on the magnifier and leaned forward to look; he had emerged into normal time in the year 10 of the Atomic Era, a decade after the first uranium-pile had gone into operation, and seven years after the first atomic bombs had been exploded in warfare. The altimeter showed that he was hovering at eight thousand feet above ground-level.

Slowly, he cut out the antigrav, letting the time-machine down easily. He knew that there had been no danger of materializing inside anything; the New Tower had been built to put it above anything that had occupied that space-point at any moment within history, or legend, or even the geological knowledge of man. What lay below, however, was uncertain. It was night—the visi-screen showed only a star-dusted, moonless sky, and dark shadows below. He snapped another switch; for a few microseconds a beam of intense light was turned on, automatically photographing the landscape under him. A second later, the developed picture was projected upon another screen; it showed only wooded mountains and a barren, brush-grown valley.

The time-machine came to rest with a soft jar and a crashing of broken bushes that was audible through the sound pickup.

Hradzka pulled the main switch; there was a click as the shielding went out and the door opened. A breath of cool night air drew into the hollow sphere.

Then there was a loud *bang* inside the mechanism, and a flash of blue-white light which turned to pinkish flame with a nasty crackling. Curls of smoke began to rise from the square black box that housed the time-shift mechanism, and from behind the instrument-board. In a moment, everything was glowing-hot; driblets of aluminum and silver were running down from the instruments. Then the whole interior of the time-machine was afire; there was barely time for Hradzka to leap through the open door.

The brush outside impeded him, and he used his blaster to clear a path for himself away from the big sphere, which was now glowing faintly on the outside. The heat grew in intensity, and the brush outside was taking fire. It was not until he had gotten two hundred yards from the machine that he stopped, realizing what had happened.

The machine, of course, had been sabotaged. That would have been young Zoldy, whom he had killed, or that old billy-goat, Kradzy Zago; the latter, most likely. He cursed both of them for having marooned him in this savage age, at the very beginning of atomic civilization, with all his printed and recorded knowledge destroyed. Oh, he could still gain mastery over these barbarians; he knew enough to fashion a crude blaster, or a heat-beam gun, or an atomic-electric conversion unit. But without his books and records, he could never build an antigrav unit, and the secret of the temporal shift was lost.

For Time is not an object, or a medium which can be travelled along. The Time-Machine was not a vehicle; it was a mechanical process of displacement within the space-time continuum, and those who constructed it knew that it could not be used with the sort of accuracy that the dials indicated. Hradzka had ordered his scientists to produce a ''Time Machine,'' and they had combined the possible— displacement within the space-time continuum—with the sort of fiction the dictator demanded, for their own well-being. Even had there been no sabotage, his return to his own time was nearly of zero probability.

The fire, spreading from the time-machine, was blowing toward him; he observed the wind-direction and hurried around out of the path of the flames. The light enabled him to pick his way through the brush, and, after crossing a small stream, he found a rutted road, and followed it up the mountainside until he came to a place where he could rest concealed until morning.

2

It was broad daylight when he woke, and there was a strange throbbing sound; Hradzka lay motionless under the brush where he had slept, his blaster ready. In a few minutes, a vehicle came into sight, following the road down the mountainside.

It was a large thing, four-wheeled, with a projection in front which probably housed the engine and a cab for the operator. The body of the vehicle was simply an open rectangular box. There were two men in the cab, and about twenty or thirty more crowded into the box-body. They were dressed in faded and nondescript garments of blue and gray and brown; all were armed with crude weapons—axes, billhooks, long-handled instruments with serrated edges, and what looked like broad-bladed spears. The vehicle itself, which seemed to be propelled by some sort of chemical-explosion engine, was dingy and mud-splattered; the men in it were ragged and unshaven. Hradzka snorted in contempt; they were probably warriors of the local tribe, going to the fire in the belief that it had been started by raiding enemies. When they found the wreckage of the time-machine, they would no doubt believe that it was the chariot of some god, and drag it home to be venerated.

A plan of action was taking shape in his mind. First, he must get clothing of the sort worn by these people, and find a safe hiding-place for his own things. Then, pretending to be a deaf-mute, he would go among them to learn something of their customs and pick up the language. When he had done that, he would move on to another tribe or village, able to tell a credible story for himself. For a while, it would be necessary for him to do menial work, but in the end, he would establish himself among these people. Then he could gather around him a faction of those who were dissatisfied with whatever conditions existed, organize a conspiracy, make arms for his followers, and start his program of power-seizure.

The matter of clothing was attended to shortly after he had crossed the mountain and descended into the valley on the other side. Hearing a clinking sound some distance from the road, as of metal striking stone, Hradzka stole cautiously through the woods until he came within sight of a man who was digging with a mattock, uprooting small bushes of a particular sort, with rough gray bark and three-pointed leaves. When he had dug one up, he would cut off the roots and then slice away the root-bark with a knife, putting it into a sack. Hradzka's lip curled contemptuously; the fellow was gathering the stuff for medicinal use. He had heard of the use of roots and herbs for such purposes by the ancient savages.

The blaster would be no use here; it was too powerful, and would destroy the clothing that the man was wearing. He unfastened a strap from his belt and attached it to a stone to form a hand-loop, then, inched forward behind the lone herb-gatherer. When he was close enough, he straightened and rushed forward, swinging his improvised weapon. The man heard him and turned, too late.

After undressing his victim, Hradzka used the mattock to finish him, and then to dig a grave. The fugitive buried his own clothes with the murdered man, and donned the faded blue shirt, rough shoes, worn trousers and jacket. The blaster he concealed under the jacket, and he kept a few other Hundredth Century gadgets; these he would hide somewhere closer to his center of operations.

He had kept, among other things, a small box of food-concentrate capsules, and in one pocket of the newly acquired jacket he found a package containing food. It was rough and unappetizing fare—slices of cold cooked meat between slices of some cereal substance. He ate these before filling in the grave, and put the paper wrappings in with the dead man. Then, his work finished, he threw the mattock into the brush and set out again, grimacing disgustedly and scratching himself. The clothing he had appropriated was verminous.

Crossing another mountain, he descended into a second valley, and, for a time, lost his way among a tangle of narrow ravines. It was dark by the time he mounted a hill and found himself looking down another valley, in which a few scattered lights gave evidence of human habitations. Not wishing to arouse suspicion by approaching these in the night-time, he found a place among some young evergreens where he could sleep.

The next morning, having breakfasted on a concentrate capsule, he found a hiding-place for his blaster in a hollow tree. It was in a sufficiently prominent position so that he could easily find it again, and at the same time unlikely to be discovered by some native. Then he went down into the inhabited valley.

He was surprised at the ease with which he established contact with the natives. The first dwelling which he approached, a cluster of farm-buildings at the upper end of the valley, gave him shelter. There was a man, clad in the same sort of rough garments Hradzka had taken from the body of the herb-gatherer, and a woman in a faded and shapeless dress. The man was thin and work-bent; the woman short and heavy. Both were past middle age.

He made inarticulate sounds to attract their attention, then gestured to his mouth and ears to indicate his assumed affliction. He rubbed his stomach to portray hunger. Looking above, he saw an ax sticking in a chopping-block, and a pile of wood near it, probably the fuel used by these people. He took the ax, split up some of the wood, then repeated the hunger-signs. The man and the woman both nodded, laughing; he was shown a pile of tree-limbs, and the man picked up a short billet of wood and used it like a measuring-rule, to indicate that all the wood was to be cut to that length.

Hradzka fell to work, and by mid-morning, he had all the wood cut. He had seen a circular stone, mounted on a trestle with a metal axle through it, and judged it to be some sort of a grinding-wheel, since it was fitted with a foot-pedal and a rusty metal can was set above it to spill water onto the grinding-edge. After chopping the wood, he carefully sharpened the ax, handing it to the man for inspection. This seemed to please the man; he clapped Hradzka on the shoulder, making commendatory sounds.

It required considerable time and ingenuity to make himself a more or less permanent member of the household. Hradzka had made a survey of the farmyard, noting the sorts of work that would normally be performed on the farm, and he pantomimed this work in its simpler operations. He pointed to the east, where the sun would rise, and to the zenith, and to the west. He made signs indicative of eating, and of sleeping, and of rising, and of working. At length, he succeeded in conveying his meaning.

There was considerable argument between the man and the woman, but his proposal was accepted as he expected it would be. It was easy to see that the work of the farm was hard for this aging couple; now, for a place to sleep and a little food, they were able to acquire a strong and intelligent slave.

In the days that followed, he made himself useful to the farm people; he fed the chickens and the livestock, milked the cow, worked in the fields. He slept in a small room at the top of the house, under the eaves, and ate with the man and woman in the farmhouse kitchen.

It was not long before he picked up a few words which he had heard his employers using, and related them to the things or acts spoken of. And he began to notice that these people, in spite of the crudities of their own life, enjoyed some of the advantages of a fairly complex civilization. Their implements were not hand-craft products, but showed machine workmanship. There were two objects hanging on hooks on the kitchen wall which he was sure were weapons. Both had wooden shoulder-stocks, and wooden forepieces; they had long tubes extending to the front, and triggers like blasters. One had double tubes mounted side-by-side, and double triggers; the other had an octagonal tube mounted over a round tube, and a loop extension on the trigger-guard. Then, there was a box on the kitchen wall, with a mouthpiece and a cylindrical tube on a cord. Sometimes a bell would ring out of the box, and the woman would go to this instrument, take down the tube and hold it to her ear, and talk into the mouthpiece. There was another box from which voices would issue, of people conversing, or of orators, or of singing, and sometimes instrumental music. None of these were objects made by savages; these people probably traded with some fairly high civilization. They were not illiterate; he found printed matter, indicating the use of some phonetic alphabet, and paper pamphlets containing printed reproductions of photographs as well as verbal text.

There was also a vehicle on the farm, powered, like the one he had seen on the road, by an engine in which a hydrocarbon liquid-fuel was exploded. He made it his business to examine this minutely, and to study its construction and operation until he was thoroughly familiar with it.

It was not until the third day after his arrival that the chickens began to die. In the morning, Hradzka found three of them dead when he went to feed them, the rest drooping unhealthily; he summoned the man and showed him what he had found. The next morning, they were all dead, and the cow was sick. She gave bloody milk, that evening, and the next morning she lay in her stall and would not get up.

The man and the woman were also beginning to sicken, though both of them tried to continue their work. It was the woman who first noticed that the plants around the farmhouse were withering and turning yellow.

The farmer went to the stable with Hradzka and looked at the cow. Shaking his head, he limped back to the house, and returned carrying one of the weapons from the kitchen—the one with the single trigger and the octagonal tube. As he entered the stable, he jerked down and up on the loop extension of the trigger-guard, then put the weapon to his shoulder and pointed it at the cow. It made a flash, and roared louder even than a hand-blaster, and the cow jerked convulsively and was dead. The man then indicated by signs that Hradzka was to drag the dead cow out of the stable, dig a hole, and bury it. This Hradzka did, carefully examining the wound in the cow's head—the weapon, he decided, was not an energy-weapon, but a simple solid-missile projector.

By evening, neither the man nor the woman were able to eat, and both seemed to be suffering intensely. The man used the communicating-instrument on the wall, probably calling on his friends for help. Hradzka did what he could to make them comfortable, cooked his own meal, washed the dishes as he had seen the woman doing, and tidied up the kitchen.

It was not long before people, men and women whom he had seen on the road or who had stopped at the farmhouse while he had been there, began arriving, some carrying baskets of food; and shortly after Hradzka had eaten, a vehicle like the farmer's, but in better condition and of better quality, arrived and a young man got out of it and entered the house, carrying a leather bag. He was apparently some sort of a scientist; he examined the man and his wife, asked many questions, and administered drugs. He also took samples for blood-tests and urinalysis. This, Hradzka considered, was another of the many contradictions he had encountered among these people—this man behaved like an educated scientist, and seemingly had nothing in common with the peasant herb-gatherer on the mountainside.

The fact was that Hradzka was worried. The strange death of the animals, the blight which had smitten the trees and vegetables around the farm, and the sickness of the farmer and his woman, all mystified him. He did not know of any disease which would affect plants and animals and humans; he wondered if some poisonous gas might not be escaping from the earth near the farmhouse. However, he had not, himself, been affected. He also disliked the way in which the doctor and the neighbors seemed to be talking about him. While he had come to a considerable revision of his original opinion about the culture-level of these people, it was not impossible that they might suspect him of having caused the whole thing by witchcraft; at any moment, they might fall upon him and put him to death. In any case, there was no longer any use in his staying here, and it might be wise if he left at once.

Accordingly, he filled his pockets with food from the pantry and slipped out of the farmhouse; before his absence was discovered he was well on his way down the road.

3

That night, Hradzka slept under a bridge across a fairly wide stream; the next morning, he followed the road until he came to a town. It was not a large place; there were perhaps four or five hundred houses and other buildings in it. Most of these were dwellings like the farmhouse where he had been staying, but some were much larger, and seemed to be places of business. One of these latter was a concrete structure with wide doors at the front; inside, he could see men working on the internal-combustion vehicles which seemed to be in almost universal use. Hradzka decided to obtain employment here.

It would be best, he decided, to continue his pretense of being a deaf-mute. He did not know whether a world-language was in use at this time or not, and even if not, the pretense of being a foreigner unable to speak the local dialect might be dangerous. So he entered the vehicle-repair shop and accosted a man in a clean shirt who seemed to be issuing instructions to the workers, going into his pantomime of the homeless mute seeking employment.

The master of the repair-shop merely laughed at him, however. Hradzka became more insistent in his manner,

making signs to indicate his hunger and willingness to work.
The other men in the shop left their tasks and gathered
around; there was much laughter and unmistakably ribald and
derogatory remarks. Hradzka was beginning to give up hope
of getting employment here when one of the workmen approached the master and whispered something to him.

The two of them walked away, conversing in low voices.
Hradzka thought he understood the situation; no doubt the
workman, thinking to lighten his own labor, was urging that
the vagrant be employed, for no other pay than food and
lodging. At length, the master assented to his employee's
urgings; he returned, showed Hradzka a hose and a bucket,
and sponges and cloths, and set him to work cleaning the mud
from one of the vehicles. Then, after seeing that the work was
being done properly, he went away, entering a room at one
side of the shop.

About twenty minutes later, another man entered the shop.
He was not dressed like any of the other people whom
Hradzka had seen; he wore a gray tunic and breeches,
polished black boots, and a cap with a visor and a metal
insignia on it; on a belt, he carried a holstered weapon like a
blaster.

After speaking to one of the workers, who pointed
Hradzka out to him, he approached the fugitive and said
something. Hradzka made gestures at his mouth and ears and
made gargling sounds; the newcomer shrugged and motioned
him to come with him, at the same time producing a pair of
handcuffs from his belt and jingling them suggestively.

In a few seconds, Hradzka tried to analyze the situation
and estimate its possibilities. The newcomer was a soldier,
or, more likely, a policeman, since manacles were a part of
his equipment. Evidently, since the evening before, a warning had been made public by means of communicating de-
vices such as he had seen at the farm, advising people that a
man of his description, pretending to be a deaf-mute, should
be detained and the police notified; it had been for that reason
that the workman had persuaded his master to employ

Hradzka. No doubt he would be accused of causing the conditions at the farm by sorcery.

Hradzka shrugged and nodded, then went to the water-tap to turn off the hose he had been using. He disconnected it, coiled it and hung it up, and then picked up the water-bucket. Then, without warning, he hurled the water into the policeman's face, sprang forward, swinging the bucket by the bale, and hit the man on the head. Releasing his grip on the bucket, he tore the blaster or whatever it was from the holster.

One of the workers swung a hammer, as though to throw it. Hradzka aimed the weapon at him and pulled the trigger; the thing belched fire and kicked back painfully in his hand, and the man fell. He used it again to drop the policeman, then thrust it into the waistband of his trousers and ran outside. The thing was not a blaster at all, he realized—only a missile projector like the big weapons at the farm, utilizing the force of some chemical explosive.

The policeman's vehicle was standing outside. It was a small single-seat, two wheeled affair. Having become familiar with the principles of these hydro-carbon engines from examination of the vehicle of the farm, and accustomed as he was to far more complex mechanisms than this crude affair, Hradzka could see at a glance how to operate it. Springing onto the saddle, he kicked away the folding support and started the engine. Just as he did, the master of the repair-shop ran outside, one of the small hand-weapons in his hand, and fired several shots. They all missed, but Hradzka heard the whining sound of the missiles passing uncomfortably close to him.

It was imperative that he recover the blaster he had hidden in the hollow tree at the head of the valley. By this time, there would be a concerted search under way for him, and he needed a better weapon than the solid-missile projector he had taken from the policeman. He did not know how many shots the thing contained, but if it propelled solid missiles by chemical explosion, there could not have been more than five or six such charges in the cylindrical part of the weapon which he had assumed to be the charge-holder. On the other hand, his blaster, a weapon of much greater power, contained enough energy for five hundred blasts, and with it were eight extra energy-capsules, giving him a total of four thousand five hundred blasts.

Handling the two-wheeled vehicle was no particular problem; although he had never ridden on anything of the sort before, it was child's play compared to controlling a Hundredth Century strato-rocket, and Hradzka was a skilled rocket-pilot.

Several times he passed vehicles on the road—the passenger vehicles with enclosed cabins, and cargo-vehicles piled high with farm produce. Once he encountered a large number of children, gathered in front of a big red building with a flagstaff in front, from which a queer flag, with horizontal red and white stripes and a white-spotted blue device in the corner, flew. They scattered off the road in terror at his approach; fortunately, he hit none of them, for at the speed at which he was travelling, such a collision would have wrecked his light vehicle.

As he approached the farm where he had spent the past few days, he saw two passenger-vehicles standing by the road. One was a black one, similar to the one in which the physician had come to the farm, and the other was white with black trimmings and bore the same device he had seen on the cap of the policeman. A policeman was sitting in the driver's seat of this vehicle, and another policeman was standing beside it, breathing smoke with one of the white paper cylinders these people used. In the farm-yard, two men were going about with a square black box; to this box, a tube was connected by a wire, and they were passing the tube about over the ground.

The policeman who was standing beside the vehicle saw him approach, and blew his whistle, then drew the weapon from his belt. Hradzka, who had been expecting some attempt to halt him, had let go the right-hand steering handle and drawn his own weapon; as the policeman drew, he fired at him. Without observing the effect of the shot, he sped on;

before he had rounded the bend above the farm, several shots were fired after him.

A mile beyond, he came to the place where he had hidden the blaster. He stopped the vehicle and jumped off, plunging into the brush and racing toward the hollow tree. Just as he reached it, he heard a vehicle approach and stop, and the door of the police vehicle slam. Hradzka's fingers found the belt of his blaster; he dragged it out and buckled it on, tossing away the missile weapon he had been carrying.

Then, crouching behind the tree, he waited. A few moments later, he caught a movement in the brush toward the road. He brought up the blaster, aimed and squeezed the trigger. There was a faint bluish glow at the muzzle, and a blast of energy tore through the brush, smashing the molecular structure of everything that stood in the way. There was an involuntary shout of alarm from the direction of the road; at least one of the policemen had escaped the blast. Hradzka holstered his weapon and crept away for some distance, keeping under cover, then turned and waited for some sign of the presence of his enemies. For some time nothing happened; he decided to turn hunter against the men who were hunting him. He started back in the direction of the road, making a wide circle, flitting silently from rock to bush and from bush to tree, stopping often to look and listen.

This finally brought him upon one of the policemen, and almost terminated his flight at the same time. He must have grown over-confident and careless; suddenly a weapon roared, and a missile smashed through the brush inches from his face. The shot had come from his left and a little to the rear. Whirling, he blasted four times, in rapid succession, then turned and fled for a few yards, dropping and crawling behind a rock. When he looked back, he could see wisps of smoke rising from the shattered trees and bushes which had absorbed the energy-output of his weapon, and he caught a faint odor of burned flesh. One of his pursuers, at least, would pursue him no longer.

He slipped away, down into the tangle of ravines and hollows in which he had wandered the day before his arrival at the farm. For the time being, he felt safe, and finally confident that he was not being pursued, he stopped to rest. The place where he stopped seemed familiar, and he looked about. In a moment, he recognized the little stream, the pool where he had bathed his feet, the clump of seedling pines under which he had slept. He even found the silver-foil wrapping from the food-concentrate capsule.

But there had been a change since the night when he had slept here. Then, the young pines had been green and alive; now they were blighted, and their needles had turned brown. Hradzka stood for a long time, looking at them. It was the same blight that had touched the plants around the farmhouse. And here, among the pine needles on the ground, lay a dead bird.

It took some time for him to admit, to himself, the implications of what this meant; vegetation, the chickens, the cow, the farmer and his wife, had all sickened and died. He had been in this place, and now, when he had returned, he found that death had followed him here, too.

During the early centuries of the Atomic Era, he knew, there had been great wars, the stories of which had survived even to the Hundredth Century. Among the weapons that had been used, there had been artificial plagues and epidemics, caused by new types of bacteria developed in laboratories, against which the victims had possessed no protection. Those germs and viruses had persisted for centuries, and gradually had lost their power to harm mankind. Suppose, now, that he had brought some of them back with him, to a century before they had been developed. Suppose, that was, that he were a human plague-carrier. He thought of the vermin that had infested the clothing he had taken from the man he had killed on the other side of the mountain; they had not troubled him after the first day.

There was a throbbing mechanical sound somewhere in the air; he looked about, and finally identified its source. A small aircraft had come over the valley from the other side of the mountain and was circling lazily overhead. He froze, shrinking back under a pine tree; as long as he remained motionless, he would not be seen, and soon the thing would go away. He was beginning to understand why the search for him was being pressed so relentlessly; as long as he remained alive, he was a menace to everybody in this First Century world.

He got out his supply of food concentrates, saw that he had only three capsules left, and put them away again. For a long time, he sat under the dying tree, chewing on a twig and thinking. There must be some way in which he could overcome, or even utilize, his inherent deadliness to these people. He might find some isolated community, conceal himself near it, invade it at night and infect it, and then, when everybody was dead, move in and take it for himself. But was there any such isolated community? The farmhouse where he had worked had been fairly remote, yet its inhabitants had been in communication with the outside world, and the physician had come immediately in response to their call for help.

The little aircraft had been circling overhead, directly above the place where he lay hidden. For a while, Hradzka was afraid it had spotted him, and was debating the advisability of using his blaster on it. Then it banked, turned and went away. He watched it circle over the valley on the other side of the mountain, and got to his feet.

4

Almost at once, there was a new sound—a multiple throbbing, at a quick, snarling tempo that hinted at enormous power, growing louder each second. Hradzka stiffened and drew his blaster; as he did, five more aircraft swooped over the crest of the mountain and came rushing down toward him; not aimlessly, but as though they knew exactly where he was. As they approached, the leading edges of their wings sparkled with light, branches began flying from the trees about him, and there was a loud hammering noise.

He aimed a little in front of them and began blasting. A wing flew from one of the aircraft, and it plunged downward. Another came apart in the air; a third burst into flames. The other two zoomed upward quickly. Hradzka swung his blaster after them, blasting again and again. He hit a fourth with a blast of energy, knocking it to pieces, and then the fifth was out of range. He blasted at it twice, but without effect; a hand-blaster was only good for a thousand yards at the most.

Holstering his weapon, he hurried away, following the stream and keeping under cover of trees. The last of the attacking aircraft had gone away, but the little scout-plane was still circling about, well out of blaster-range.

Once or twice, Hradzka was compelled to stay hidden for some time, not knowing the nature of the pilot's ability to detect him. It was during one of these waits that the next phase of the attack developed.

It began, like the last one, with a distant roar that swelled in volume until it seemed to fill the whole world. Then, fifteen or twenty thousand feet out of blaster-range, the new attackers swept into sight.

There must have been fifty of them, huge tapering things with wide-spread wings, flying in close formation, wave after V-shaped wave. He stood and stared at them, amazed; he had never imagined that such aircraft existed in the First Century. Then a high-pitched screaming sound cut through the roar of the propellers, and for an instant he saw countless small specs in the sky, falling downward.

The first bomb-salvo landed in the young pines, where he had fought against the first air attack. Great gouts of flame shot upward, and smoke, and flying earth and debris. Hradzka turned and started to run. Another salvo fell in front of him; he veered to the left and plunged on through the undergrowth. Now the bombs were falling all about him, deafening him with their thunder, shaking him with concussion. He dodged, frightened, as the trunk of a tree came crashing down beside him. Then something hit him across the back, knocking him flat. For a moment, he lay stunned, then tried to rise. As he did, a searing light filled his eyes and a wave of intolerable heat swept over him. Then darkness . . .

"No, Zarvas Pol," Kradzy Zago repeated. "Hradzka will not return; the time-machine was sabotaged."

"So? By you?" the soldier asked.

The scientist nodded. "I knew the purpose for which he intended it. Hradzka was not content with having enslaved a whole Solar System; he hungered to bring tyranny and serfdom to all the past and all the future as well; he wanted to be master not only of the present but of the centuries that were and were to be, as well. I never took part in politics, Zarvas Pol; I had no hand in this revolt. But I could not be party to such a crime as Hradzka contemplated when it lay within my power to prevent it."

"The machine will take him out of our space-time continuum, or back to a time when this planet was a swirling cloud of flaming gas?" Zarvas Pol asked.

Kradzy Zago shook his head. "No, the unit is not powerful enough for that. It will only take him about ten thousand years into the past. But then, when it stops, the machine will destroy itself. It may destroy Hradzka with it, or he may escape. But if he does, he will be left stranded ten thousand years ago, when he can do us no harm.

"Actually, it did not operate as he imagined and there is an infinitely small chance that he could have returned to our time, in any event. But I wanted to insure against even so small a chance."

"We can't be sure of that," Zarvas Pol objected. "He may know more about the machine than you think; enough more to build another like it. So you must build me a machine, and I'll take back a party of volunteers and hunt him down."

"That would not be necessary, and you would only share his fate." Then, apparently changing the subject, Kradzy Zago asked: "Tell me, Zarvas Pol; have you never heard the legends of the Deadly Radiations?"

General Zarvas smiled. "Who has not? Every cadet at the Officers' College dreams of re-discovering them, to use as a weapon, but nobody ever has. We hear these tales of how, in the early days, atomic engines and piles and fission-bombs emitted particles which were utterly deadly, which would make anything with which they came in contact deadly, which would bring a horrible death to any human being. But these are only myths. All the ancient experiments have been duplicated time and again, and the deadly-radiation effect has never been observed. Some say that it is a mere old-wives' terror-tale; some say that the deaths were caused by fear of atomic energy, when it was still unfamiliar; others contend that the fundamental nature of atomic energy has altered by the degeneration of the fissionable matter. For my own part, I'm not enough of a scientist to have an opinion.''

The old one smiled wanly. ''None of these theories is correct. In the beginning of the Atomic Era, the Deadly Radiations existed. They still exist, but they are no longer deadly, because all life on this planet has adapted itself to such radiations, and all living things are now immune to them.''

''And Hradzka has returned to a time when such immunity did not exist? But would that not be to his advantage?''

''Remember, General, that man has been using atomic energy for ten thousand years. Our whole world has become drenched with radioactivity. The planet, the seas, the atmosphere, and every living thing, are all radioactive, now. Radioactivity is as natural to us as the air we breathe. Now, you remember hearing of the great wars of the first centuries of the Atomic Era, in which whole nations were wiped out, leaving only hundreds of survivors out of millions. You, no doubt, think that such tales are products of ignorant and barbaric imagination, but I assure you, they are literally true. It was not the blast-effect of a few bombs which created such holocausts, but the radiations released by the bombs. And those who survived to carry on the race were men and women whose systems resisted the radiations, and they transmitted to their progeny that power of resistance. In many cases their children were mutants—not monsters, although there were many of them, too, which did not survive—but humans who were immune to radioactivity.''

''An interesting theory, Kradzy Zago,'' the soldier commented. ''And one which conforms both to what we know of atomic energy and to the ancient legends. Then you would say that those radiations are still deadly—to the non-immune?''

"Exactly. And Hradzka, his body emitting those radiations, has returned to the First Century of the Atomic Era—to a world without immunity."

General Zarvas' smile vanished. "Man!" he cried in horror. "You have loosed a carrier of death among those innocent people of the past!"

Kradzy Zago nodded. "That is true. I estimate that Hradzka will probably cause the death of a hundred or so people, before he is dealt with. But dealt with he will be. Tell me, General; if a man should appear now, out of nowhere, spreading a strange and horrible plague wherever he went, what would you do?"

"Why, I'd hunt him down and kill him," General Zarvas replied. "Not for anything he did, but for the menace he was. And then, I'd cover his body with a mass of concrete bigger than this place."

"Precisely." Kradzy Zago smiled. "And the military commanders and political leaders of the First Century were no less ruthless or efficient than you. You know how atomic energy was first used? There was an ancient nation, upon the ruins of whose cities we have built our own, which was famed for its idealistic humanitarianism. Yet that nation, treacherously attacked, created the first atomic bombs in self-defense, and used them. It is among the people of that nation that Hradzka has emerged."

"But would they recognize him as the cause of the calamity he brings among them?"

"Of course. He will emerge at the time when atomic energy is first being used. They will have detectors for the Deadly Radiations—detectors we know nothing of, today, for a detection instrument must be free from the thing it is intended to detect, and today everything is radioactive. It will be a day or so before they discover what is happening to them, and not a few will die in that time, I fear; but once they have found out what is killing their people, Hradzka's days—no, his hours—will be numbered."

"A mass of concrete bigger than this place," Tobbh the Slave repeated General Zarvas' words. "*The Ancient Spaceport!*"

Prince Burvanny clapped him on the shoulder. "Tobbh, man! You've hit it!"

"You mean . . . ?" Kradzy Zago began.

"Yes. You all know of it. It's stood for nobody knows how many millennia, and nobody's ever decided what it was, to begin with, except that somebody, once, filled a valley with concrete, level from mountain-top to mountain-top. The accepted theory is that it was done for a firing-stand for the first Moon-rocket. But gentlemen, our friend Tobbh's explained it. It is the tomb of Hradzka, and it has been the tomb of Hradzka for ten thousand years before Hradzka was born!"

OPERATION R.S.V.P.

In "Operation R.S.V.P.," Piper again examines the theme of nuclear power, but with a different emphasis. Thirty years of further study have taught us much about nuclear physics, but Piper was second-to-none on the subject of nuclear brinksmanship.

Vladmir N. Dzhoubinsky, Foreign Minister, Union of East European Soviet Republics, to Wu Fung Tung, Foreign Minister, United People's Republics of East Asia:

15 Jan., 1984

Honored Sir:

Pursuant to our well-known policy of exchanging military and scientific information with the Governments of friendly Powers, my Government takes great pleasure in announcing the completely successful final tests of our new nuclear-rocket guided missile *Marxist Victory*. The test launching was made from a position south of Lake Balkash; the target was located in the East Siberian Sea.

In order to assist you in appreciating the range of the new guided missile *Marxist Victory*, let me point out that the distance from launching-site to target is somewhat over 50 percent greater than the distance from launching-site to your capital, Nanking.

My Government is still hopeful that your Government will revise its present intransigent position on the Khakum River dispute.

I have the honor, etc., etc., etc.,

V. N. Dzhoubinsky

Wu Fung Tung, to Vladmir N. Dzhoubinsky:

7 Feb., 1984

Estimable Sir:

My Government was most delighted to learn of the splendid triumph of your Government in developing the new guided missile *Marxist Victory,* and at the same time deeply relieved. We had, of course, detected the release of nuclear energy incident to the test, and inasmuch as it had obviously originated in the disintegration of a quantity of uranium 235, we had feared that an explosion had occurred at your Government's secret uranium plant at Khatanga. We have long known of the lax security measures in effect at this plant, and have, as a consequence, been expecting some disaster there.

I am therefore sure that your Government will be equally gratified to learn of the perfection, by my Government, of our own new guided missile *Celestial Destroyer,* which embodies, in greatly improved form, many of the features of your own Government's guided missile *Marxist Victory.* Naturally, your own scientific warfare specialists have detected the release of energy incident to the explosion of our own improved thorium-hafnium interaction bomb; this bomb was exploded over the North Polar ice cap, about two hundred miles south of the Pole, on about 35 degrees East Longitude, almost due north of your capital city of Moscow. The launching was made from a site in Tibet.

Naturally, my Government cannot deviate from our present just and reasonable attitude in the Khakum River question. Trusting that your Government will realize this, I have the honor to be, Your obedient and respectful servant.

Wu Fung Tung

From N. Y. Times, *Feb 20, 1984:*

AFGHAN RULER FETED AT NANKING
Ameer Shere Ali Abdallah Confers With
UPREA Pres. Sung Li-Yin

UEESR Foreign Minister Dzhoubinsky to Maxim G. Krylenkoff, Ambassador at Nanking:

3 March, 1984

Comrade Ambassador:

It is desired that you make immediate secret and confidential, repeat, secret and confidential inquiry as to the whereabouts of Dr. Dimitri O. Voronoff, the noted Soviet rocket expert, designer of the new guided missile *Marxist Victory*, who vanished a week ago from the Josef Vissarionovitch Djugashvli Reaction-Propulsion Laboratories at Molotovgorod. It is feared in Government circles that this noted scientist has been abducted by agents of the United People's Republics of East Asia, possibly to extract from him, under torture, information of a secret technical nature.

As you know, this is but the latest of a series of such disappearances, beginning about five years ago, when the Khakum River question first arose.

Your utmost activity in this matter is required.

Dzhoubinsky

Ambassador Krylenkoff to Foreign Minister Dzhoubinsky:

Comrade Foreign Minister:

Since receipt of yours of 3/3/'84, I have been utilizing

all resources at my disposal in the matter of the noted scientist D. O. Voronoff, and availing myself of all sources of information, e.g., spies, secret agents, disaffected elements of the local population, and including two UPREA Cabinet Ministers on my payroll. I regret to report that results of this investigation have been entirely negative. No one here appears to know anything of the whereabouts of Dr. Voronoff.

At the same time, there is considerable concern in UPREA Government circles over the disappearances of certain prominent East Asian scientists, e.g., Dr. Hong Foo, the nuclear physicist; Dr. Hin Yang-Woo, the great theoretical mathematician; Dr. Mong Shing, the electronics expert. I am informed that UPREA Government sources are attributing these disappearances to us.

I can only say that I am sincerely sorry that is is not the case.

Krylenkoff

Wu Fung Tung to Vladmir N. Dzhoubinsky:

21 April, 1984

Estimable Sir:

In accordance with our established policy of free exchange with friendly Powers of scientific information, permit me to inform your Government that a new mutated disease-virus has been developed in our biological laboratories, causing a highly contagious disease similar in symptoms to bubonic plague, but responding to none of the treatments for this latter disease. This new virus strain was accidentally produced in the course of some experiments with radioactivity.

In spite of the greatest care, it is feared that this virus has spread beyond the laboratory in which it was developed. We warn you most urgently of the dange that it may have spread to the UEESR; enclosed is a list of symptoms, etc.

My Government instructs me to advise your Government that the attitude of your Government in the Khakum River question is utterly unacceptable, and will require considerable revision before my Government can even consider negotiation with your Government on the subject.

Your obedient and respectful servant,

Wu Fung Tung

From N. Y. Times, *May 12, 1984:*

AFGHAN RULER FETED AT MOSCOW
Ameer sees Red Square Troop Review; Confers with
Premier-President Mouzorgin

Sing Yat, UPREA Ambassador at Moscow, to Wu Fung Tung:

26 June, 1984

Venerable and Honored Sir:

I regret humbly that I can learn nothing whatever about the fate of the learned scholars of science of whom you inquire, namely: Hong Foo, Hin Yang-Woo, Mong Shing, Yee Ho Li, Wong Fat and Bao Hu-Shin. This inability may be in part due to incompetence of my unworthy self, but none of my many sources of information, including Soviet Minister of Police Morgodoff, who is on my payroll, can furnish any useful data whatever. I am informed, however, that the UEESR Government is deeply concerned about similar disappearances of some of the foremost of their own scientists, including Voronoff, Jirnikov, Kagorinoff, Bakhorin, Himmelfarber and Pavlovinsky, all of whose dossiers are on file with our Bureau of Foreign Intelligence. I am further informed that the Government of the UEESR ascribes these disappearances to our own activities.

Ah, Venerable and Honored Sir, if this were only true!

Kindly condescend to accept compliments of,

Sing Yat

Dzhoubinsky to Wu Fung Tung:

6 October, 1984

Honored Sir:

Pursuant to our well-known policy of exchanging scientific information with the Governments of friendly Powers, my Government takes the greatest pleasure in announcing a scientific discovery of inestimable value to the entire world. I refer to nothing less than a positive technique for liquidating rats as a species.

This technique involves treatment of male rats with certain types of hard radiations, which not only renders them reproductively sterile but leaves the rodents so treated in full possession of all other sexual functions and impulses. Furthermore, this condition of sterility is venereally contagious, so that one male rat so treated will sterilize all female rats with which it comes in contact, and these, in turn, will sterilize all male rats coming in contact with them. Our mathematicians estimate that under even moderately favorable circumstances, the entire rat population of the world could be sterilized from one male rat in approximately two hundred years.

Rats so treated have already been liberated in the granaries at Odessa; in three months, rat-trappings there have fallen by 26.4 percent, and grain-losses to rats by 32.09 percent.

We are shipping you six dozen sterilized male rats, which you can use for sterilization stock, and, by so augmenting their numbers, may duplicate our own successes.

Curiously enough, this effect of venereally-contagious sterility was discovered quite accidentally, in connection with the use of hard radiations for human sterilization (criminals, mental defectives, etc.). Knowing the disastrous possible effects of an epidemic of contagious human sterility, all persons so sterilized were liquidated as soon as the contagious nature of their sterility had been discovered, with the exception of a dozen or so convicts, who had been released before this discovery was made. It is believed that at least some of them have made their way over the border and into the territory of the United People's Republics of East Asia. I must caution your Government to be on the lookout for them. Among a people still practicing ancestor-worship, an epidemic of sterility would be a disaster indeed.

My Government must insist that your Government take some definite step toward the solution of the Khakum River question; the present position of the Government of the United People's Republics of East Asia on this subject is utterly unacceptable to the Government of the Union of East European Soviet Republics, and must be revised very considerably.

I have the honor, etc., etc.,

Vladmir N. Dzhoubinsky

Coded radiogram, Dzhoubinsky to Krylenkoff:

25 OCTOBER, 1984

ASCERTAIN IMMEDIATELY CAUSE OF RELEASE OF NUCLEAR ENERGY VICINITY OF NOVA ZEMBLA THIS AM

DZHOUBINSKY

Coded radiogram, Wu Fung Tung to Sing Yat:

25 OCTOBER, 1984

ASCERTAIN IMMEDIATELY CAUSE OF RELEASE OF NUCLEAR ENERGY VICINITY OF NOVA ZEMBLA THIS AM

WU

*Letter from the Ameer of Afghanistan to UEESR Premier-
President Mouzorgin and UPREA President Sung Lin-Yin:*

26 October, 1984

SHERE ALI ABDALLAH, Ameer of Afghanistan,
Master of Kabul, Lord of Herat and Kandahar, Keeper
of Khyber Pass, Defender of the True Faith, Servant of
the Most High and Sword-Hand of the Prophet; Ph. D.
(Princeton); Sc. B. (Massachusetts Institute of Technology); M. A. (Oxford): to their Excellencies A. A.
Mouzorgin, Premier-President of the Union of East
European Soviet Republics and Sung Li-Yin, President
of the United People's Republics of East Asia.

Greetings, in the name of Allah!

For the past five years, I have watched, with growing
concern, the increasing tensions between your Excellencies' respective Governments, allegedly arising out
of the so-called Khakum River question. It is my conviction that this Khakum River dispute is the utterly fraudulent device by which both Governments hope to create a
pretext for the invasion of India, each ostensibly to
rescue that unhappy country from the rapacity of the
other. Your Excellencies must surely realize that this is
a contingency which the Government of the Kingdom of
Afghanistan cannot and will not permit; it would mean
nothing short of the national extinction of the Kingdom
of Afghanistan, and the enslavement of the Afghan
people.

Your Excellencies will recall that I discussed this
matter most urgently on the occasions of my visits to
your respective capitals of Moscow and Nanking, and
your respective attitudes, on those occasions, have firm-
ly convinced me that neither of your Excellencies is by
nature capable of adopting a rational or civilized attitude
toward this question. It appears that neither of your
Excellencies has any intention of abandoning your present war of mutual threats and blackmail until forced to
do so by some overt act on the part of one or the other of
your Excellencies' Governments, which would result in

physical war of pan-Asiatic scope and magnitude. I am further convinced that this deplorable situation arises out of the megalomaniac ambitions of the Federal Governments of the UEESR and the UPREA, respectively, and that the different peoples of what you unblushingly call your "autonomous" republics have no ambitions except, on a rapidly diminishing order of probability, to live out their natural span of years in peace. Therefore:

> *In the name of ALLAH, the Merciful, the Compassionate: We, Shere Ali Abdallah, Ameer of Afghanistan, etc., do decree and command that the political entities known as the Union of East European Soviet Republics and the United People's Republics of East Asia respectively, are herewith abolished and dissolved into their constituent autonomous republics, each one of which shall hereafter enjoy complete sovereignty within its own borders as is right and proper.*

Now, in case either of you gentlemen feel inclined to laugh this off, let me remind you of the series of mysterious disappearances of some of the most noted scientists of both the UEESR and the UPREA, and let me advise your Excellencies that these scientists are now residents and subjects of the Kingdom of Afghanistan, and are here engaged in research and development work for my Government. These gentlemen were not abducted, as you gentlemen seem to believe; they came here of their own free will, and ask nothing better than to remain here, where they are treated with dignity and honor, given material rewards—riches, palaces, harems, retinues of servants, etc.—and are also free from the intellectual and ideological restraints which make life so intolerable in your respective countries to any man above the order of intelligence of a cretin. In return for these benefactions, these eminent scientists have developed, for my Government, certain weapons. For example:

1.) A nuclear-rocket guided missile, officially designated as the *Sword of Islam*, vastly superior to your Excellencies' respective guided missiles *Marxist Victory* and *Celestial Destroyer*. It should be; it was the product of the joint efforts of Dr. Voronoff and Dr. Bao Hu-Shin, whom your Excellencies know.

2.) A new type of radar-radio-electronic defense screen, which can not only detect the approach of a guided missile, at any velocity whatever, but will automatically capture and redirect same. In case either of your Excellencies doubt this statement, you are invited to aim a rocket at some target in Afghanistan and see what happens.

3.) Both the UPREA mutated virus and the UEESR contagious sterility, with positive vaccines against the former and means of instrumental detection of the latter.

4.) A technique for initiating and controlling the Bethe carbon-hydrogen cycle. We are now using this as a source of heat for industrial and even domestic purposes, and we also have a carbon-hydrogen cycle bomb. Such a bomb, delivered by one of our *Sword of Islam* Mark IV's, was activated yesterday over the northern tip of Nova Zembla, at an altitude of four miles. I am enclosing photographic reproductions of views of this test, televised to Kabul by an accompanying *Sword of Islam* Mark V observation rocket. I am informed that expeditions have been sent by both the UEESR and the UPREA to investigate; they should find some very interesting conditions. For one thing, they won't need their climbing equipment to get over the Nova Zembla Glacier; the Nova Zembla Glacier isn't there, anymore.

5.) A lithium bomb. This has not been tested, yet. A lithium bomb is nothing for a country the size of Afghanistan to let off inside its own borders. We intend making a test with it within the next ten days, however. If your Excellencies will designate a target, which must be at the center of an uninhabited area at least five hundred miles square, the test can be made in perfect safety. If not, I cannot answer the results; that will be in the hands of Allah, Who has ordained all things. No doubt Allah has ordained the destruction of either Moscow or Nanking; whichever city Allah has elected to erase, I will make it my personal responsibility to see to it that the other isn't slighted, either.

However, if your Excellencies decide to accede to my modest and reasonable demands, not later than one week from today, this test-launching will be cancelled as unnecessary. Of course, that would leave unsettled a bet I have made with Dr. Hong Foo—a star sapphire against his favorite Persian concubine—that the explosion of a lithium bomb will not initiate a chain reaction in the Earth's crust and so disintegrate this planet. This, of course, is a minor consideration, unworthy of Your notice.

Of course, I am aware that both your Excellencies have, in the past, fomented mutual jealousies and suspicions among the several "autonomous" republics under your respective jurisdictions, as an instrument of policy. If these peoples were, at this time, to receive full independence, the present inevitability of a pan-Asiatic war on a grand scale would be replaced only by the inevitability of a pan-Asiatic war by detail. Obviously, some single supra-national sovereignty is needed to maintain peace, and such a sovereignty should be established under some leadership not hitherto associated with either the former UEESR or the former UPREA. I humbly offer myself as President of such a supranational organization, counting as a matter of course upon the whole-hearted support and cooperation of both your Excellencies. It might be well if both your Excellencies were to come here to Kabul to confer with me on this subject at your very earliest convenience.

The Peace of Allah be upon both your Excellencies!
Shere Ali Abdallah,
Ph. D., Sc. B., M. A.

From N.Y. Times, *Oct. 30, 1984:*

MOUZORGIN, SUNG LI-YIN,
FETED AT KABUL
Confer With Ameer;
Discuss Peace Plans
Surprise Developments Seen . . .

GENESIS

In his Paratime series, Piper divided the Paratime alternate worlds into five different levels, based on the Martians' varying degrees of success in their attempt to colonize Terra, 75,000 to 100,000 years ago. For example, they were completely successful on Level One—the only level possessing the secret of Paratime travel to alternate worlds.

The Euro-American Sector—our own time line—is located on the maximum probability time-line, the Fourth Level. It is on this level that a disaster occurred of such magnitude that all Martian technology and civilization were completely lost. Most Fourth Level inhabitants believe they are an indigenous race with a long history of savagery.

"Genesis" is the long-unavailable story of the disaster that struck these Martian colonists, and their fight for survival.

1

ABOARD THE SHIP, there was neither day nor night; the hours slipped gently by, as vistas of star-gemmed blackness slid across the visiscreens. For the crew, time had some

147

meaning—one watch on duty and two off. But for the thousand-odd colonists, the men and women who were to be the spearhead of migration to a new and friendlier planet, it had none. They slept, and played, worked at such tasks as they could invent, and slept again, while the huge ship followed her plotted trajectory.

Kalvar Dard, the army officer who would lead them in their new home, had as little to do as any of his followers. The ship's officers had all the responsibility for the voyage, and, for the first time in over five years, he had none at all. He was finding the unaccustomed idleness more wearying than the hectic work of loading the ship before the blastoff from Doorsha. He went over his landing and security plans again, and found no probable emergency unprepared for. Dard wandered about the ship, talking to groups of his colonists, and found morale even better than he had hoped. He spent hours staring into the forward visiscreens, watching the disk of Tareesh, the planet of his destination, grow larger and clearer ahead.

Now, with the voyage almost over, he was in the cargo-hold just aft of the Number Seven bulkhead, with six girls to help him, checking construction material which would be needed immediately after landing. The stuff had all been checked two or three times before, but there was no harm in going over it again. It furnished an occupation to fill in the time; it gave Kalvar Dard an excuse for surrounding himself with half a dozen charming girls, and the girls seemed to enjoy being with him. There was tall blonde Olva, the electromagnetician; pert little Varnis, the machinist's helper; Kyna, the surgeon's-aide; dark-haired Analea; Dorita, the accountant; plump little Eldra, the armament technician. At the moment, they were all sitting on or around the desk in the corner of the storeroom, going over the inventory when they were not just gabbling.

"Well, how about the rock-drill bitts?" Dorita was asking earnestly, trying to stick to business. "Won't we need them almost as soon as we're off?"

"Yes, we'll have to dig temporary magazines for our explosives, small-arms and artillery ammunition, and storage-pits for our fissionables and radioactives,'' Kalvar Dard replied. "We'll have to have safe places for that stuff ready before it can be unloaded; and if we run into hard rock near the surface, we'll have to drill holes for blasting-shots.''

"The drilling machinery goes into one of those prefabricated sheds,'' Eldra considered. "Will there be room in it for all the bitts, too?''

Kalvar Dard shrugged. "Maybe. If not, we'll cut poles and build racks for them outside. The bitts are nono-steel; they can be stored in the open.''

"If there are poles to cut,'' Olva added.

"I'm not worrying about that,'' Kalvar Dard replied. "We have a pretty fair idea of conditions on Tareesh; our astronomers have been making telescopic observations for the past fifteen centuries. There's a pretty big Arctic ice-cap, but it's been receding slowly, with a wide belt of what's believed to be open grassland to the south of it, and a belt of what's assumed to be evergreen forest south of that. We plan to land somewhere in the northern hemisphere, about the grassland-forest line. And since Tareesh is richer in water than Doorsha, you mustn't think of grassland in terms of our brush thickets. The vegetation should be much more luxuriant.''

"If there's such a large polar ice-cap, the summers ought to be fairly cool, and the winters cold,'' Varnis reasoned. "I'd think that would mean fur-bearing animals. Colonel, you'll have to shoot me something with a nice soft fur; I like furs.''

Kalvar Dard chuckled. "Shoot you nothing, you can shoot your own furs. I've seen your carbine and pistol scores,'' he began.

There was a sudden suck of air, disturbing the papers on the desk. They all turned to see one of the ship's rocket-boat bays open; a young Air Force lieutenant named Seldar Glav, who would be staying on Tareesh with them to pilot their aircraft, emerged from an open airlock.

"Don't tell me you've been to Tareesh and back in that thing,'' Olva greeted him.

Seldar Glav grinned at her. "I could have been, at that;

we're only twenty or thirty planetary calibers away, now. We ought to be entering Tareeshan atmosphere by the middle of the next watch. I was only checking the boats, to make sure they'll be ready to launch . . . Colonel Kalvar, would you mind stepping over here? There's something I think you should look at, sir.''

Kalvar Dard took one arm from around Analea's waist and lifted the other from Varnis' shoulder, sliding off the desk. He followed Glav into the boat-bay; as they went through the airlock, the cheerfulness left the young lieutenant's face.

''I didn't want to say anything in front of the girls, sir,'' he began, ''but I've been checking boats to make sure we can make a quick getaway. Our meteor-security's gone out. The detectors are deader than the Fourth Dynasty, and the blasters won't synchronize. . . . Did you hear a big thump, about a half an hour ago, Colonel?''

''Yes, I thought the ship's labor-crew was shifting heavy equipment in the hold aft of us. What was it, a meteor-hit?''

''It was. Just aft of Number Ten bulkhead. A meteor about the size of the nose of that rocket-boat.''

Kalvar Dard whistled softly. ''Great Gods of Power! The detectors must be dead, to pass up anything like that . . . Why wasn't a boat-stations call sent out?''

''Captain Vlazil was unwilling to risk starting a panic, sir,'' the Air Force officer replied. ''Really, I'm exceeding my orders in mentioning it to you, but I thought you should now . . .''

Kalvar Dard swore. ''It's a blasted pity Captain Vlazil didn't try thinking! Gold-braided quarter-wit! Maybe his crew might panic, but my people wouldn't . . . I'm going to call the control-room and have it out with him. By the Ten Gods . . .!''

He ran through the airlock and back into the hold, starting toward the intercom-phone beside the desk. Before he could reach it, there was another heavy jar, rocking the entire ship. He, and Seldar Glav, who had followed him out of the boat-bay, and the six girls, who had risen on hearing their commander's angry voice, were all tumbled into a heap.

Dard surged to his feet, dragging Kyna up along with him; together, they helped the others to rise. The ship was suddenly filled with jangling bells, and the red danger-lights on the ceiling were flashing on and off.

"Attention! Attention!" the voice of some officer in the control-room blared out of the intercom-speaker. "The ship has just been hit by a large meteor! All compartments between bulkheads Twelve and Thirteen are sealed off. All persons between bulkheads Twelve and Thirteen put on oxygen helmets and plug in at the nearest phone connection. Your air is leaking, and you can't get out, but if you put on oxygen equipment immediately, you'll be all right. We'll get you out as soon as we can, and in any case, we are only a few hours out of Tareeshan atmosphere. All persons in Compartment Twelve, put on . . ."

Kalvar Dard was swearing evilly. "That does it! That does it for good! . . . Anybody else in this compartment, below the living quarter level?"

"No, we're the only ones," Analea told him.

"The people above have their own boats; they can look after themselves. You girls, get in that boat, in there. Glav, you and I'll try to warn the people above . . ."

There was another jar, heavier than the one which had preceded it, throwing them all down again. As they rose, a new voice was shouting over the public-address system:

"*Abandon ship! Abandon ship!* The converters are back-firing, and rocket-fuel is leaking back toward the engine-rooms! An explosion is imminent! Abandon ship, all hands!"

Kalvar Dard and Seldar Glav grabbed the girls and literally threw them through the hatch, into the rocket-boat. Dard pushed Glav in ahead of him, then jumped in. Before he had picked himself up, two or three of the girls were at the hatch, dogging the cover down.

"All right, Glav, blast off!" Dard ordered. "We've got to be at least a hundred miles from this ship when she blows, or we'll blow with her!"

"Don't I know!" Seldar Glav retorted over his shoulder, racing for the controls. "Grab hold of something, everybody;

I'm going to fire all jets at once!''

An instant later, while Kalvar Dard and the girls clung to stanchions and pieces of fixed furniture, the boat shot forward out of its housing. When Dard's head had cleared, they were in free flight.

"How was that?" Glav yelled. "Everybody all right?" He hesitated for a moment. "I think I blacked out for about ten seconds."

Kalvar Dard looked the girls over. Eldra was using a corner of her smock to stanch a nosebleed, and Olva had a bruise over one eye. Otherwise, everybody was in good shape.

"Wonder we didn't all black out, permanently," he said. "Well, put on the visiscreens, and let's see what's going on outside. Olva, get on the radio and try to see if anybody else got away."

"Set course for Tareesh?" Glav asked. "We haven't fuel enough to make it back to Doorsha."

"I was afraid of that," Dard nodded. "Tareesh it is; northern hemisphere, daylight side. Try to get about the edge of the temperate zone, as near water as you can . . ."

2

They were flung off their feet again, this time backward along the boat. As they picked themselves up, Seldar Glav was shaking his head, sadly. "That was the ship going up," he said; "the blast must have caught us dead astern."

"All right." Kalvar Dard rubbed a bruised forehead. "Set course for Tareesh, then cut out the jets till we're ready to land. And get the screens on, somebody; I want to see what's happened."

The screens glowed; then full vision came on. The planet on which they would land loomed huge before them, its north pole toward them, and its single satellite on the port side. There was no sign of any rocket-boat in either side screen, and the rear-view screen was a blur of yellow flame from the jets.

"Cut the jets, Glav," Dard repeated. "Didn't you hear me?"

"But I did, sir!" Seldar Glav indicated the firing-panel. Then he glanced at the rear-view screen. "The gods help us! It's *yellow* flame; the jets are burning out!"

Kalvar Dard had not boasted idly when he had said that his people would not panic. All the girls went white, and one or two gave low cries of consternation, but that was all.

"What happens next?" Analea wanted to know. "Do we blow, too?"

"Yes, as soon as the fuel-line burns up to the tanks."

"Can you land on Tareesh before then?" Dard asked.

"I can try. How about the satellite? It's closer."

"It's also airless. Look at it and see for yourself," Kalvar Dard advised. "Not enough mass to hold an atmosphere."

Glav looked at the army officer with new respect. He had always been inclined to think of the Frontier Guards as a gang of scientifically illiterate dirk-and-pistol bravos. He fiddled for a while with instruments on the panel; an automatic computer figured the distance to the planet, the boat's velocity, and the time needed for a landing.

"We have a chance, sir," he said. "I think I can set down in about thirty minutes; that should give us about ten minutes to get clear of the boat, before she blows up."

"All right; get busy, girls," Kalvar Dard said. "Grab everything we'll need. Arms and ammunition first; all of them you can find. After that, warm clothing, bedding, tools and food."

With that, he jerked open one of the lockers and began pulling out weapons. He buckled on a pistol and dagger, and handed other weapon-belts to the girls behind him. He found two of the heavy big-game rifles, and several bandoliers of ammunition for them. He tossed out carbines, and boxes of carbine and pistol cartridges. He found two bomb-bags, each containing six light anti-personnel grenades and a big demolition-bomb. Glancing, now and then, at the forward screen, he caught glimpses of blue sky and green-tinted plains below.

"All right!" the pilot yelled. "We're coming in for a

landing! A couple of you stand by to get the hatch open.''

There was a jolt, and all sense of movement stopped. A cloud of white smoke drifted past the screens. The girls got the hatch open; snatching up weapons and bedding-wrapped bundles they all scrambled up out of the boat.

There was fire outside. The boat had come down upon a grassy plain; now the grass was burning from the heat of the jets. One by one, they ran forward along the top of the rocket-boat, jumping down to the ground clear of the blaze. Then, with every atom of strength they possessed, they ran away from the doomed boat.

The ground was rough, and the grass high, impeding them. One of the girls tripped and fell; without pausing, two others pulled her to her feet, while another snatched up and slung the carbine she had dropped. Then, ahead, Kalvar Dard saw a deep gully, through which a little stream trickled.

They huddled together at the bottom of it, waiting, for what seemed like a long while. Then a gentle tremor ran through the ground, and swelled to a sickening, heaving shock. A roar of almost palpable sound swept over them, and a flash of blue-white light dimmed the sun above. The sound, the shock, and the searing light did not pass away at once; they continued for seconds that seemed like an eternity. Earth and stones pelted down around them; choking dust rose. Then the thunder and the earth-shock were over; above, incandescent vapors swirled, and darkened into an overhanging pall of smoke and dust.

For a while, they crouched motionless, too stunned to speak. Then shaken nerves steadied and jarred brains cleared. They all rose weakly. Trickles of earth were still coming down from the sides of the gully, and the little stream, which had been clear and sparkling, was roiled with mud. Mechanically, Kalvar Dard brushed the dust from his clothes and looked to his weapons.

"That was just the fuel-tank of a little Class-3 rocket-boat," he said. "I wonder what the explosion of the ship was like." He thought for a moment before continuing. "Glav, I think I know why our jets burned out. We were stern-on to the ship when she blew; the blast drove our flame right back through the jets.''

"Do you think the explosion was observed from Doorsha?'' Dorita inquired, more concerned about the practical aspects of the situation. ''The ship, I mean. After all, we have no means of communication, of our own.''

"Oh, I shouldn't doubt it; there were observatories all around the planet watching our ship,'' Kalvar Dard said. "They probably know all about it, by now. But if any of you are thinking about the chances of rescue, forget it. We're stuck here.''

"That's right. There isn't another human being within fifty million miles,'' Seldar Glav said. ''And that was the first and only space-ship ever built. It took fifty years to build her, and even allowing twenty for research that wouldn't have to be duplicated, you can figure when we can expect another one.''

"The answer to that one is, never. The ship blew up in space; fifty years' effort and fifteen hundred people gone, like that.'' Kalvar Dard snapped his fingers. ''So now, they'll try to keep Doorsha habitable for a few more thousand years by irrigation, and forget about immigrating to Tareesh.''

"Well, maybe, in a hundred thousand years, our descendants will build a ship and go to Doorsha, then,'' Olva considered.

"Our descendants?'' Eldra looked at her in surprise. ''You mean, then . . .?''

Kyna chuckled. ''Eldra, you are an awful innocent, about anything that doesn't have a breech-action or a recoil-mechanism,'' she said. ''Why do you think the women on this expedition outnumbered the men seven to five, and why do you think there were so many obstetricians and pediatricians in the med staff? We were sent out to put a human population on Tareesh, weren't we? Well, here we are.''

"But . . . Aren't we ever going to . . .?'' Varnis began. "Won't we ever see anybody else, or do anything but just live here, like animals, without machines or ground-cars or aircraft or houses or anything?'' Then she began to sob bitterly.

Analea, who had been cleaning a carbine that had gotten covered with loose earth during the explosion, laid it down and went to Varnis, putting her arm around the other girl and comforting her. Kalvar Dard picked up the carbine she had laid down.

''Now, let's see,'' he began. ''We have two heavy rifles, six carbines, and eight pistols, and these two bags of bombs. How much ammunition, counting what's in our belts, do we have?''

They took stock of their slender resources, even Varnis joining in the task, as he had hoped she would. There were over two thousand rounds for the pistols, better than fifteen hundred for the carbines, and four hundred for the two big-game guns. They had some spare clothing, mostly space-suit undergarments, enough bed-robes, one hand-axe, two flashlights, a first-aid kit, and three atomic lighters. Each one had a combat-dagger. There was enough tinned food for about a week.

''We'll have to begin looking for game and edible plants, right away,'' Glav considered. ''I suppose there is game, of some sort; but our ammunition won't last forever.''

''We'll have to make it last as long as we can; and we'll have to begin improvising weapons,'' Dard told him. ''Throwing-spears, and throwing-axes. If we can find metal, or any recognizable ore that we can smelt, we'll use that; if not, we'll use chipped stone. Also, we can learn to make snares and traps, after we learn the habits of the animals on this planet. By the time the ammunition's gone, we ought to have learned to do without firearms.''

''Think we ought to camp here?''

Kalvar Dard shook his head. ''No wood here for fuel, and the blast will have scared away all the game. We'd better go upstream; if we go down, we'll find the water roiled with mud and unfit to drink. And if the game on this planet behave like the game-herds on the wastelands of Doorsha, they'll run for high ground when frightened.''

Varnis rose from where she had been sitting. Having

mastered her emotions, she was making a deliberate effort to show it.

"Let's make up packs out of this stuff," she suggested. "We can use the bedding and spare clothing to bundle up the food and ammunition."

They made up packs and slung them, then climbed out of the gully. Off to the left, the grass was burning in a wide circle around the crater left by the explosion of the rocket-boat. Kalvar Dard, carrying one of the heavy rifles, took the lead. Beside and a little behind him, Analea walked, her carbine ready. Glav, with the other heavy rifle, brought up the rear, with Olva covering for him, and between, the other girls walked, two and two.

Ahead, on the far horizon, was a distance-blue line of mountains. The little company turned their faces toward them and moved slowly away, across the empty sea of grass.

3

They had been walking, now, for five years. Kalvar Dard still led, the heavy rifle cradled in the crook of his left arm and a sack of bombs slung from his shoulder, his eyes forever shifting to right and left searching for hidden danger. The clothes in which he had jumped from the rocket-boat were patched and ragged; his shoes had been replaced by high-laced buskins of smoke-tanned hide. He was bearded, now, and his hair had been roughly trimmed with the edge of his dagger.

Analea still walked beside him, but her carbine was slung, and she carried three spears with chipped flint heads, one heavy weapon, to be thrown by hand or used for stabbing, and two light javelins to be thrown with the aid of the hooked throwing-stick Glav had invented. Beside her trudged a four-year-old boy, hers and Dard's, and on her back, in a fur-lined net bag, she carried their six-month-old baby.

In the rear, Glav still kept his place with the other big-game gun, and Olva walked beside him with carbine and spears in front of them, their three-year-old daughter toddled. Between vanguard and rearguard, the rest of the party walked: Varnis, carrying her baby on her back, and Dorita, carrying a baby and leading two other children. The baby on her back had cost the life of Kyna in childbirth; one of the others had been left motherless when Eldra had been killed by the Hairy People.

That had been two years ago, during the winter when they had used one of their two demolition-bombs to blast open a cavern in the mountains. It had been a hard winter; two children had died, then—Kyna's firstborn, and the little son of Kalvar Dard and Dorita. It had been their first encounter with the Hairy People, too.

Eldra had gone outside the cave with one of the skin water-bags, to fill it at the spring. It had been after sunset, but she had carried her pistol, and no one had thought of danger until they heard the two quick shots, and the scream. They had all rushed out, to find four shaggy, manlike things tearing at Eldra with hands and teeth, another lying dead, and a sixth huddled at one side, clutching its abdomen and whimpering. There had been a quick flurry of shots that had felled all four of the assailants, and Seldar Glav had finished the wounded creature with his dagger, but Eldra was dead. They had built a cairn of stones over her body, as they had done over the bodies of the two children killed by the cold. But, after an examination to see what sort of things they were, they had tumbled the bodies of the Hairy People over the cliff. These had been too bestial to bury as befitted human dead, but too manlike to skin and eat as game.

Since then, they had often found traces of the Hairy People, and when they met with them, they killed them without mercy. These were great shambling parodies of humanity, long-armed, short-legged, twice as heavy as men, with close-set reddish eyes and heavy bone-crushing jaws. They may have been incredibly debased humans, or perhaps beasts on the very threshold of manhood. From what he had seen of conditions on this planet, Kalvar Dard suspected the latter to be the case. In a million or so years, they might evolve into something like humanity. Already, the Hairy Ones had learned the use of fire, and of chipped crude stone implements—mostly heavy triangular choppers to be used in the hand, without helves.

Twice, after that night, the Hairy People had attacked them—once while they were on the march, and once in camp. Both assaults had been beaten off without loss to themselves, but at cost of precious ammunition. Once they had caught a band of ten of them swimming a river on logs; they had picked them all off from the bank with their carbines. Once, when Kalvar Dard and Analea had been scouting alone, they had come upon a dozen of them huddled around a fire and had wiped them out with a single grenade. Once, a large band of Hairy People hunted them for two days, but only twice had they come close, and both times, a single shot had sent them all scampering. That had been after the bombing of the group around the fire. Dard was convinced that the beings possessed the rudiments of language, enough to communicate a few simple ideas, such as the fact that this little tribe of aliens was dangerous in the extreme.

There were Hairy People about now; for the past five days, moving northward through the forest to the open grasslands, the people of Kalvar Dard had found traces of them. Now, as they came out among the seedling growth of the edge of the open plains, everybody was on the alert.

They emerged from the big trees and stopped among the young growth, looking out into the open country. About a mile away, a herd of game was grazing slowly westward. In the distance, they looked like the little horselike things, no higher than a man's waist and heavily maned and bearded, that had been one of their most important sources of meat. For the ten thousandth time, Dard wished, as he strained his eyes, that somebody had thought to secure a pair of binoculars when they had abandoned the rocket-boat. He studied the grazing herd for a long time.

The seedling pines extended almost to the game-herd and would offer concealment for the approach, but the animals were grazing into the wind, and their scent was much keener than their vision. This would preclude one of their favorite hunting techniques, that of lurking in the high grass ahead of the quarry. It had rained heavily in the past few days, and the undermat of dead grass was soaked, making a fire-hunt impossible. Kalvar Dard knew that he could stalk to within easy carbine-shot, but he was unwilling to use cartridges on game; and in view of the proximity of Hairy People, he did not want to divide his band for a drive-hunt.

"What's the scheme?" Analea asked him, realizing the problem as well as he did. "Do we try to take them from behind?"

"We'll take them from an angle," he decided. "We'll start from here and work in, closing on them at the rear of the herd. Unless the wind shifts on us, we ought to get within spear-cast. You and I will use the spears; Varnis can come along and cover for us with a carbine. Glav, you and Olva and Dorita stay here with the children and the packs. Keep a sharp lookout; Hairy People around, somewhere." He unslung his rifle and exchanged it for Olva's spears. "We can only eat about two of them before the meat begins to spoil, but kill all you can," he told Analea; "we need the skins."

Then he and the two girls began their slow, cautious, stalk. As long as the grassland was dotted with young trees, they walked upright, making good time, but the last five hundred yards they had to crawl, stopping often to check the wind, while the horse-herd drifted slowly by. Then they were directly behind the herd, with the wind in their faces, and advanced more rapidly.

"Close enough?" Dard whispered to Analea.

"Yes; I'm taking the one that's lagging a little behind."

"I'm taking the one on the left of it." Kalvar Dard fitted a javelin to the hook of his throwing-stick. "Ready? Now!"

He leaped to his feet, drawing back his right arm and hurling, the throwing-stick giving added velocity to the spear. Beside him, he was conscious of Analea rising and propelling her spear. His missile caught the little bearded pony in the chest; it stumbled and fell forward to its front knees. He snatched another light spear, set it on the hook of the stick and darted it at another horse, which reared, biting at the spear with its teeth. Grabbing the heavy stabbing-spear, he ran forward, finishing it off with a heart-thrust. As he did, Varnis slung her carbine, snatched a stone-headed throwing axe from her belt, and knocked down another horse, then ran forward with her dagger to finish it.

By this time, the herd, alarmed, had stampeded and was galloping away, leaving the dead and dying behind. He and Analea had each killed two; with the one Varnis had knocked down, that made five. Using his dagger, he finished off one that was still kicking on the ground, and then began pulling out the throwing-spears. The girls, shouting in unison, were announcing the successful completion of the hunt; Glav, Olva and Dorita were coming forward with the children.

It was sunset by the time they had finished the work of skinning and cutting up the horses and had carried the hide-wrapped bundles of meat to the little brook where they had intended camping. There was firewood to be gathered, and the meal to be cooked, and they were all tired.

"We can't do this very often, any more," Kalvar Dard told them, "but we might as well, tonight. Don't bother rubbing sticks for fire; I'll use the lighter."

He got it from a pouch on his belt—a small, gold-plated, atomic lighter, bearing the crest of his old regiment of the Frontier Guards. It was the last one they had in working order. Piling a handful of dry splinters under the firewood, he held the lighter to it, pressed the activator, and watched the fire eat into the wood.

The greatest achievement of man's civilization, the mastery of the basic, cosmic, power of the atom—being used to kindle a fire of a natural fuel, to cook unseasoned meat killed with stone-tipped spears. Dard looked sadly at the twinkling little gadget, then slipped it back into its pouch. Soon it would be worn out, like the other two, and then they would gain fire only by rubbing dry sticks, or hacking spears from bits of flint or pyrites. Soon, too, the last cartridge would be fired, and then they would perforce depend for protection, as they were already doing for food, upon their spears.

And they were so helpless. Six adults, burdened with seven little children, all of them requiring momently care and watchfulness. If the cartridges could be made to last until they were old enough to fend for themselves . . . If they could avoid collisions with the Hairy People . . . Some day, they would be numerous enough for effective mutual protection and support; some day, the ratio of helpless children to able adults would redress itself. Until then, all that they could do would be to survive; day after day, they must follow the game-herds.

4

For twenty years, now, they had been following the game. Winters had come, with driving snow, forcing horses and deer into the woods, and the little band of humans to the protection of mountain caves. Springtime followed, with fresh grass on the plains and plenty of meat for the people of Kalvar Dard. Autumns followed summers, with fire-hunts, and the smoking and curing of meat and hides. Winters followed autumns, and springtimes came again, and thus until the twentieth year after the landing of the rocket-boat.

Kalvar Dard still walked in the lead, his hair and beard flecked with gray, but he no longer carried the heavy rifle; the last cartridge for that had been fired long ago. He carried the hand-axe, fitted with a long helve, and a spear with a steel head that had been worked painfully from the receiver of a useless carbine. He still had his pistol, with eight cartridges in the magazine, and his dagger, and the bomb-bag, containing the big demolition-bomb and one grenade. The last shred of clothing from the ship was gone, now; he was clad in a sleeveless tunic of skin and horsehide buskins.

Analea no longer walked beside him; eight years before, she had broken her back in a fall. It had been impossible to move her, and she stabbed herself with her dagger to save a cartridge. Seldar Glav had broken through the ice while crossing a river, and had lost his rifle; the next day he died of the chill he had taken. Olva had been killed by the Hairy People, the night they had attacked the camp, when Varnis' child had been killed.

They had beaten off that attack, shot or speared ten of the huge sub-men, and the next morning they buried their dead after their custom, under cairns of stone. Varnis had watched the burial of her child with blank, uncomprehending eyes, then she had turned to Kalvar Dard and said something that had horrified him more than any wild outburst of grief could have.

"Come on, Dard; what are we doing this for? You promised you'd take us to Tareesh, where we'd have good houses, and machines, and all sorts of lovely things to eat and wear. I don't like this place, Dard; I want to go to Tareesh."

From that day on, she had wandered in merciful darkness. She had not been idiotic, or raving mad; she had just escaped from a reality that she could no longer bear.

Varnis, lost in her dream-world, and Dorita, hard-faced and haggard, were the only ones left, beside Kalvar Dard, of the original eight. But the band had grown, meanwhile, to more than fifteen. In the rear, in Seldar Glav's old place, the son of Kalvar Dard and Analea walked. Like his father, he wore a pistol, for which he had six rounds, and a dagger, and in his hand he carried a stone-headed killing-maul with a three-foot handle which he had made for himself. The woman who walked beside him and carried his spears was the daughter of Glav and Olva; in a net-bag on her back she carried their infant child, the first Tareeshan born of Tareeshan parents; Kalvar Dard often looked at his little grandchild during nights in camp and days on the trail, seeing, in that tiny fur-swaddled morsel of humanity, the meaning and purpose of all that he did. Of the older girls, one or two were already pregnant, now; this tiny threatened beachhead of humanity was expanding, gaining strength. Long after man had died out on Doorsha and the dying planet itself had become an arid waste, the progeny of this little band would continue to grow and to dominate the younger planet, nearer the sun. Some day, an even mightier civilization than the one he had left would rise here . . .

All day, the trail had wound upward into the mountains. Great cliffs loomed above them, and little streams spumed and dashed in rocky gorges below. All day, the Hairy People had followed, fearful to approach too close, unwilling to allow their enemies to escape. It had started when they had rushed the camp, at daybreak; they had been beaten off, at cost of almost all the ammunition, and the death of one child. No sooner had the tribe of Kalvar Dard taken the trail, however, than they had been pressing after them. Dard had determined to cross the mountains, and had led his people up a game-trail, leading toward the notch of a pass high against the skyline.

The shaggy ape-things seemed to have divined his purpose. Once or twice, he had seen hairy brown shapes dodging among the rocks and stunted trees to the left. They were trying to reach the pass ahead of him. Well, if they did . . . He made a quick mental survey of his resources. His pistol, and his son's, and Dorita's, with eight, and six, and seven rounds. One grenade, and the big demolition bomb, too powerful to be thrown by hand, but which could be set for delayed explosion and dropped over a cliff or left behind to explode among pursuers. Five steel daggers, and plenty of spears and slings and axes. Himself, his son and his son's woman, Dorita, and four or five of the older boys and girls, who would make effective front-line fighters. And Varnis, who might come out of her private dream-world long enough to give account for herself, and even the tiniest of the walking children could throw stones or light spears. Yes, they could force the pass, if the Hairy People reached it ahead of them, and then seal it shut with the heavy bomb. What lay on the other side, he did not know; he wondered how much game there would be, and if there were Hairy People on that side, too.

Two shots slammed quickly behind him. He dropped his axe and took a two-handed grip on his stabbing-spear as he turned. His son was hurrying forward, his pistol drawn, glancing behind as he came.

"Hairy People. Four," he reported. "I shot two; she threw a spear and killed another. The other ran."

The daughter of Seldar Glav and Olva nodded in agreement.

"I had no time to throw again," she said, "and Bo-Bo would not shoot the one that ran."

Kalvar Dard's son, who had no other name than the one his mother had called him as a child, defended himself. "He was running away. It is the rule: *use bullets only to save life, where a spear will not serve.*"

Kalvar Dard nodded. "You did right, son," he said, taking out his own pistol and removing the magazine, from which he extracted two cartridges. "Load these into your pistol; four rounds aren't enough. Now we each have six. Go back to the rear, keep the little ones moving, and don't let Varnis get behind."

"That is right. *We must all look out for Varnis, and take care of her,*" the boy recited obediently. "That is the rule."

He dropped to the rear. Kalvar Dard holstered his pistol and picked up his axe, and the column moved forward again. They were following a ledge, now; on the left, there was a sheer drop of several hundred feet, and on the right a cliff rose above them, growing higher and steeper as the trail slanted upward. Dard was worried about the ledge; if it came to an end, they would all be trapped. No one would escape. He suddenly felt old and unutterably weary. It was a frightful weight that he bore—responsibility for an entire race.

Suddenly, behind him, Dorita fired her pistol upward. Dard sprang forward—there was no room for him to jump aside— and drew his pistol. The boy, Bo-Bo, was trying to find a target from his position in the rear. Then Dard saw the two Hairy People; the boy fired, and the stone fell, all at once.

It was a heavy stone, half as big as a man's torso, and it almost missed Kalvar Dard. If it had hit him directly, it would have killed him instantly, mashing him to a bloody pulp; as it was, he was knocked flat, the stone pinning his legs.

At Bo-Bo's shot, a hairy body plummeted down, to hit the ledge. Bo-Bo's woman instantly ran it through with one of her spears. The other ape-thing, the one Dorita had shot, was still clinging to a rock above. Two of the children scampered up to it and speared it repeatedly, screaming like little furies. Dorita and one of the older girls got the rock off Kalvar

Dard's legs and tried to help him to his feet, but he collapsed, unable to stand. Both his legs were broken.

This was it, he thought, sinking back. "Dorita, I want you to run ahead and see what the trail's like," he said. "See if the ledge is passable. And find a place, not too far ahead, where we can block the trail by exploding that demolition-bomb. It has to be close enough for a couple of you to carry or drag me and get me there in one piece."

"What are you going to do?"

"What do you think?" he retorted. "I have both legs broken. You can't carry me with you; if you try it, they'll catch us and kill us all. I'll have to stay behind; I'll block the trail behind you, and get as many of them as I can, while I'm at it. Now, run along and do as I said."

She nodded. "I'll be back as soon as I can," she agreed.

The others were crowding around Dard. Bo-Bo bent over him, perplexed and worried. "What are you going to do, father?" he asked. "You are hurt. Are you going to go away and leave us, as mother did when she was hurt?"

"Yes, son, I'll have to. You carry me on ahead a little, when Dorita gets back, and leave me where she shows you to. I'm going to stay behind and block the trail, and kill a few Hairy People. I'll use the big bomb."

"The *big* bomb? The one nobody dares throw?" The boy looked at his father in wonder.

"That's right. Now, when you leave me, take the others and get away as fast as you can. Don't stop till you're up to the pass. Take my pistol and dagger, and the axe and the big spear, and take the little bomb, too. Take everything I have, only leave the big bomb with me. I'll need that."

Dorita rejoined them. "There's a waterfall ahead. We can get around it, and up to the pass. The way's clear and easy; if you put off the bomb just this side of it, you'll start a rock-slide that'll block everything."

"All right. Pick me up, a couple of you. Don't take hold of me below the knees. And hurry."

A hairy shape appeared on the ledge below them; one of the older boys used his throwing-stick to drive a javelin into it.

Two of the girls picked up Dard; Bo-Bo and his woman gathered up the big spear and the axe and the bomb-bag.

They hurried forward, picking their way along the top of a talus of rubble at the foot of the cliff, and came to where the stream gushed out of a narrow gorge. The air was wet with spray there, and loud with the roar of the waterfall. Kalvar Dard looked around; Dorita had chosen the spot well. Not even a sure-footed mountain-goat could make the ascent, once that gorge was blocked.

"All right; put me down here," he directed. "Bo-Bo, take my belt, and give me the big bomb. You have one light grenade; know how to use it?"

"Of course, you have often showed me. I turn the top, and then press in the little thing on the side, and hold it in till I throw. I throw it at least a spear-cast, and drop to the ground or behind something."

"That's right. And use it only in greatest danger, to save everybody. Spare your cartridges; use them only to save life. And save everything of metal, no matter how small."

"Yes. Those are the rules. I will follow them, and so will the others. And we will always take care of Varnis."

"Well, goodbye, son." He gripped the boy's hand. "Now get everybody out of here; don't stop till you're at the pass."

"You're not staying behind!" Varnis cried. "Dard, you promised us! I remember, when we were all in the ship together—you and I and Analea and Olva and Dorita and Eldra and, oh, what was that other girl's name, Kyna! And we were all having such a nice time, and you were telling us how we'd all come to Tareesh, and we were having such fun talking about it . . ."

"That's right, Varnis," he agreed. "And so I will. I have something to do, here, but I'll meet you on top of the mountain, after I'm through, and in the morning we'll all go to Tareesh."

She smiled—the gentle, childlike smile of the harmlessly mad—and turned away. The son of Kalvar Dard made sure that she and all the children were on the way, and then he, too, turned and followed them, leaving Dard alone.

Alone, with a bomb and a task. He'd borne that task for

twenty years, now; in a few minutes, it would be ended, with an instant's searing heat. He tried not to be too glad; there were so many things he might have done, if he had tried harder. Metals, for instance. Somewhere there surely must be ores which they could have smelted, but he had never found them. And he might have tried catching some of the little horses they hunted for food, to break and train to bear burdens. And the alphabet—why hadn't he taught it to Bo-Bo and the daughter of Seldar Glav, and laid on them an obligation to teach the others? And the grass-seeds they used for making flour sometimes; they should have planted fields of the better kinds, and patches of edible roots, and returned at the proper time to harvest them. There were so many things, things that none of those young savages or their children would think of in ten thousand years . . .

Something was moving among the rocks, a hundred yards away. He straightened, as much as his broken legs would permit, and watched. Yes, there was one of them, and there was another, and another. One rose from behind a rock and came forward at a shambling run, making bestial sounds. Then two more lumbered into sight, and in a moment the ravine was alive with them. They were almost upon him when Kalvar Dard pressed in the thumbpiece of the bomb; they were clutching at him when he released it. He felt a slight jar . . .

When they reached the pass, they all stopped as the son of Kalvar Dard turned and looked back. Dorita stood beside him, looking toward the waterfall too; she also knew what was about to happen. The others merely gaped in blank incomprehension, or grasped their weapons, thinking that the enemy was pressing close behind and that they were making a stand here. A few of the smaller boys and girls began picking up stones.

Then a tiny pin-point of brilliance winked, just below where the snow-fed stream vanished into the gorge. That was all, for an instant, and then a great fire-shot cloud swirled upward, hundreds of feet into the air; there was a crash, louder than any sound any of them except Dorita and Varnis had ever heard before.

"He did it!" Dorita said softly.

"Yes, he did it. My father was a brave man," Bo-Bo replied. "We are safe, now."

Varnis, shocked by the explosion, turned and stared at him, and then she laughed happily. "Why, there you are, Dard!" she exclaimed. "I was wondering where you'd gone. What did you do, after we left?"

"What do you mean?" The boy was puzzled, not knowing how much he looked like his father, when his father had been an officer of the Frontier Guards, twenty years before.

His puzzlement worried Varnis vaguely. "You . . . You are Dard, aren't you?" she asked. "But that's silly; of course you're Dard! Who else could you be?"

"Yes, I am Dard," the boy said, remembering that it was the rule for everybody to be kind to Varnis and to pretend to agree with her. Then another thought struck him. His shoulders straightened. "Yes. I am Dard, son of Dard," he told them all. "I lead, now. Does anybody say no?"

He shifted his axe and spear to his left hand and laid his right hand on the butt of his pistol, looking sternly at Dorita. If any of them tried to dispute his claim, it would be she. But instead, she gave him the nearest thing to a real smile that had crossed her face in years.

"You are Dard," she told him. "You lead us, now."

"But of course Dard leads! Hasn't he always led us?" Varnis wanted to know. "Then what's all the argument about? And tomorrow he's going to take us to Tareesh, and we'll have houses and ground-cars and aircraft and gardens and lights, and all the lovely things we want. Aren't you, Dard?"

"Yes, Varnis; I will take you all to Tareesh, to all the wonderful things," Dard, son of Dard, promised, for such was the rule about Varnis.

Then he looked down from the pass into the country beyond. There were lower mountains, below, and foothills, and a wide blue valley, and, beyond that, distant peaks reared

jaggedly against the sky. He pointed with his father's axe.
"We go down that way," he said.

So they went, down, and on, and on, and on. The last
cartridge was fired; the last silver of Doorshan metal wore out
or rusted away. By then, however, they had learned to make
chipped stone, and bone, and reindeer-horn serve their
needs. Century after century, millennium after millennium,
they followed the game-herds from birth to death, and birth
replenished their numbers faster than death depleted. Bands
grew in numbers and split; young men rebelled against the
rule of the old and took their women and children elsewhere.

They hunted down the hairy Neanderthalers, and extermi-
nated them ruthlessly, the origin of their implacable hatred
lost in legend. All that they remembered, in the misty,
confused, way that one remembers a dream, was that there
had once been a time of happiness and plenty, and that there
was a goal to which they would some day attain. They left the
mountains—were they the Caucasus? The Alps? The
Pamirs?—and spread outward, conquering as they went.

We find their bones, and their stone weapons, and their
crude paintings, in the caves of Cro-Magnon and Grimaldi
and Altimira and Mas-d'Azil; the deep layers of horse and
reindeer and mammoth bones at their feasting-place at Sol-
utre. We wonder how and whence a race so like our own
came into a world of brutish sub-humans.

Just as we wonder, too, at the network of canals which
radiate from the polar caps of our sister planet, and speculate
on the possibility that they were the work of hands like our
own. And we concoct elaborate jokes about the "Men From
Mars"—*ourselves*.

THE ANSWER

In most of Piper's stories—including those in his Terro-Human Future History—man does survive the nuclear holocaust, although not in the areas where civilization thrives today. Instead, the Southern Hemisphere becomes the new cradle of civilization.

In "The Answer," we learn what happens to two survivors—one Russian, one American—who are now working for the Argentines on an investigation of negative matter. Unfortunately, as often happens when the genie of science is summoned, they learn far more than they wanted to know . . .

FOR A MOMENT, after the screen door snapped and wakened him, Lee Richardson sat breathless and motionless, his eyes still closed, trying desperately to cling to the dream and print it upon his conscious memory before it faded.

"Are you there, Lee?" he heard Alexis Pitov's voice.

"Yes, I'm here. What time is it?" he asked, and then added, "I fell asleep. I was dreaming."

It was all right; he was going to be able to remember. He could still see the slim woman with the graying blonde hair, playing with the little dachshund among the new-fallen leaves on the lawn. He was glad they'd both been in this dream together; these dream-glimpses were all he'd had for the last fifteen years, and they were too precious to lose. He opened his eyes. The Russian was sitting just outside the light from the open door of the bungalow, lighting a cigarette. For a moment, he could see the blocky, high-cheeked face, now pouched and wrinkled, and then the flame went out and there was only the red coal glowing in the darkness. He closed his eyes again, and the dream picture came back to him, the woman catching the little dog and raising her head as though to speak to him.

"Plenty of time, yet." Pitov was speaking German instead of Spanish, as they always did between themselves. "They're still counting down from minus three hours. I just phoned the launching site for a jeep. Eugenio's been there ever since dinner; they say he's running around like a cat looking for a place to have her first litter of kittens."

He chuckled. This would be something new for Eugenio Galvez—for which he could be thankful.

"I hope the generators don't develop any last-second bugs," he said. "We'll only be a mile and a half away, and that'll be too close to fifty kilos of negamatter if the field collapses."

"It'll be all right," Pitov assured him. "The bugs have all been chased out years ago."

"Not out of those generators in the rocket. They're new." He fumbled in his coat pocket for his pipe and tobacco. "I never thought I'd run another nuclear-bomb test, as long as I lived."

"Lee!" Pitov was shocked. "You mustn't call it that. It isn't that, at all. It's purely a scientific experiment."

"Wasn't that all any of them were? We made lots of experiments like this, back before 1969." The memories of all those other tests, each ending in an Everest-high mushroom column, rose in his mind. And the end result—the United States and the Soviet Union blasted to rubble, a whole hemisphere pushed back into the Dark Ages, a quarter of a billion dead. Including a slim woman with graying blonde hair, and a little red dog, and a girl from Odessa whom Alexis Pitov had been going to marry. "Forgive me, Alexis. I just couldn't help remembering. I suppose it's this shot we're going to make, tonight. It's so much like the other ones, before—" He hesitated slightly. "Before the Auburn Bomb."

There; he'd come out and said it. In all the years they'd worked together at the *Instituto Argentino de Ciencia Fisica*, that had been unmentioned between them. The families of hanged cutthroats avoid mention of ropes and knives. He thumbed the old-fashioned American lighter and held it to his pipe. Across the veranda, in the darkness, he knew that Pitov was looking intently at him.

"You've been thinking about that, lately, haven't you?" the Russian asked, and then, timidly: "Was that what you were dreaming of?"

"Oh, no, thank heaven!"

"I think about it, too, always. I suppose—" He seemed relieved, now that it had been brought out into the open and could be discussed. "You saw it fall, didn't you?"

"That's right. From about thirty miles away. A little closer than we'll be to this shot, tonight. I was in charge of the investigation at Auburn, until we had New York and Washington and Detroit and Mobile and San Francisco to worry about. Then what had happened to Auburn wasn't important, any more. We were trying to get evidence to lay before the United Nations. We kept at it for about twelve hours after the United Nations had ceased to exist."

"I could never understand about that, Lee. I don't know what the truth is; I probably never shall. But I know that my government did not launch that missile. During the first days after yours began coming in, I talked to people who had been in the Kremlin at the time. One had been in the presence of Klyzenko himself when the news of your bombardment arrived. He said that Klyzenko was absolutely stunned. We always believed that your government decided upon a preventive surprise attack, and picked out a town, Auburn, New

York, that had been hit by one of our first retaliation missiles, and claimed that it had been hit first.''

He shook his head. ''Auburn was hit an hour before the first American missile was launched. I know that to be a fact. We could never understand why you launched just that one, and no more until after ours began landing on you; why you threw away the advantage of surprise and priority of attack—''

''Because we didn't do it, Lee!'' The Russian's voice trembled with earnestness. ''You believe me when I tell you that?''

''Yes, I believe you. After all that happened, and all that you, and I, and the people you worked with, and the people I worked with, and your government, and mine, have been guilty of, it would be a waste of breath for either of us to try to lie to the other about what happened fifteen years ago.'' He drew slowly on his pipe. ''But who launched it, then? It had to be launched by somebody.''

''Don't you think I've been tormenting myself with that question for the last fifteen years?'' Pitov demanded. ''You know, there were people inside the Soviet Union—not many, and they kept themselves well hidden—who were dedicated to the overthrow of the Soviet regime. They, or some of them, might have thought that the devastation of both our countries, and the obliteration of civilization in the Northern Hemisphere, would be a cheap price to pay for ending the rule of the Communist Party.''

''Could they have built an ICBM with a thermonuclear warhead in secret?'' he asked. There were also fanatical nationalist groups in Europe, both sides of the Iron Curtain, who might have thought our mutual destruction would be worth the risks involved.''

''There was China, and India. If your country and mine wiped each other out, they could go back to the old ways and the old traditions. Or Japan, or the Moslem States. In the end, they all went down along with us, but what criminal ever expects to fall?''

''We have too many suspects, and the trail's too cold,

Alexis. That rocket wouldn't have had to have been launched anywhere in the Northern Hemisphere. For instance, our friends here in the Argentine have been doing very well by themselves since *El Coloso del Norte* went down."

And there were the Australians, picking themselves up bargains in real-estate in the East Indies at gunpoint, and there were the Boers, trekking north again, in tanks instead of ox-wagons. And Brazil, with a not-too-implausible pretender to the Braganza throne, calling itself the Portuguese Empire and looking eastward. And, to complete the picture, here were Professor Doctor Lee Richardson and Comrade Professor Alexis Petrovitch Pitov, getting ready to test a missile with a matter-annihilation warhead.

No. This thing just wasn't a weapon.

A jeep came around the corner, lighting the dark roadway between the bungalows, its radio on and counting down—*Twenty-two minutes. Twenty-one fifty-nine, fifty-eight, fifty-seven*— It came to a stop in front of their bungalow, at exactly minus two hours, twenty-one minutes, fifty-four seconds. The driver called out in Spanish:

"Doctor Richardson; Doctor Pitov! Are you ready?"

"Yes, ready. We're coming."

They both got to their feet, Richardson pulling himself up reluctantly. The older you get, the harder it is to leave a comfortable chair. He settled himself beside his colleague and former enemy, and the jeep started again, rolling between the buildings of the living-quarters area and out onto the long, straight road across the pampas, toward the distant blaze of electric lights.

He wondered why he had been thinking so much, lately, about the Auburn Bomb. He'd questioned, at times, indignantly, of course, whether Russia *had* launched it—but it wasn't until tonight, until he had heard what Pitov had to say, that he seriously doubted it. Pitov wouldn't lie about it, and Pitov would have been in a position to have known the truth, if the missile had been launched from Russia. Then he stopped thinking about what was water—or blood—a long time over the dam.

The special policeman at the entrance to the launching site reminded them that they were both smoking. When they extinguished respectively, their cigarette and pipe, he waved the jeep on and went back to his argument with a carload of tourists who wanted to get a good view of the launching.

"There, now, Lee; do you need anything else to convince you that this isn't a weapon project?" Pitov asked.

"No, now that you mention it. I don't. You know, I don't believe I've had to show an identity card the whole time I've been here."

"I don't believe I have an identity card," Pitov said. "Think of that."

The lights blazed everywhere around them, but mostly about the rocket that towered above everything else, so thick that it seemed squat. The gantry-cranes had been hauled away, now, and it stood alone, but it was still wreathed in thick electric cables. They were pouring enough current into that thing to light half the street-lights in Buenos Aires; when the cables were blown free by separation charges at the blastoff, the generators powered by the rocket-engines had better be able to take over, because if the magnetic field collapsed and that fifty-kilo chunk of negative-proton matter came in contact with natural positive-proton matter, an old fashioned H-bomb would be a firecracker compared to what would happen. Just one hundred kilos of pure, two-hundred proof MC^2.

The driver took them around the rocket, dodging assorted trucks and mobile machinery that were being hurried out of the way. The countdown was just beyond two hours five minutes. The jeep stopped at the edge of a crowd surrounding three more trucks, and Doctor Eugenio Galvez, the director of the Institute, left the crowd and approached at an awkward half-run as they got down.

"Is everything checked, gentlemen?" he wanted to know.

"It was this afternoon at 1730," Pitov told him. "And nobody's been burning my telephone to report anything different. Are the balloons and the drone planes ready?"

"The Air Force just finished checking; they're ready. Captain Urquiola flew one of the planes over the course and made a guidance-tape; that's been duplicated and all the planes are equipped with copies.''

"How's the wind?" Richardson asked.

"Still steady. We won't have any trouble about fallout or with the balloons.''

"Then we'd better go back to the bunker and make sure everybody there is on the job.''

The loudspeaker was counting down to two hours one minute.

"Could you spare a few minutes to talk to the press?" Eugenio Galvez asked. "And perhaps say a few words for telecast? This last is most important; we can't explain too many times the purpose of this experiment. There is still much hostility, arising from fear that we are testing a nuclear weapon.''

The press and telecast services were well represented; there were close to a hundred correspondents, from all over South America, from South Africa and Australia, even one from Ceylon. They had three trucks, with mobile-telecast pickups, and when they saw who was approaching, they released the two rocketry experts they had been quizzing and pounced on the new victims.

Was there any possibility that negative-proton matter might be used as a weapon?

"Anything can be used as a weapon; you could stab a man to death with that lead pencil you're using," Pitov replied. "But I doubt if negamatter will ever be so used. We're certainly not working on weapons design here. We started, six years ago, with the ability to produce negative protons, reverse-spin neutrons, and positrons, and the theoretical possibility of assembling them into negamatter. We have just gotten a fifty kilogramme mass of nega-iron assembled. In those six years, we had to invent all our techniques, and design all our equipment. If we'd been insane enough to want to build a nuclear weapon, after what we went through up North, we could have done so from memory, and designed a better—which is to say a worse—one from memory in a few days.''

"Yes, and building a negamatter bomb for military purposes would be like digging a fifty-foot shaft to get a rock to bash somebody's head in, when you could do the job better with the shovel you're digging with," Richardson added. "The time, money, energy and work we put in on this thing would be ample to construct twenty thermonuclear bombs. And that's only a small part of it." He went on to tell them about the magnetic bottle inside the rocket's warhead, mentioning how much electric current was needed to keep up the magnetic field that insulated the negamatter from contact with posimatter.

"Then what was the purpose of this experiment, Doctor Richardson?"

"Oh, we were just trying to find out a few basic facts about natural structure. Long ago, it was realized that the nucleonic particles—protons, neutrons, mesons and so on—must have structure of their own. Since we started constructing negative-proton matter, we've found out a few things about neuclonic structure. Some rather odd things, including fractions of Planck's constant."

A couple of the correspondents—a man from La Prensa, and an Australian—whistled softly. The others looked blank. Pitov took over:

"You see, gentlemen, most of what we learned, we learned from putting negamatter atoms together. We annihilated a few of them—over there in that little concrete building, we have one of the most massive steel vaults in the world, where we do that—but we assembled millions of them for every one we annihilated, and that chunk of nega-iron inside the magnetic bottle kept growing. And when you have a piece of negamatter you don't want, you can't just throw it out on the scrap-pile. We might have rocketed it into escape velocity and let it blow up in space, away from the Moon or any of the artificial satellites, but why waste it? So we're going to have the rocket eject it, and when it falls, we can see, by our telemetered instruments, just what happens."

"Well, won't it be annihilated by contact with atmosphere?" somebody asked.

"That's one of the things we want to find out," Pitov said. "We estimate about twenty percent loss from contact with atmosphere, but the mass that actually lands on the target area should be about forty kilos. It should be something of a spectacle, coming down.''

"You say you had to assemble it, after creating the negative protons and neutrons and the positrons. Doesn't any of this sort of matter exist in nature?''

The man who asked that knew better himself. He just wanted the answer on the record.

"Oh no; not on this planet, and probably not in the Galaxy. There may be whole galaxies composed of nothing but negamatter. There may even be isolated stars and planetary systems inside our Galaxy composed of negamatter, though I think that very improbable. But when negamatter and posimatter come into contact with one another, the result is immediate mutual annihilation.''

They managed to get away from the press, and returned as far as the bunkers, a mile and a half away. Before they went inside, Richardson glanced up at the sky, fixing the location of a few of the more conspicuous stars in his mind. There were almost a hundred men and women inside, each at his or her instruments—view-screens, radar indicators, detection instruments of a dozen kinds. The reporters and telecast people arrived shortly afterward, and Eugenio Galvez took them in tow. While Richardson and Pitov were making their last-minute rounds, the countdown progressed past minus one hour, and at minus twenty minutes all the overhead lights went off and the small instrument operators' lights came on.

Pitov turned on a couple of view-screens, one from a pickup on the roof of the bunker and another from the launching-pad. They sat down side by side and waited. Richardson got his pipe out and began loading it. The loudspeaker was saying: *"Minus two minutes, one fifty-nine, fifty-eight, fifty-seven—"*

He let his mind drift away from the test, back to the world that had been smashed around his ears in the autumn of 1969. He was doing that so often, now, when he should be thinking about—

"Two seconds, one second, FIRING!"

It was a second later that his eyes focused on the left-hand view-screen. Red and yellow flames were gushing out at the bottom of the rocket, and it was beginning to tremble. Then the upper jets, the ones that furnished power for the generators, began firing. He looked anxiously at the meters; the generators were building up power. Finally, when he was sure that the rocket would be blasting off anyhow, the separator-charges fired and the heavy cables fell away. An instant later, the big missile started inching upward, gaining speed by the second, first slowly and jerkily, and then more rapidly, until it passed out of the field of the pickup. He watched the rising spout of fire from the other screen until it passed from sight.

By that time, Pitov had twisted a dial and gotten another view on the left-hand screen, this time from close to the target. That camera was radar-controlled; it had fastened onto the approaching missile, which was still invisible. The stars swung slowly across the screen until Richardson recognized the ones he had spotted at the zenith. In a moment, now, the rocket, a hundred miles overhead, would be nosing down, and then the warhead would open and the magnetic field inside would alter and the mass of negamatter would be ejected.

The stars were blotted out by a sudden glow of light. Even at a hundred miles, there was enough atmospheric density to produce considerable energy release. Pitov, beside him, was muttering, partly in German and partly in Russian; most of what Richardson caught was figures. Trying to calculate how much of the mass of unnatural iron would get down for the ground blast. Then the right-hand screen broke into a wriggling orgy of color, and at the same time every scrap of radio-transmitted apparatus either went out or began reporting erratically. The left-hand screen, connected by wiring to the pickup on the roof, was still functioning. For a moment, Richardson wondered what was going on, and then shocked recognition drove that from his mind as he stared at the ever-brightening glare in the sky.

It was the Auburn Bomb again! He was back, in memory, to the night on the shore of Lake Ontario; the party breaking up in the early hours of morning; he and Janet and the people with whom they had been spending a vacation week, standing on the lawn as the guests were getting into their cars. And then the sudden light in the sky. The cries of surprise, and then of alarm as it seemed to be rushing straight down upon them. He and Janet, clutching each other and staring up in terror at the falling blaze from which there seemed no escape. Then relief, as it curved away from them and fell to the south. And then the explosion, lighting the whole southern sky.

There was a similar explosion on the screen, when the mass of nega-iron landed—a sheet of pure white light, so bright and so quick as to almost pass above the limit of visibility, and then a moment's darkness that was in his stunned eyes more than on the screen, and then the rising glow of updrawn incandescent dust.

Before the sound-waves had reached them, he had been legging it into the house. The television had been on, and it had been acting as insanely as the screen on his right, now. He had called the State Police—the telephones had been working all right—and told them who he was, and they had told him to stay put and they'd send a car for him. They did, within minutes. Janet and his host and hostess had waited with him on the lawn until it came, and after he had gotten into it, he had turned around and looked back through the rear window, and seen Janet standing under the front light, holding the little dog in her arms, flopping one of its silly little paws up and down with her hand to wave goodbye to him.

He had seen her and the dog like that every day of his life for the last fifteen years.

"What kind of radiation are you getting?" he could hear Alexis Pitov asking into a phone. "What? Nothing else? Oh; yes, of course. But mostly cosmic. That shouldn't last long." He turned from the phone. "A devil's own dose of cosmic, and some gamma. It was the cosmic radiation that put the radios and telescreens out. That's why I insisted that the drone planes be independent of radio control."

They always got cosmic radiation from the micro-annihilations in the test-vault. Well, now they had an idea of what produced natural cosmic rays. There must be quite a bit

of negamatter and posimatter going into mutual annihilation
and total energy release through the Universe.

"Of course, there were no detectors set up in advance
around Auburn," he said. "We didn't really begin to find
anything out for half an hour. By that time, the cosmic
radiation was over and we weren't getting anything but
gamma."

"What— What has Auburn to do—?" The Russian
stopped short. "You think this was the same thing?" He gave
it a moment's consideration. "Lee, you're crazy! There
wasn't an atom of artificial negamatter in the world in 1969.
Nobody had made any before us. We gave each other some
scientific surprises, then, but nobody surprised both of us.
You and I, between us, knew everything that was going on in
nuclear physics in the world. And you know as well as I
do—"

A voice came out of the public-address speaker. "Some of
the radio equipment around the target area, that wasn't
knocked out by blast, is beginning to function again. There is
an increasingly heavy gamma radiation, but no more cosmic
rays. They were all prompt radiation from the annihilation;
the gamma is secondary effect. Wait a moment; Captain
Urquiola, of the Air Force, says that the first drone plane is
about to take off."

It had been two hours after the blast that the first drones had
gone over what had been Auburn, New York. He was trying
to remember, as exactly as possible, what had been learned
from them. Gamma radiation; a great deal of gamma. But it
didn't last long. It had been almost down to a safe level by the
time the investigation had been called off, and, two months
after there had been no more missiles, and no way of producing more, and no targets to send them against if they'd had
them, rather—he had been back at Auburn on his hopeless
quest, and there had been almost no trace of radiation. Nothing but a wide, shallow crater, almost two hundred feet in
diameter and only fifteen at its deepest, already full of water,
and a circle of flattened and scattered rubble for a mile and a
half all around it. He was willing to bet anything that that was

what they'd find where the chunk of nega-iron had landed, fifty miles away on the pampas.

Well, the first drone ought to be over the target area before long, and at least one of the balloons that had been sent up was reporting its course by radio. The radios in the others were silent, and the recording counters had probably jammed in all of them. There'd be something of interest when the first drone came back. He dragged his mind back to the present, and went to work with Alexis Pitov.

They were at it all night, checking, evaluating, making sure that the masses of data that were coming in were being promptly processed for programming the computers. At each of the increasingly frequent coffee-breaks, he noticed Pitov looking curiously. He said nothing, however, until, long after dawn, they stood outside the bunker, waiting for the jeep that would take them back to their bungalow and watching the line of trucks—Argentine army engineers, locally-hired laborers, load after load of prefab-huts and equipment—going down toward the target-area, where they would be working for the next week.

"Lee, were you serious?" Pitov asked. "I mean, about this being like the one at Auburn?"

"It was exactly like Auburn; even that blazing light that came rushing down out of the sky. I wondered about that at the time—what kind of a missile would produce an effect like that. Now I know. We just launched one like it."

"But that's impossible! I told you, between us we knew everything that was happening in nuclear physics then. Nobody in the world knew how to assemble atoms of negamatter and build them into masses."

"Nobody, and nothing, on this planet built that mass of negamatter. I doubt if it even came from this Galaxy. But we didn't know that, then. When that negamatter meteor fell, the only thing anybody could think of was that it had been a Soviet missile. If it had hit around Leningrad or Moscow or Kharkov, who would you have blamed it on?"

CROSSROADS OF DESTINY

---

*In this nifty little tale, Piper again weaves a new pattern
into one of his favorite themes, parallel worlds. In the process, he creates a television show that might have rivaled
Twilight Zone.*

I STILL HAVE the dollar bill. It's in my box at the bank, and I
think that's where it will stay. I simply won't destroy it, but I
can think of nobody to whom I'd be willing to show it—
certainly nobody at the college, my History Department
colleagues least of all. Merely to tell the story would brand
me irredeemably as a crackpot, but crackpots are tolerated,
even on college faculties. It's only when they begin producing physical evidence that they get themselves actively re-
sented.

When I went into the club-car for a nightcap before going
back to my compartment to turn in, there were five men
there, sitting together.

One was an Army officer, with the insignia and badges of a
Staff Intelligence colonel. Next to him was a man of about

my own age, with sandy hair and a bony, Scottish-looking face, who sat staring silently into a highball which he held in both hands. Across the aisle, an elderly man, who could have been a lawyer or a banker, was smoking a cigar over a glass of port, and beside him sat a plump and slightly too well groomed individual who had a tall colorless drink, probably gin-and-tonic. The fifth man, separated from him by a vacant chair, seemed to be dividing his attention between a book on his lap and the conversation, in which he was taking no part. I sat down beside the sandy-haired man; as I did so and rang for the waiter, the colonel was saying:

"No, that wouldn't. I can think of a better one. Suppose you have Columbus get his ships from Henry the Seventh of England and sail under the English instead of the Spanish flag. You know, he did try to get English backing, before he went to Spain, but King Henry turned him down. That could be changed."

I pricked up my ears. The period from 1492 to the Revolution is my special field of American history, and I knew, at once, the enormous difference that would have made. It was a moment later that I realized how oddly the colonel had expressed the idea, and by that time the plump man was speaking.

"Yes, that would work," he agreed. "Those kings made decisions, most of the time, on whether or not they had a hangover, or what some court favorite thought." He got out a notebook and pen and scribbled briefly. "I'll hand that to the planning staff when I get to New York. That's Henry the Seventh, not Henry the Eighth? Right. We'll fix it so that Columbus will catch him when he's in a good humor."

That was too much. I turned to the man beside me.

"What goes on?" I asked. "Has somebody invented a time machine?"

He looked up from the drink he was contemplating and gave me a grin.

"Sounds like it, doesn't it? Why, no; our friend here is getting up a television program. Tell the gentleman about it," he urged the plump man across the aisle.

The waiter arrived at that moment. The plump man, who seemed to need little urging, waited until I had ordered a drink and then began telling me what a positively sensational idea it was.

"We're calling it *Crossroads of Destiny*," he said. "It'll be a series, one half-hour show a week; in each episode, we'll take some historic event and show how history could have been changed if something had happened differently. We dramatize the event up to that point just as it really happened, and then a commentary-voice comes on and announces that this is the Crossroads of Destiny; this is where history could have been completely changed. Then he gives a resumé of what really did happen, and then he says, '*But*—suppose so and so had done this and that, instead of such and such.' Then we pick up the dramatization at that point, only we show it the way it might have happened. Like this thing about Columbus; we'll show how it could have happened, and end with Columbus wading ashore with his sword in one hand and a flag in the other, just like the painting, only it'll be the English flag, and Columbus will shout: 'I take possession of this new land in the name of His Majesty, Henry the Seventh of England!' " He brandished his drink, to the visible consternation of the elderly man beside him. "And then, the sailors all sing *God Save the King.*"

"Which wasn't written till about 1745," I couldn't help mentioning.

"Huh?" The plump man looked startled. "Are you sure?" Then he decided that I was, and shrugged. "Well, they can all shout, 'God Save King Henry!' or 'St. George for England!' or something. Then, at the end, we introduce the program guest, some history expert, a real name, and he tells how he thinks history would have been changed if it had happened this way.

The conservatively-dressed gentleman beside him wanted to know how long he expected to keep the show running.

"The crossroads will give out before long," he added.

"The sponsor'll give out first," I said. "History is just one damn crossroads after another." I mentioned, in passing, that I taught the subject. ''Why, since the beginning of this century, we've had enough of them to keep the show running for a year.''

''We have about twenty already written and ready to produce,'' the plump man said comfortably, ''and ideas for twice as many that the planning staff is working on now.''

· The elderly man accepted that and took another cautious sip of wine.

''What I wonder, though, is whether you can really say that history can be changed.''

''Well, of course—'' The television man was taken aback; one always seems to be when a basic assumption is questioned. ''Of course, we only know what really did happen, but it stands to reason if something had happened differently, the results would have been different, doesn't it?''

''But it seems to me that everything would work out the same in the long run. There'd be some differences at the time, but over the years wouldn't they all cancel out?''

''*Non, non, Monsieur!*'' the man with the book, who had been outside the conversation until now, told him earnestly. ''Make no mistake; 'istoree can be shange'!''

I looked at him curiously. The accent sounded French, but it wasn't quite right. He was some kind of a foreigner, though; I'd swear that he never bought the clothes he was wearing in this country—the way the suit fitted, and the cut of it, and the shirt-collar, and the necktie. The book he was reading was Langmuir's *Social History of the American People*—not one of my favorites, a bit too much on the doctrinaire side, but what a bookshop clerk would give a foreigner looking for something to explain America.

''What do you think, Professor?'' the plump man was asking me.

''It would work out the other way. The differences wouldn't cancel out; they'd accumulate. Say something happened a century ago, to throw a presidential election the other way. You'd get different people at the head of the government, opposite lines of policy taken, and eventually we'd be getting into different wars with different enemies at different times, and different batches of young men killed before they could marry and have families—different people being born or not being born. That would mean different ideas, good or bad, being advanced; different books written; different inventions, and different social and economic problems as a consequence."

"Look, he's only giving himself a century," the colonel added. "Think of the changes if this thing we were discussing, Columbus sailing under the English flag, had happened. Or suppose Leif Ericson had been able to plant a permanent colony in America in the Eleventh Century, or if the Saracens had won the Battle of Tours. Try to imagine the world today if any of those things had happened. One thing you can be sure of—any errors you make in trying to imagine such a world will be on the side of over-conservatism."

The sandy-haired man beside me, who had been using his highball for a crystall ball, must have glimpsed in it what he was looking for. He finished the drink, set the empty glass on the stand-tray beside him, and reached back to push the button.

"I don't think you realize just how good an idea you have, here," he told the plump man abruptly. "If you did, you wouldn't ruin it with such timid and unimaginative treatment."

I thought he'd been staying out of the conversation because it was over his head. Instead, he had been taking the plump man's idea apart, examining all the pieces, and considering what was wrong with it and how it could be improved. The plump man looked startled, and then angry—timid and unimaginative were the last things he'd expected his idea to be called. Then he became uneasy. Maybe this fellow was a typical representative of his lord and master, the faceless abstraction called the Public.

"What do you mean?" he asked.

"Misplaced emphasis. You shouldn't emphasize the event that could have changed history; you should emphasize the changes that could have been made. You're going to end this show you were talking about with a shot of Columbus wading up to the beach with an English flag, aren't you?"

"Well, that's the logical ending."

"That's the logical beginning," the sandy-haired man contradicted. "And after that, your guest historian comes on; how much time will he be allowed?"

"Well, maybe three or four minutes. We can't cut the dramatization too short—"

"And he'll have to explain, a couple of times, and in words of one syllable, that what we have seen didn't really happen, because if he doesn't, the next morning half the twelve-year-old kids in the country will be rushing wild-eyed into school to slip the teacher the real inside about the discovery of America. By the time he gets that done, he'll be able to mumble a couple of generalities about vast and incalculable effects, and then it'll be time to tell the public about Widgets, the really safe cigarettes, all filter and absolutely free from tobacco."

The waiter arrived at this point, and the sandy-haired man ordered another rye highball. I decided to have another bourbon on the rocks, and the TV impresario said, "Gin-and-tonic," absently, and went into a reverie which lasted until the drinks arrived. Then he came awake again.

"I see what you mean," he said. "Most of the audience would wonder what difference it would have made where Columbus would have gotten his ships, as long as he got them and America got discovered. I can see it would have made a hell of a big difference. But how could it be handled any other way? How could you figure out just what the difference would have been?"

"Well, you need a man who'd know the historical background, and you'd need a man with a powerful creative imagination, who is used to using it inside rigorously defined limits. Don't try to get them both in one; a collaboration would really be better. Then you work from the known situation in Europe and in America in 1492, and decide on the immediate effects. And from that, you have to carry it along, step by step, down to the present. It would be a lot of hard and very exacting work, but the result would be worth it." He took a sip from his glass and added: "Remember, you don't have to prove that the world today would be the way you set it up. All you have to do is make sure that nobody else would be able to prove that it wouldn't.''

"Well, how could you present that?''

"As a play, with fictional characters and a plot; time, the present, under the changed conditions. The plot—the reason the coward conquers his fear and becomes a hero, the obstacle to the boy marrying the girl, the reason the innocent man is being persecuted—will have to grow out of this imaginary world you've constructed, and be impossible in our real world. As long as you stick to that, you're all right.''

"Sure. I get that.'' The plump man was excited again; he was about half sold on the idea. "But how will we get the audience to accept it? We're asking them to start with an assumption they know isn't true.''

"Maybe it is, in another time-dimension,'' the colonel suggested. "You can't prove it isn't. For that matter, you can't prove there aren't other time-dimensions.''

"Hah, that's it!'' the sandy-haired man exclaimed. "World of alternate probability. That takes care of that.''

He drank about a third of his highball and sat gazing into the rest of it, in an almost yogic trance. The plump man looked at the colonel in bafflement.

"Maybe this alternate probability time-dimension stuff means something to you,'' he said. "Be damned if it does to me.''

"Well, as far as we know, we live in a four-dimensional universe,'' the colonel started.

The elderly man across from him groaned. "Fourth dimension! Good God, are we going to talk about that?''

"It isn't anything to be scared of. You carry an instrument for measuring in the fourth dimension all the time. A watch.''

"You mean it's just time? But that isn't—''

"We know of three dimensions of space,'' the colonel told him, gesturing to indicate them. "We can use them for coordinates to locate things, but we also locate things in time. I wouldn't like to ride on a train or a plane if we didn't. Well, let's call the time we know, the time your watch registers, Time-A. Now, suppose the entire, infinite extent of Time-A is only an instant in another dimension of time, which we'll call Time-B. The next instant of Time-B is also the entire extent of Time-A, and the next and the next. As in Time-A, different things are happening at different instants. In one of these instants of Time-B, one of the things that's happening is that King Henry the Seventh of England is furnishing ships to Christopher Columbus.''

The man with the odd clothes was getting excited again.

''Zees—'ow you say—zees alternate probabeelitay; eet ees a theory zhenerally accept' een zees countree?''

''Got it!'' the sandy-haired man said, before anybody could answer. He set his drink on the stand-tray and took a big jackknife out of his pocket, holding it unopened in his hand. ''How's this sound?'' he asked, and hit the edge of the tray with the back of the knife, *Bong!*

''Crossroads—of—*Destiny!*'' he intoned, and hit the edge of the tray again, *Bong!* ''This is the year 1959—but not the 1959 of our world, for we are in a world of alternate probability, in another dimension of time; a world parallel to and coexistent with, but separate from our own, in which history has been completely altered by a single momentous event.'' He shifted back to his normal voice.

''Not bad; only twenty-five seconds,'' the plump man said, looking up from his wrist watch. ''And a trained announcer could maybe shave five seconds off that. Yes, something like that, and at the end we'll have another thirty seconds, and we can do without the guest.''

''But zees alternate probabeelitay, in anozzer dimension,'' the stranger was insisting. ''Ees zees a concept original weet you?'' he asked the colonel.

''Oh, no; that idea's been around for a long time.''

''I never heard of it before now,'' the elderly man said, as though that completely demolished it.

''Zen eet ees zhenerally accept' by zee scienteest'?''

''Umm, no,'' the sandy-haired man relieved the colonel. ''There's absolutely no evidence to support it, and scientists don't accept unsupported assumptions unless they need them to explain something, and they don't need this assumption for anything. Well, it would come in handy to make some of these reports of freak phenomena, like mysterious appearances and disappearances, or flying-object sightings, or reported falls of nonmeteoric matter, theoretically respectable. Reports like that usually get the ignore-and-forget treatment, now."

"Zen you believe zat zeese ozzer world of zee alternate probabeelitay, zey exist?"

"No. I don't disbelieve it, either. I've no reason to, one way or another." He studied his drink for a moment, and lowered the level in the glass slightly. "I've said that once in a while things get reported that look as though such other worlds, in another time-dimension, may exist. There have been whole books published by people who collect stories like that. I must say that academic science isn't very hospitable to them."

"You mean, zings sometimes, 'ow-you-say, leak in from one of zees ozzer worlds? Zat has been known to 'appen?"

"Things have been said to have happened that might, if true, be cases of things leaking through from another time-world," the sandy-haired man corrected. "Or leaking away to another time-world." He mentioned a few of the more famous cases of unexplained mysteries—the English diplomat in Prussia who vanished in plain sight of a number of people, the ship found completely deserted by her crew, the lifeboats all in place; stories like that. "And there's this rash of alleged sightings of unidentified flying objects. I'd sooner believe that they came from another dimension than from another planet. But, as far as I know, nobody's seriously advanced this other-time-dimension theory to explain them."

"I think the idea's familiar enough, though, that we can use it as an explanation, or pseudo-explanation, for the program," the television man said. "Fact is, we aren't married to this Crossroads title, yet; we could just as easily call it *Fifth Dimension*. That would lead the public to expect something out of the normal before the show started."

That got the conversation back onto the show, and we talked for some time about it, each of us suggesting possibilities.

The stranger even suggested one—that the Civil War had started during the Jackson Administration. Fortunately, nobody else noticed that. Finally, a porter came through and inquired if any of us were getting off at Harrisburg, saying that we would be getting in in five minutes.

The stranger finished his drink hastily and got up, saying that he would have to get his luggage. He told us how much he had enjoyed the conversation, and then followed the porter toward the rear of the train. After he had gone out, the TV man chuckled.

"Was that one an oddball!" he exclaimed. "Where the hell do you suppose he got that suit?"

"It was a tailored suit," the colonel said. "A very good one. And I can't think of any country in the world in which they cut suits just like that. And did you catch his accent?"

"Phony," the television man pronounced. "The French accent of a Greek waiter in a fake French restaurant. In the Bronx."

"Not quite. The pronunciation was all right for French accent, but the cadence, the way the word-sounds were strung together, was German."

The elderly man looked at the colonel keenly. "I see you're Intelligence," he mentioned. "Think he might be somebody up your alley, Colonel?"

The colonel shook his head. "I doubt it. There are agents of unfriendly powers in this country—a lot of them, I'm sorry to have to say. But they don't speak accented English, and they don't dress eccentrically. You know there's an enemy agent in a crowd; pick out the most normally American type in sight and you usually won't have to look further."

The train ground to a stop. A young couple with hand-luggage came in and sat at one end of the car, waiting until other accommodations could be found for them. After a while, it started again. I dallied over my drink, and then got up and excused myself, saying that I wanted to turn in early.

In the next car behind, I met the porter who had come in just before the stop. He looked worried, and after a moment's hesitation, he spoke to me.

''Pardon, sir. The man in the club-car who got off at Harrisburg; did you know him?''

''Never saw him before. Why?''

''He tipped me with this.''

He showed it to me, and I didn't blame him for looking unhappy. It was marked *One Dollar*, and *United States of America*, but outside that there wasn't a thing right about it. One side was gray, all right, but the other side was green. The picture wasn't the right one. And there were a lot of other things about it, some of them absolutely ludicrous. It wasn't counterfeit—it wasn't even an imitation of a United States bill.

And then it hit me, like a bullet in the chest. Not a bill of *our* United States. No wonder he had been so interested in whether our scientists accepted the theory of other time-dimensions and other worlds of alternate probability!

On an impulse, I got out two ones and gave them to the porter—perfectly good United States Bank gold-certificates.

''You'd better let me keep this,'' I said, trying to make it sound the way he'd think a Federal Agent would say it. He took the bills, smiling, and I folded his bill and put it into my vest pocket.

''Thank you, sir,'' he said. ''I have no wish to keep it.''

Some part of my mind below the level of consciousness must have taken over and guided me back to the right car and compartment; I didn't realize where I was going till I put on the light and recognized my own luggage. Then I sat down, as dizzy as though the two drinks I had had, had been a dozen. For a moment, I was tempted to rush back to the club-car and show the thing to the colonel and the sandy-haired man. On second thought, I decided against that.

The next thing I banished from my mind was the adjective ''incredible.'' I had to credit it; I had the proof in my vest pocket. The coincidence arising from our topic of conversation didn't bother me too much, either. It was the topic which had drawn him into it. And, as the sandy-haired man had pointed out, we know nothing, one way or another, about these other worlds; we certainly don't know what barriers separate them from our own, or how often those barriers may fail. I might have thought more about that if I'd been in physical science. I wasn't; I was in American history. So what I thought about was what sort of country that other United States must be, and what its history must have been.

The man's costume was basically the same as ours—same general style, but many little differences of fashion. I had the impression that it was the costume of a less formal and conservative society than ours and a more casual way of life. It could be the sort of costume into which ours would evolve in another thirty or so years. There was another odd thing. I'd noticed him looking curiously at both the waiter and the porter, as though something about them surprised him. The only thing they had in common was their race, the same as every other passenger-car attendant. But he wasn't used to seeing Chinese working in railway cars.

And there had been that remark about the Civil War and the Jackson Administration. I wondered what Jackson he had been talking about; not Andrew Jackson, the Tennessee militia general who got us into war with Spain in 1810, I hoped. And the Civil War; that baffled me completely. I wondered if it had been a class-war, or a sectional conflict. We'd had plenty of the latter, during our first century, but all of them had been settled peacefully and constitutionally. Well, some of the things he'd read in Langmuir's *Social History* would be surprises for him, too.

And then I took the bill out for another examination. It must have gotten mixed with his spendable money—it was about the size of ours—and I wondered how he had acquired enough of our money to pay his train fare. Maybe he'd had a diamond and sold it, or maybe he'd had a gun and held somebody up. If he had, I didn't know that I blamed him, under the circumstances. I had an idea that he had some realization of what had happened to him—the book, and the fake accent, to cover any mistakes he might make. Well, I wished him luck, and then I unfolded the dollar bill and looked at it again.

In the first place, it had been issued by the United States Department of Treasury itself, not the United States Bank or one of the State Banks. I'd have to think over the implications of that carefully. In the second place, it was a silver certificate; why, in this other United States, silver must be an acceptable monetary metal; maybe equally so with gold, though I could hardly believe that. Then I looked at the picture on the gray obverse side, and had to strain my eyes on the fine print under it to identify it. It was Washington, all right, but a much older Washington than any of the pictures of him I had ever seen. Then I realized that I knew just where the Crossroads of Destiny for his world and mine had been.

As every schoolchild among us knows, General George Washington was shot dead at the Battle of Germantown, in 1777, by an English, or, rather Scottish, officer, Patrick Ferguson—the same Patrick Ferguson who invented the breech-loading rifle that smashed Napoleon's armies. Washington, today, is one of our lesser national heroes, because he was our first military commander-in-chief. But in this other world, he must have survived to lead our armies to victory and become our first President, as was the case with the man who took his place when he was killed.

I folded the bill and put it away carefully among my identification cards, where it wouldn't a second time get mixed with the money I spent, and as I did, I wondered what sort of a President George Washington had made, and what part, in the history of that other United States, had been played by the man whose picture appears on our dollar bills—General and President Benedict Arnold.

DAY OF THE MORON

In light of the Three-Mile Island incident, this story is topical enough—other than the dates—for a current issue of Analog. *As we are beginning to learn, it is not the nuclear piles, but rather the people who run them that pose the greatest threat.*

In "Day of the Moron," Piper shows us that in a centralized civilization such as ours, we can no longer tolerate the mistakes of half-wits and blunderers—no matter how well-intentioned.

THERE WERE STILL, in 1968, a few people who were afraid of the nuclear power plant. Oldsters, in whom the term "atomic energy" produced semantic reactions associated with Hiroshima. Those who saw, in the towering steam-column above it, a tempting target for enemy—which still meant Soviet—bombers and guided missiles. Some of the Central Intelligence and F.B.I. people, who realized how futile even the most elaborate security measures were against a resourceful and suicidally determined saboteur. And a minority of engineers and nuclear physicists who remained unpersuaded that accidental blowups at nuclear-reaction plants were impossible.

Scott Melroy was among these last. He knew, as a matter of fact, that there had been several nasty, meticulously unpublicized, near-castastrophes at the Long Island Nuclear Reaction Plant, all involving the new Doernberg-Giardano breeder-reactors, and that there had been considerable carefully-hushed top-level acrimony before the Melroy Engineering Corporation had been given the contract to install the fully cybernetic control system intended to prevent a recurrence of such incidents.

That had been three months ago. Melroy and his people had moved in, been assigned sections of a couple of machine shops, set up an assembly shop and a set of plyboard-partitioned offices in a vacant warehouse just outside the reactor area, and tried to start work, only to run into the almost interminable procedural disputes and jurisdictional wranglings of the sort which he privately labeled "bureau bunk." It was only now that he was ready to begin work on the reactors.

He sat at his desk, in the inner of three successively smaller offices on the second floor of the converted warehouse, checking over a symbolic-logic analysis of a relay system and, at the same time, sharpening a pencil, his knife paring off tiny feathery shavings of wood. He was a tall, sparely-built man of indeterminate age, with thinning sandy hair, a long Gaelic upper lip, and a wide, half-humorous, half-weary mouth; he wore an open-necked shirt, and an old and shabby leather jacket, on the left shoulder of which a few clinging flecks of paint showed where some military emblem had been, long ago. While his fingers worked with the jackknife and his eyes traveled over the page of closely-written symbols, his mind was reviewing the eight different ways in which one of the efficient but treacherous Doernberg-Giardano reactors could be allowed to reach critical mass, and he was wondering if there might not be some unsuspected ninth way. That was a possibility which always lurked in the back of his mind, and lately it had been giving him surrealistic nightmares.

"Mr. Melroy!" the box on the desk in front of him said

suddenly, in a feminine voice. "Mr. Melroy, Dr. Rives is here."

Melroy picked up the handphone, thumbing on the switch.
"Dr. Rives?" he repeated.

"The psychologist who's subbing for Dr. von Heyden-reich," the box told him patiently.

"Oh, yes. Show him in," Melroy said.

"Right away, Mr. Melroy," the box replied.

Replacing the handphone, Melroy wondered, for a moment, why there had been a hint of suppressed amusement in his secretary's voice. Then the door opened and he stopped wondering. Dr. Rives wasn't a him; she was a her. Very attractive looking her, too—dark hair and eyes, rather long oval features, clear, lightly tanned complexion, bright red lipstick put on with a micrometric exactitude that any engineer could appreciate. She was tall, within four inches of his own six-foot mark, and she wore a black tailored outfit, perfectly plain, which had probably cost around five hundred dollars and would have looked severe and mannish except that the figure under it curved and bulged in just the right places and to just the right degree.

Melroy rose, laying down knife and pencil and taking his pipe out of his mouth.

"Good afternoon," he greeted. "Dr. von Heydenreich gave me quite a favorable account of you—as far as it went. He might have included a few more data and made it more so . . . Won't you sit down?"

The woman laid her handbag on the desk and took the visitor's chair, impish mirth sparking in her eyes.

"He probably omitted mentioning that the D. is for Doris," she suggested. "Suppose I'd been an Englishman with a name like Evelyn or Vivian?"

Melroy tried to visualize her as a male Englishman named Vivian, gave up, and grinned at her.

"Let this be a lesson," he said. "Inferences are to be drawn from objects, or descriptions of objects; never from verbal labels. Do you initial your first name just to see how people react when they meet you?''

"Well, no, though that's an amusing and sometimes instructive by-product. It started when I began contributing to some of the professional journals. There's still a little of what used to be called male sex-chauvinism among my colleagues, and some who would be favorably impressed with an article signed D. Warren Rives might snort in contempt at the same article signed Doris Rives.''

"Well, fortunately, Dr. von Heydenreich isn't one of those,'' Melroy said. "How is the Herr Doktor, by the way, and just what happened to him? Miss Kourtakides merely told me that he'd been injured and was in a hospital in Pittsburgh.''

"The Herr Doktor got shot,'' Doris Rives informed him. "With a charge of BB's, in a most indelicate portion of his anatomy. He was out hunting, the last day of small-game season, and somebody mistook him for a turkey. Nothing really serious, but he's face down in bed, cursing hideously in German, English, Russian, Italian and French, mainly because he's missing deer hunting.''

"I might have known it,'' Melroy said in disgust. "The ubiquitous lame-brain with a dangerous mechanism. . . . I suppose he briefed you on what I want done, here?''

"Well, not too completely. I gathered that you want me to give intelligence tests, or aptitude tests, or something of the sort, to some of your employees. I'm not really one of these so-called industrial anthropologists,'' she explained. "Most of my work, for the past few years, has been for public-welfare organizations, with subnormal persons. I told him that, and he said that was why he selected me. He said one other thing. He said, 'I used to think Melroy had an obsession about fools; well, after stopping this load of shot, I'm beginning to think it's a good subject to be obsessed about.' ''

Melroy nodded. " 'Obsession' will probably do. 'Phobia' would be more exact. I'm afraid of fools, and the chance that I have one working for me, here, affects me like having a cobra crawling around my bedroom in the dark. I want you to locate any who might be in a gang of new men I've had to hire, so that I can get rid of them.''

"And just how do you define the term 'fool,' Mr. Melroy?" she asked. "Remember, it has no standard meaning. Republicans apply it to Democrats, and vice versa."

"Well, I apply it to people who do things without considering possible consequences. People who pepper distinguished Austrian psychologists in the pants-seat with turkey-shot, for a starter. Or people who push buttons to see what'll happen, or turn valves and twiddle with dial-knobs because they have nothing else to do with their hands. Or shoot insulators off power lines to see if they can hit them. People who don't know it's loaded. People who think warning signs are purely ornamental. People who play practical jokes. People who—"

"I know what you mean. Just day-before-yesterday, I saw a woman toss a cocktail into an electric heater. She didn't want to drink it, and she thought it would just go up in steam. The result was slightly spectacular."

"Next time, she won't do that. She'll probably throw her drink into a lead-ladle, if there's one around. Well, on a statistical basis, I'd judge that I have three or four such dud rounds among this new gang I've hired. I want you to put the finger on them, so I can bounce them before they blow the whole plant up, which could happen quite easily."

"That," Doris Rives said, "is not going to be as easy as it sounds. Ordinary intelligence-testing won't be enough. The woman I was speaking of has an I.Q. well inside the meaning of normal intelligence. She just doesn't use it."

"Sure." Melroy got a thick folder out of his desk and handed it across. "Heydenreich thought of that, too. He got this up for me, about five years ago. The intelligence test is based on the new French Sûreté test for mentally deficient criminals. Then there's a memory test, and tests for judgment and discrimination, semantic reactions, temperamental and emotional makeup, and general mental attitude."

She took the folder and leafed through it. "Yes, I see. I always liked this Sûreté test. And this memory test is a honey—'One hen, two ducks, three squawking geese, four corpulent porpoises, five Limerick oysters, six pairs of Don Alfonso tweezers . . .' I'd like to see some of these memory-course boys trying to make visual images of six pairs of Don Alfonso tweezers. And I'm going to make a copy of this word-association list. It's really a semantic reaction test; Korzybski would have loved it. And, of course, our old friend, the Rorschach Ink-Blots. I've always harbored the impious suspicion that you can prove almost anything you want to with that. But these question-suggestions for personal interview are really crafty. Did Heydenreich get them up himself?''

"Yes. And we have stacks and stacks of printed forms for the written portion of the test, and big cards to summarize each subject on. And we have a disk-recorder to use in the oral tests. There'll have to be a pretty complete record of each test, in case—''

The office door opened and a bulky man with a black mustache entered, beating the snow from his overcoat with a battered porkpie hat and commenting blasphemously on the weather. He advanced into the room until he saw the woman in the chair beside the desk, and then started to back out.

"Come on in, Sid," Melroy told him. "Dr. Rives, this is our general foreman, Sid Keating. Sid, Dr. Rives, the new dimwit detector. Sid's in direct charge of personnel," he continued, "so you two'll be working together quite a bit."

"Glad to know you, doctor," Keating said. Then he turned to Melroy. "Scott, you're really going through with this, then?" he asked. "I'm afraid we'll have trouble, then."

"Look, Sid," Melroy said. "We've been all over that. Once we start work on the reactors, you and Ned Puryear and Joe Ricci and Steve Chalmers can't be everywhere at once. A cybernetic system will only do what it's been assembled to do, and if some quarter-wit assembles one of these things wrong—'' He left the sentence dangling; both men knew what he meant.

Keating shook his head. "This union's going to bawl like a branded calf about it," he predicted. "And if any of the dear sirs and brothers get washed out—'' That sentence didn't need to be completed, either.

"We have a right," Melroy said, "to discharge any worker who is, quote, of unsound mind, deficient mentality or emotional instability, unquote. It says so right in our union contract, in nice big print."

"Then they'll claim the tests are wrong."

"I can't see how they can do that," Doris Rives put in, faintly scandalized.

"Neither can I, and they probably won't either," Keating told her. "But they'll go ahead and do it. Why, Scott, they're pulling the Number One Doernberg-Giardano, tonight. By oh-eight-hundred, it ought to be cool enough to work on. Where will we hold the tests? Here?"

"We'll have to, unless we can get Dr. Rives security-cleared." Melroy turned to her. "Were you ever security-cleared by any Government agency?"

"Oh, yes. I was with Armed Forces Medical, Psychiatric Division, in Indonesia in '62 and '63, and I did some work with mental fatigue cases at Tonto Basin Research Establishment in '64."

Melroy looked at her sharply. Keating whistled.

"If she could get into Tonto Basin she can get in here," he declared.

"I should think so. I'll call Colonel Bradshaw, the security officer."

"That way, we can test them right on the job," Keating was saying. "Take them in relays. I'll talk to Ben about it, and we'll work up some kind of a schedule." He turned to Doris Rives. "You'll need a wrist-Geiger, and a dosimeter. We'll furnish them," he told her. "I hope they don't try to make you carry a pistol, too."

"A pistol?" For a moment, she must have thought he was using some technical-jargon term, and then it dawned on her that he wasn't. "You mean—?" She cocked her thumb and crooked her index finger.

"Yeah. A rod. Roscoe. The Equalizer. We all have to." He half-lifted one out of his side pocket. "We're all United States deputy marshals. They don't bother much with counterespionage, here, but they don't fool when it comes to countersabotage. Well, I'll get an order cut and posted. Be seeing you, Doctor.''

"You think the union will make trouble about these tests?" she asked, after the general foreman had gone out.

''They're sure to,'' Melroy replied. ''Here's the situation. I have about fifty of my own men, from Pittsburgh, here, but they can't work on the reactors because they don't belong to the Industrial Federation of Atomic Workers, and I can't just pay their initiation fees and union dues and get union cards for them, because admission to this union is on an annual quota basis, and this is December, and the quota's full. So I have to use them outside the reactor area, on fabrication and assembly work. And I have to hire through the union, and that's handled on a membership seniority basis, so I have to take what's thrown at me. That's why I was careful to get that clause I was quoting to Sid written into my contract.

''Now, here's what's going to happen. Most of the men'll take the test without protest, but a few of them'll raise the roof about it. Nothing burns a moron worse than to have somebody question his fractional intelligence. The odds are that the ones that yell the loudest about taking the test will be the ones who get scrubbed out, and when the test shows that they're deficient, they won't believe it. A moron simply cannot conceive of his being anything less than perfectly intelligent, and more than a lunatic can conceive of his being less than perfectly sane. So they'll claim we're framing them, as an excuse to fire them. And the union will have to back them up, right or wrong, at least on the local level. That goes without saying. In any dispute, the employer is always wrong and the worker is always right, until proven otherwise. And that takes a lot of doing, believe me!''

''Well, if they're hired through the union, on a seniority basis, wouldn't they be likely to be experienced and competent workers?'' she asked.

''Experienced, yes. That is, none of them has ever been caught doing anything downright calamitous . . . yet,'' Melroy replied. ''The moron I'm afraid of can go on for years, doing routine work under supervision, and nothing'll happen. Then, some day, he does something on his own lame-brained initiative, and when he does, it's only at the whim of whatever gods there be that the result isn't a wholesale catastrophe. And people like that are the most serious threat facing our civilization today, atomic war not excepted.''

Dr. Doris Rives lifted a delicately penciled eyebrow over that. Melroy, pausing to relight his pipe, grinned at her.

''You think that's the old obsession talking?'' he asked. ''Could be. But look at this plant, here. It generates every kilowatt of current used between Trenton and Albany, the New York metropolitan area included. Except for a few little storage-battery or Diesel generator systems, that couldn't handle one tenth of one per cent of the barest minimum load, it's been the only source of electric current here since 1962, when the last coal-burning power plant was dismantled. Knock this plant out and you darken every house and office and factory and street in the area. You immobilize the elevators—think what that would mean in lower and midtown Manhattan alone. And the subways. And the new endless-belt conveyors that handle eighty per cent of the city's freight traffic. And the railroads—there aren't a dozen steam or Diesel locomotives left in the whole area. And the pump stations for water and gas and fuel oil. And seventy per cent of the space-heating is electric, now. Why, you can't imagine what it'd be like. It's too gigantic. But what you can imagine would be a nightmare.

''You know, it wasn't so long ago, when every home lighted and heated itself, and every little industry was a self-contained unit, that a fool couldn't do great damage unless he inherited a throne or was placed in command of an army, and that didn't happen nearly as often as our leftist social historians would like us to think. But today, everything we depend upon is centralized, and vulnerable to blunder-damage. Even our food—remember that poisoned soft-drink horror in Chicago, in 1963; three thousand hospitalized and six hundred dead because of one man's stupid mistake at a bottling plant.'' He shook himself slightly, as though to throw off some shadow that had fallen over him, and looked at his watch. "Sixteen hundred. How did you get here? Fly your own plane?"

"No; I came by T.W.A. from Pittsburgh. I have a room at the new Midtown City hotel, on Forty-seventh Street; I had my luggage sent on there from the airport and came out on the Long Island subway."

"Fine. I have a room at Midtown City, myself, though I sleep here about half the time." He nodded toward a door on the left. "Suppose we go in and have dinner together. This cafeteria, here, is a horrible place. It's run by a dietitian instead of a chef, and everything's so white-enamel antiseptic that I swear I smell belladonna-icthyol ointment every time I go in the place. Wait here till I change clothes."

At the Long Island plant, no one was concerned about espionage—neither the processes nor the equipment used there were secret—but the countersabotage security was fantastically thorough. Every person or scrap of material entering the reactor area was searched; the life-history of every man and woman employed there was known back to the cradle. A broad highway encircled it outside the fence, patrolled night and day by twenty General Stuart cavalry-tanks. There were a thousand soldiers, and three hundred Atomic Power Authority police, and only God knew how many F.B.I. and Central Intelligence undercover agents. Every supervisor and inspector and salared technician was an armed United States deputy marshal. And nobody, outside the Department of Defense, knew how much radar and counter-rocket and fighter protection the place had, but the air-defense zone extended from Boston to Philadelphia and as far inland as Wilkes-Barre, Pennsylvania.

The Long Island Nuclear Power Plant, Melroy thought, had all the invulnerability of Achilles—and no more.

The six new Doernberg-Giardano breeder-reactors clustered in a circle inside a windowless concrete building at the center of the plant. Beside their primary purpose of plutonium production, they furnished heat for the sea-water distillation and chemical extraction system, processing the water that was run through the steam boilers at the main power reactors, condensed, redistilled, and finally pumped, pure, into the water mains of New York. Safe outside the shielding, in a corner of a high-ceilinged room, was the plyboard-screened on-the-job office of the Melroy Engineering Corporation's timekeepers and foremen. Beyond, along the far wall, were the washroom and locker room and lunch room of the workmen.

Sixty or seventy men, mostly in white coveralls and all wearing identification badges and carrying dosimeters in their breast pockets and midget Geigers strapped to their wrists, were crowded about the bulletin-board in front of the makeshift office. There was a hum of voices—some perplexed or angry; but mostly good-humored and bantering. As Melroy and Doris Rives approached, the talking died out and the men turned. In the sudden silence, one voice, harshly strident, continued:

". . . do they think this is, anyhow? We don't hafta take none of that."

Somebody must have nudged the speaker, trying without success to hush him. The bellicose voice continued, and Melroy spotted the speaker—short, thick-set, his arms jutting out at an angle from his body, his heavy features soured with anger.

"Like we was a lotta halfwits, 'r nuts, 'r some'n! Well, we don't hafta stand for this. They ain't got no right—"

Doris Rives clung tigher to Melroy's arm as he pushed a way for himself and her through the crowd and into the temporary office. Inside, they were met by a young man with a deputy marshal's badge on his flannel shirt and a .38 revolver on his hip.

"Ben Puryear; Dr. Rives," Melroy introduced. "Who's the mouthy character outside?"

"One of the roustabouts; name's Burris," Puryear replied. "Washroom lawyer."

Melroy nodded. "You always get one or two like that. How're the rest taking it?"

Puryear shrugged. "About how you'd expect. A lot of kidding about who's got any intelligence to test. Burris seems to be the only one who's trying to make an issue out of it."

"Well, what are they doing ganged up here?" Melroy wanted to know. "It's past oh-eight-hundred; why aren't they at work?"

"Reactor's still too hot. Temperature and radioactivity both too high; radioactivity's still up around eight hundred REM's."

"Well, then, we'll give them all the written portion of the test together, and start the personal interviews and oral tests as soon as they're through." He turned to Doris Rives. "Can you give all of them the written test together?" he asked. "And can Ben help you—distributing forms, timing the test, seeing that there's no fudging, and collecting the forms when they're done?"

"Oh, yes; all they'll have to do is follow the printed instructions." She looked around. "I'll need a desk, and an extra chair for the interview subject."

"Right over here, Doctor," Puryear said. "And here are the forms and cards, and the sound-recorder, and blank sound-disks."

"Yes," Melroy added. "Be sure you get a recording of every interview and oral test; we may need them for evidence."

He broke off as a man in white coveralls came pushing into the office. He was a scrawny little fellow with a wide, loose-lipped mouth and a protuberant Adam's apple; beside his identity badge, he wore a two-inch celluloid button lettered: I.F.A.W. STEWARD.

"Wanta use the phone," he said. "Union business."

Melroy gestured toward a telephone on the desk beside him. The newcomer shook his head, twisting his mouth into a smirk.

"Not that one; the one with the whisper mouthpiece," he said. "This is private union business."

Melroy shrugged and indicated another phone. The man with the union steward's badge picked it up, dialed, and held a lengthy conversation into it, turning his head away in case Melroy might happen to be a lip reader. Finally he turned.

''Mr. Crandall wants to talk to you,'' he said, grinning triumphantly, the phone extended to Melroy.

The engineer picked up another phone, snapping a button on the base of it.

''Melroy here,'' he said.

Something on the line started going *beep-beep-beep* softly.

''Crandall, executive secretary, I.F.A.W.,'' the man on the other end of the line identified himself. ''Is there a recorder going on this line?''

''Naturally,'' Melroy replied. ''I record all business conversations; office routine.''

''Mr. Melroy, I've been informed that you propose forcing our members in your employ to submit to some kind of a mental test. Is that correct?''

''Not exactly. I'm not able to force anybody to submit to anything against his will. If anybody objects to taking these tests, he can say so, and I'll have his time made out and pay him off.''

''That's the same thing. A threat of dismissal is coercion, and if these men want to keep their jobs they'll have to take this test.''

''Well, that's stated more or less correctly,'' Melroy conceded. ''Let's just put it that taking—and passing—this test is a condition of employment. My contract with your union recognizes my right to establish standards of intelligence; that's implied by my recognized right to dismiss any person of unsound mind, deficient mentality or emotional instability. Psychological testing is the only means of determining whether or not a person is classifiable in those terms.''

''Then, in case the test purports to show that one of these men is, let's say, mentally deficient, you intend dismissing him?''

''With the customary two weeks' severance-pay, yes.''

''Well, if you do dismiss anybody on those grounds, the union will have to insist on reviewing the grounds for dismissal.''

''My contract with your union says nothing whatever

about any right of review being reserved by the union in such cases. Only in cases of disciplinary dismissal, which this is not. I take the position that certain minimum standards of intelligence and mental stability are essentials in this sort of work, just as, say, certain minimum standards of literacy are essential in clerical work.''

''Then you're going to make these men take these tests, whatever they are?''

''If they want to work for me, yes. And anybody who fails to pass them will be dropped from my payroll.''

''And who's going to decide whether or not these men have successfully passed these tests?'' Crandall asked. ''You?''

''Good Lord, no! I'm an electronics engineer, not a psychologist. The tests are being given, and will be evaluated, by a graduate psychologist, Dr. D. Warren Rives, who has a diploma from the American Board of Psychiatry and Neurology and is a member of the American Psychological Association. Dr. Rives will be the final arbiter on who is or is not disqualified by these tests.''

''Well, our man Koffler says you have some girl there to give the tests,'' Crandall accused.

''I suppose he means Dr. Rives,'' Melroy replied. ''I can assure you, she is an extremely competent psychologist, however. She came to me most highly recommended by Dr. Karl von Heydenreich, who is not inclined to be careless with his recommendations.''

''Well, Mr. Melroy, we don't want any more trouble with you than we have to have,'' Crandall told him, ''but we will insist on reviewing any dismissals which occur as a result of these tests.''

''You can do that. I'd advise, first, that you read over the contract you signed with me. Get a qualified lawyer to tell you what we've agreed to and what we haven't. Was there anything else you wanted to talk about? . . . No? . . . Then good morning, Mr. Crandall.''

He hug up. ''All right; let's get on with it,'' he said. ''Ben, you get them into the lunch room; there are enough tables and

benches in there for everybody to take the written test in two
relays.''

"The union's gotta be represented while these tests is
going on,'' the union steward announced. ''Mr. Crandall
says I'm to stay here an' watch what you do to these guys.''

"This man working for us?'' Melroy asked Puryear.

"Yes. Koffler, Julius. Electrical fitter; Joe Ricci's gang.''

"All right. See to it that he gets placed in the first relay for
the written test, and gets first turn for the orals. That way he
can spend the rest of his time on duty here for the union, and
will know in advance what the test is like.'' He turned to
Koffler. ''But understand this. You keep your mouth out of
it. If you see anything that looks objectionable, make a note
of it, but don't try to interfere.''

The written tests, done on printed forms, required about
twenty minutes. Melroy watched the process of oral testing
and personal interviewing for a while, then picked up a big
flashlight and dropped it into his overcoat pocket, prepara-
tory to going out to inspect some equipment that had been
assembled outside the reactor area and brought in. As he went
out, Koffler was straddling a chair, glowering at Doris Rives
and making occasional ostentatious notes on a pad.

For about an hour, he poked around the newly assembled
apparatus, checking the wiring, and peering into it. When he
returned to the temporary office, the oral testing was still
going on; Koffler was still on duty as watcher for the union,
but the sport had evidently palled on him, for he was now
studying a comic book.

Melroy left the reactor area and returned to the office in the
converted area. During the midafternoon, somebody named
Leighton called him from the Atomic Power Authority
executive office, wanting to know what was the trouble
between him and the I.F.A.W. and saying that a protest
against his alleged high-handed and arbitrary conduct had
been received from the union.

Melroy explained, at length. He finished: ''You people
have twenty Stuart tanks, and a couple of thousand soldiers

and cops and undercover-men, here, guarding against sabotage. Don't you realize that a workman who makes stupid or careless or impulsive mistakes is just as dangerous to the plant as any saboteur? If somebody shoots you through the head, it doesn't matter whether he planned to murder you for a year or just didn't know the gun was loaded; you're as dead one way as the other. I should think you'd thank me for trying to eliminate a serious source of danger."

"Now, don't misunderstand my position, Mr. Melroy," the other man hastened to say. "I sympathize with your attitude, entirely. But these people are going to make trouble."

"If they do, it'll be my trouble. I'm under contract to install this cybernetic system for you; you aren't responsible for my labor policy," Melroy replied. "Oh, have you had much to do with this man Crandall, yourself?"

"Have I had—!" Leighton sputtered for a moment. "I'm in charge of personnel, here; that makes me his top-priority target, all the time."

"Well, what sort of a character is he, anyhow? When I contracted with the I.F.A.W., my lawyer and their lawyer handled everything; I never even met him."

"Well—He has his job to do, the same as I have," Leighton said. "He does it conscientiously. But it's like this— anything a workman tells him is the truth, and anything an employer tells him is a dirty lie. Until proven differently, of course, but that takes a lot of doing. And he goes off half-cocked a lot of times. He doesn't stop to analyze situations very closely."

"That's what I was afraid of. Well, you tell him you don't have any control over my labor relations. Tell him to bring his gripes to me."

At sixteen-thirty, Doris Rives came in, finding him still at his desk.

"I have the written tests all finished, and I have about twenty of the tests and interviews completed," she said. "I'll have to evaluate the results, though. I wonder if there's a vacant desk around here, anywhere, and a record player."

"Yes, sure. Ask Joan to fix you up; she'll find a place for you to work. And if you're going to be working late, I'll order some dinner for you from the cafeteria. I'm going to be here all evening, myself."

Sid Keating came in, a short while later, peeling out of his overcoat, jacket and shoulder holster.

"I don't think they got everything out of that reactor," he said. "Radioactivity's still almost active-normal—about eight hundred REM's—and the temperature's way up, too. That isn't lingering radiation; that's prompt radiation."

"Radioactivity hasn't dropped since morning; I'd think so, too," Melroy said. "What are they getting on the breakdown counter?"

"Mostly neutrons and alpha-particles. I talked to Fred Hausinger, the maintenance boss; he doesn't like it, either."

"Well, I'm no nuclear physicist," Melroy disclaimed, "but all that alpha stuff looks like a big chunk of Pu-239 left inside. What's Fred doing about it?"

"Oh, poking around inside the reactor with telemetered scanners and remote-control equipment. When I left, he had a gang pulling out graphite blocks with RC-tongs. We probably won't get a chance to work on it much before thirteen-hundred tomorrow." He unzipped a bulky brief case he had brought in under his arm and dumped papers onto his desk. "I still have this stuff to get straightened out, too."

"Had anything to eat? Then call the cafeteria and have them send up three dinners. Dr. Rives is eating here, too. Find out what she wants; I want pork chops."

"Uh-huh; Li'l Abner Melroy; po'k chops unless otherwise specified." Keating got up and went out into the middle office. As he opened the door, Melroy could hear a recording of somebody being given a word-association test.

Half an hour later, when the food arrived, they spread their table on a relatively clear desk in the middle office. Doris Rives had finished evaluating the completed tests; after dinner, she intended going over the written portions of the uncompleted tests.

"How'd the finished tests come out?" Melroy asked her.

"Better than I'd expected. Only two washouts," she replied. "Harvey Burris and Julius Koffler."

"Oh, *no!*" Keating wailed. "The I.F.A.W. steward, and the loudest-mouthed I-know-my-rights boy on the job!"

"Well, wasn't that to be expected?" Melroy asked. "If you'd seen the act those two put on—"

"They're both inherently stupid, infantile, and deficient in reasoning ability and judgment," Doris said. "Koffler is a typical adolescent problem-child show-off type, and Burris is an almost perfect twelve-year-old schoolyard bully. They both have inferiority complexes long enough to step on. If the purpose of this test is what I'm led to believe it is, I can't, in professional good conscience, recommend anything but that you get rid of both of them."

"What Bob's getting at is that they're the very ones who can claim, with the best show of plausibility, that the test is just a pretext to fire them for union activities," Melroy explained. "And the worst of it is, they're the only ones."

"Maybe we can scrub out a couple more on the written tests alone. Then they'll have company," Keating suggested.

"No, I can't do that." Doris was firm on the point. "The written part of the test was solely for ability to reason logically. Just among the three of us, I know some university professors who'd flunk on that. But if the rest of the tests show stability, sense of responsibility, good judgment, and a tendency to think before acting, the subject can be classified as a safe and reliable workman."

"Well, then, let's don't say anything till we have the tests all finished," Keating proposed.

"No!" Melroy cried. "Every minute those two are on the job, there's a chance they may do something disastrous. I'll fire them at oh-eight-hundred tomorrow."

"All right," Keating shook his head. "I only work here. But don't say I didn't warn you."

By 0930 the next morning, Keating's forebodings began to be realized. The first intimation came with a phone call to Melroy from Crandall, who accused him of having used the psychological tests as a fraudulent pretext for discharging

Koffler and Burris for union activities. When Melroy rejected his demand that the two men be reinstated, Crandall demanded to see the records of the tests.

"They're here at my office," Melroy told him. "You're welcome to look at them, and hear recordings of the oral portions of the tests. But I'd advise you to bring a professional psychologist along, because unless you're a trained psychologist yourself, they're not likely to mean much to you."

"Oh, sure!" Crandall retorted. "They'd have to be unintelligible to ordinary people, or you couldn't get away with this frame-up! Well, don't worry, I'll be along to see them."

Within ten minutes, the phone rang again. This time it was Leighton, the Atomic Power Authority man.

"We're much disturbed about this dispute between your company and the I.F.A.W.," he began.

"Well, frankly, so am I," Melroy admitted. "I'm here to do a job, not play Hatfields and McCoys with this union. I've had union trouble before, and it isn't fun. You're the gentleman who called me last evening, aren't you? Then you understand my position in the matter."

"Certainly, Mr. Melroy. I was talking to Colonel Bradshaw, the security officer, last evening. He agrees that a stupid or careless workman is, under some circumstances, a more serious threat to security than any saboteur. And we realize fully how dangerous these Doernberg-Giardanos are, and how much more dangerous they'd be if these cybernetic controls were improperly assembled. But this man Crandall is talking about calling a strike."

"Well, let him. In the first place, it'd be against me, not against the Atomic Power Authority. And, in the second place, if he does and it goes to Federal mediation, his demand for the reinstatement of those men will be thrown out, and his own organization will have to disavow his action, because he'll be calling the strike against his own contract."

"Well, I hope so." Leighton's tone indicated that the hope was rather dim. "I wish you luck; you're going to need it."

Within the hour, Crandall arrived at Melroy's office. He was a young man; he gave Melroy the impression of having recently seen military service; probably in the Indonesian campaign of '62 and '63; he also seemed a little cocky and oversure of himself.

"Mr. Melroy, we're not going to stand for this," he began, as soon as he came into the room. "You're using these so-called tests as a pretext for getting rid of Mr. Koffler and Mr. Burris because of their legitimate union activities."

"Who gave you that idea?" Melroy wanted to know. "Koffler and Burris?"

"That's the complaint they made to me, and it's borne out by the facts," Crandall replied. "We have on record at least half a dozen complaints that Mr. Koffler has made to us about different unfair work-assignments, improper working conditions, inequities in allotting overtime work, and other infractions of union-shop conditions, on behalf of Mr. Burris. Do you decided to get rid of both of them, and you think you can use this clause in our contract with your company about persons of deficient intelligence. The fact is, you're known to have threatened on several occasions to get rid of both of them."

"I am?" Melroy looked at Crandall curiously, wondering if the latter were serious, and deciding that he was. "You must believe *anything* those people tell you. Well, they lied to you if they told you that."

"Naturally that's what you'd say," Crandall replied. "But how do you account for the fact that those two men, and only those two men, were dismissed for alleged deficient intelligence?"

"The tests aren't all made," Melroy replied. "Until they are, you can't say that they are the only ones disqualified. And if you look over the records of the tests, you'll see where Koffler and Burris failed and the others passed. Here." He laid the pile of written-test forms and the summary and evaluation sheets on the desk. "Here's Koffler's, and here's Burris'; these are the ones of the men who passed the test. Look them over if you want to."

Crandall examined the forms and summaries for the two

men who had been discharged, and compared them with several random samples from the satisfactory pile.

"Why, this stuff's a lot of gibberish!" he exclaimed indignantly. "This thing, here: '. . . five Limerick oysters, six pairs of Don Alfonso tweezers, seven hundred Macedonian warriors in full battle array, eight golden crowns from the ancient, secret crypts of Egypt, nine lymphatic, sympathetic, peripatetic old men on crutches, and ten revolving heliotropes from the Ipsy-Wipsy Institute!' Great Lord, do you actually mean that you're using this stuff as an excuse for depriving men of their jobs?"

"I warned you that you should have brought a professional psychologist along," Melroy reminded him. "And maybe you ought to get Koffler and Burris to repeat their complaints on a lie-detector, while you're at it. They took the same tests, in the same manner, as any of the others. They just didn't have the mental equipment to cope with them and the others did. And for that reason, I won't run the risk of having them working on this job."

"That's just your word against theirs," Crandall insisted obstinately. "Their complaint is that you framed this whole thing up to get rid of them."

"Why, I didn't even know who either of them were, until yesterday morning."

"That's not the way they tell it," Crandall retorted. "They say you and Keating have been out to get them ever since they were hired. You and your supervisors have been persecuting both of those men systematically. The fact that Burris has had grounds for all these previous complaints proves that."

"It proves that Burris has a persecution complex, and that Koffler's credulous enough to believe him," Melroy replied. "And that tends to confirm the results of the tests they failed to pass."

"Oh, so that's the line you're taking. You persecute a man, and then say he has a persecution complex if he recognizes the fact. Well, you're not going to get away with it, that's all I have to say to you." Crandall flung the test-sheet he had been holding on to the desk. "That stuff's not worth the paper it's scribbled on!'' He turned on his heel in an automatically correct about-face and strode out of the office.

Melroy straightened out the papers and put them away, then sat down at the desk, filling and lighting his pipe. He was still working at 1215 when Ben Puryear called him.

"They walked out on us,'' he reported. "Harry Crandall was out here talking to them, and at noon the whole gang handed in their wrist-Geigers and dosimeters and cleared out their lockers. They say they aren't coming back till Burris and Koffler come back to work with them.''

"Then they aren't coming back, period,'' Melroy replied. "Crandall was here to see me, a couple of hours ago. He tells me that Burris and Koffler told him that we've been persecuting Burris; discriminating against him. You know of anything that really happened that might make them think anything like that?''

"No. Burris is always yelling about not getting enough overtime work, but you know how it is: he's just a roustabout, a common laborer. Any overtime work that has to be done is usually skilled labor on this job. We generally have a few roustabouts to help out, but he's been allowed to make overtime as much as any of the others.''

"Will the time-records show that?''

"They ought to. I don't know what he and Koffler told Crandall, but whatever it was, I'll bet they were lying.''

"That's all right, then. How's the reactor, now?''

"Hausinger says the count's down to safe limits, and the temperature's down to inactive-normal. He and his gang found a big chunk of plutonium, about one-quarter CM, inside. He got it out.''

"All right. Tell Dr. Rives to gather up all her completed or partially completed test records and come out to the office. You and the others stay on the job; we may have some men for you by this afternoon; tomorrow morning certainly.''

He hung up, then picked up the communicator phone and called his secretary.

"Joan, is Sid Keating out there? Send him in, will you?''

Keating, when he entered, was wearing the lugubriously

gratified expression appropriate to the successful prophet of disaster.

"All right, Cassandra," Melroy greeted him. "I'm not going to say you didn't warn me. Look. This strike is illegal. It's a violation of the Federal Labor Act of 1958, being called without due notice of intention, without preliminary negotiation, and without two weeks' time-allowance."

"They're going to claim that it isn't a strike. They're going to call it a 'spontaneous work-stoppage.'"

"Aah! I hope I can get Crandall on record to that effect; I'll fire every one of those men for leaving their work without permission and absence from duty without leave. How many of our own men, from Pittsburgh, do we have working in these machine shops and in the assembly shop here? About sixty?"

"Sixty-three. Why? You're not going to use them to work on the reactor, are you?"

"I just am. They're all qualified cybernetics technicians; they can do this work better than this gang we've had to hire here. Just to be on the safe side, I'm promoting all of them, as of oh-eight-hundred this morning, to assistant gang-foremen, on salaries. That'll take them outside union jurisdiction."

"But how about our contract with the I.F.A.W.?"

"That's been voided, by Crandall's own act, in interfering with the execution of our contract with the Atomic Power Authority. You know what I think? I think the I.F.A.W. front office is going to have to disavow this. It'll hurt them to do it, but they'll have to. Crandall's put them in the middle on this."

"How about security clearance for our own men?"

"Nothing to that," Melroy said. "Most of them are security-cleared, already, from the work we did installing that counter-rocket control system on the U.S.S. *Alaska*, and the work we did on that symbolic-logic computer for the Philadelphia Project. It may take all day to get the red tape unwound, but I think we can be ready to start by oh-eight-hundred tomorrow."

By the time Keating had rounded up all the regular Melroy

Engineering Corporation employees and Melroy had talked to Colonel Bradshaw about security-clearance, it was 1430. A little later, he was called on the phone by Leighton, the Atomic Power Authority man.

"Melroy, what are you trying to do?" the Power Authority man demanded. "Get this whole plant struck shut? The I.F.A.W.'s madder than a shot-stung bobcat. They claim you're going to bring in strike-breakers; they're talking about picketing the whole reactor area."

"News gets around fast, here, doesn't it?" Melroy commented. He told Leighton what he had in mind. The Power Authority man was considerably shaken before he had finished.

"But they'll call a strike on the whole plant! Have you any idea what that would mean?"

"Certainly I have. They'll either call it in legal form, in which case the whole thing will go to mediation and get aired, which is what I want, or they'll pull a Pearl Harbor on you, the way they did on me. And in that case, the President will have to intervene, and they'll fly in technicians from some of the Armed Forces plants to keep this place running. And in that case, things'll get settled that much quicker. This Crandall thinks these men I fired are martyrs, and he's preaching a crusade. He ought to carry an *advocatus diaboli* on his payroll, to scrutinize the qualifications of his martyrs, before he starts canonizing them."

A little later, Doris Rives came into the office, her hands full of papers and cards.

"I have twelve more tests completed," she reported. "Only one washout."

Melroy laughed. "Doctor, they're all washed out," he told her. "It seems there was an additional test, and they all flunked it. Evinced willingness to follow unwise leadership and allow themselves to be talked into improper courses of action. You go on in to New York, and take all the test-material, including sound records, with you. Stay at the hotel—your pay will go on—till I need you. There'll be a Federal mediation hearing in a day or so."

He had two more telephone calls. The first, at 1530, was

from Leighton. Melroy suspected that the latter had been medicating his morale with a couple of stiff drinks; his voice was almost jaunty.

"Well, the war's on," he announced. "The I.F.A.W.'s walking out on the whole plant, at oh-eight-hundred tomorrow."

"In violation of the Federal Labor Act, Section Eight, paragraphs four and five," Melroy supplemented. "Crandall really has stuck his neck in the guillotine. What's Washington doing?"

"President Hartley is ordering Navy personnel flown in from Kennebunkport Reaction Lab; they will be here by about oh-three-hundred tomorrow. And a couple of Federal mediators are coming in to La Guardia at seventeen hundred; they're going to hold preliminary hearings at the new Federal Building on Washington Square beginning twenty hundred. A couple of I.F.A.W. negotiators are coming in from the national union headquarters at Oak Ridge; they should be getting in about the same time. You'd better be on hand, and have Dr. Rives there with you. There's a good chance this thing may get cleared up in a day or so."

"I will undoubtedly be there, complete with Dr. Rives," Melroy replied. "It will be a pleasure!"

An hour later, Ben Puryear called from the reactor area, his voice strained with anger.

"Scott, do you know what those—" He gargled obscenities for a moment. "You know what they've done? They've re-packed the Number One Doernberg-Giardano; got a chain-reaction started again."

"Who?"

"Fred Hausinger's gang. Apparently at Harry Crandall's orders. The excuse was that it would be unsafe to leave the reactor in its dismantled condition during a prolonged shutdown—they were assuming, I suppose, that the strike would be allowed to proceed unopposed—but of course the real reason was that they wanted to get a chain-reaction started to keep our people from working on the reactor."

"Well, didn't Hausinger try to stop them?"

"Not very hard. I asked him what he had that deputy marshal's badge on for, but he said he had orders not to use force, for fear of prejudicing the mediators."

Melroy swore disgustedly. "All right. Gather up all our private papers, and get Steve and Joe, and come on out. We only work here—when we're able."

Doris Rives was waiting on the street level when Melroy reached the new Federal Building, in what had formerly been the Greenwich Village district of Manhattan, that evening. She had a heavy brief case with her, which he took.

"I was afraid I'd keep you waiting," she said. "I came down from the hotel by cab, and there was a frightful jam at Fortieth Street, and another one just below Madison Square."

"Yes, it gets worse every year. Pardon my obsession, but nine times out of ten—ninety-nine out of a hundred—it's the fault of some fool doing something stupid. Speaking about doing stupid things, though—I did one. Forgot to take that gun out of my overcoat pocket, and didn't notice that I had it till I was on the subway, coming in. Have a big flashlight in the other pocket, but that doesn't matter. What I'm worried about is that somebody'll find out I have a gun and raise a howl about my coming armed to a mediation hearing."

The hearing was to be held in one of the big conference rooms on the forty-second floor. Melroy was careful to remove his overcoat and lay it on a table in the corner, and then help Doris off with hers and lay it on top of his own. There were three men in the room when they arrived: Kenneth Leighton, the Atomic Power Authority man, fiftyish, acquiring a waistline bulge and losing his hair; a Mr. Lyons, tall and slender, with white hair; and a Mr. Quillen, considerably younger, with plastic-rimmed glasses. The latter two were the Federal mediators. All three had been lounging in armchairs, talking about the new plays on Broadway. They all rose when Melroy and Doris Rives came over to join them.

"We mustn't discuss business until the others get here,"

Leighton warned. "It's bad enough that all three of us got here ahead of them; they'll be sure to think we're trying to take an unfair advantage of them. I suppose neither of you have had time to see any of the new plays."

Fortunately, Doris and Melroy had gone to the theater after dinner, the evening-before-last; they were able to join the conversation. Young Mr. Quillen wanted Doris Rives' opinion, as a psychologist, of the mental processes of the heroine of the play they had seen; as nearly as she could determine, Doris replied, the heroine in question had exhibited nothing even loosely describable as mental processes of any sort. They were still on the subject when the two labor negotiators, Mr. Cronnin and Mr. Fields, arrived. Cronnin was in his sixties, with the nearsighted squint and compressed look of concentration of an old-time precision machinist; Fields was much younger, and sported a Phi Beta Kappa key.

Lyons, who seemed to be the senior mediator, thereupon called the meeting to order and they took their places at the table.

"Now, gentlemen—and Dr. Rives—this will be simply an informal discussion, so that everybody can see what everybody else's position in the matter is. We won't bother to make a sound recording. Then, if we have managed to reach some common understanding of the question this evening, we can start the regular hearing say at thirteen hundred tomorrow. Is that agreeable?"

It was. The younger mediator, Quillen, cleared his throat.

"It seems, from our information, that this entire dispute arises from the discharge, by Mr. Melroy, of two of his employees, named Koffler and Burris. Is that correct?"

"Well, there's also the question of the Melroy Engineering Corporation's attempting to use strikebreakers, and the Long Island Atomic Power Authority's having condoned this unfair employment practice," Cronnin said, acidly.

"And there's also the question of the I.F.A.W.'s calling a Pearl Harbor strike on my company," Melroy added.

"We resent that characterization!" Cronnin retorted.

"It's a term in common usage; it denotes a strike called without warning or declaration of intention, which this was," Melroy told him.

"And there's also the question of the I.F.A.W. calling a general strike, in illegal manner, at the Long Island Reaction Plant," Leighton spoke up. "On sixteen hours' notice."

"Well, that wasn't the fault of the I.F.A.W. as an organization," Fields argued. "Mr. Cronnin and I are agreed that the walk-out date should be postponed for two weeks, in accordance with the provisions of the Federal Labor Act."

"Well, how about my company?" Melroy wanted to know. "Your I.F.A.W. members walked out on me, without any notice whatever, at twelve hundred today. Am I to consider that an act of your union, or will you disavow it so that I can fire all of them for quitting without permission?"

"And how about the action of members of your union, acting on instructions from Harry Crandall, in re-packing the Number One Doernberg-Giardano breeder-reactor at our plant, after the plutonium and the U-238 and the neutron-source containers had been removed, in order to re-initiate a chain reaction to prevent Mr. Melroy's employees from working on the reactor?" Leighton demanded. "Am I to understand that the union sustains that action, too?"

"I hadn't known about that," Fields said, somewhat startled.

"Neither had I," Cronnin added. "When did it happen?"

"About sixteen hundred today," Melroy told him.

"We were on the plane from Oak Ridge, then," Fields declared. "We know nothing about that."

"Well, are you going to take the responsibility for it, or aren't you?" Leighton insisted.

Lyons, who had been toying with a small metal paperweight, rapped on the table with it.

"Gentlemen," he interrupted. "We're trying to cover too many subjects at once. I suggest that we confine ourselves, at the beginning, to the question of the dismissal of these men, Burris and Koffler. If we find that the I.F.A.W. has a legitimate grievance in what we may call the Burris-Koffler question, we can settle that and then go on to these other questions.''

''I'm agreeable to that,'' Melroy said.

''So are we,'' Cronnin nodded.

''All right, then. Since the I.F.A.W. is the complaining party in this question, perhaps you gentlemen should state the grounds for your complaints.''

Fields and Cronnin exchanged glances; Cronnin nodded to Fields and the latter rose. The two employees in question, he stated, had been the victims of discrimination and persecution because of union activities. Koffler was the union shop-steward for the men employed by the Melroy Engineering Corporation, and Burris had been active in bringing complaints about unfair employment practices. Furthermore, it was the opinion of the I.F.A.W. that the psychological tests imposed on their members had been a fraudulent pretext for dismissing these two men, and, in any case, the practice of compelling workers to submit to such tests was insulting, degrading, and not a customary condition of employment.

With that, he sat down. Melroy was on his feet at once.

''I'll deny those statements, categorically and seriatim,'' he replied. ''They are based entirely upon misrepresentations made by the two men who were disqualified by the tests and dropped from my payroll because of being, in the words of my contract with your union, 'persons of unsound mind, deficient intelligence and/or emotional instability.' What happened is that your local official, Crandall, accepted everything they told him uncritically, and you accepted everything Crandall told you, in the same spirit.

''Before I go on,'' Melroy continued, turning to Lyons, ''have I your permission to let Dr. Rives explain about these tests, herself, and tell how they were given and evaluated?''

Permission granted by Lyons, Doris Rives rose. At some length, she explained the nature and purpose of the tests, and her method of scoring and correlating them.

''Well, did Mr. Melroy suggest to you that any specific employer or employees of his were undesirable and ought to be eliminated?'' Fields asked.

"Certainly not!'' Doris Rives became angry. "And if he had, I'd have taken the first plane out of here. That suggestion is insulting! And for your information, I never met Mr. Melroy before day-before-yesterday afternoon; I am not dependent upon him for anything; I took this job as an accommodation to Dr. Karl von Heydenreich, who ordinarily does such work for the Melroy company, and I'm losing money by remaining here. Does that satisfy you?''

"Yes, it does,'' Fields admitted. He was obviously impressed by mention of the distinguished Austrian psychologist's name. "If I may ask Mr. Melroy a question: I gather that these tests were given to all your employees. Why do you demand such an extraordinary level of intelligence from your employees, even common laborers?''

"Extraordinary?'' Melroy echoed. "If the standards established by those tests are extraordinary, then God help this country; we are becoming a race of morons! I'll leave that statement to Dr. Rives for confirmation; she's already pointed out that all that is required to pass those tests is ordinary adult mental capacity.

"My company specializes in cybernetic-control systems,'' he continued. "In spite of a lot of misleading colloquial jargon about 'thinking machines' and 'giant brains,' a cybernetic system doesn't really think. It only does what it's been designed *and built* to do, and if somebody builds a mistake into it, it will automatically and infallibly repeat that mistake in practice.''

"He's right,'' Cronnin said. "The men that build a machine like that have got to be as smart as the machine's supposed to be, or the machine'll be as dumb as they are.''

Fields turned on him angrily. "Which side are you supposed to be on, anyhow?'' he demanded.

"You're probably a lawyer,'' Melroy said. "But I'll bet Mr. Cronnin's an old reaction-plant man.'' Cronnin nodded unthinkingly in confirmation. "All right, then. Ask him what those Doernberg-Giardanos are like. And then let me ask you: Suppose some moron fixed up something that would go wrong, or made the wrong kind of a mistake himself, around one of those reactors?''

It was purely a rhetorical question, but, much later, when he would have time to think about it, Scott Melroy was to wonder if ever in history such a question had been answered so promptly and with such dramatic calamitousness.

Three seconds after he stopped speaking, the lights went out.

For a moment, they were silent and motionless. Then somebody across the table from Melroy began to say, ''What the devil—?'' Doris Rives, beside him, clutched his arm. At the head of the table, Lyons was fuming impatiently, and Kenneth Leighton snapped a pocket-lighter and held it up.

The Venetian-screened windows across the room faced east. In the flicker of the lighter, Melroy made his way around to them and drew open the slats of one, looking out. Except for the headlights of cars, far down in the street, and the lights of ships in the harbor, the city was completely blacked out. But there was one other, horrible, light far away at the distant tip of Long Island—a huge ball of flame, floating upward at the tip of a column of fiery gas. As he watched, there were twinkles of unbearable brightness at the base of the pillar of fire, spreading into awesome sheet-flashes, and other fireballs soared up. Then the sound and the shock-wave of the first blast reached them.

'''The main power-reactors, too,'' Melroy said to himself, not realizing that he spoke audibly. ''Too well shielded for the blast to get them, but the heat melted the fissionables down to critical mass.''

Leighton, the lighter still burning, was beside him, now.

''That's not— God, it can't be anything else! Why, the whole plant's gone! There aren't enough other generators in this area to handle a hundredth of the demand.''

''And don't blame that on my alleged strike-breakers,'' Melroy warned. ''They hadn't got security-cleared to enter the reactor area when this happened.''

''What do you think happened?'' Cronnin asked. ''One of

the Doernberg-Giardanos let go?''

"Yes. Your man Crandall. If he survived that, it's his bad luck," Melroy said grimly. "Last night, while Fred Hausinger was pulling the fissionables and radioactives out of the Number One breeder, he found a big nugget of Pu-239, about one-quarter CM. I don't know what was done with it, but I do know that Crandall had the maintenance gang repack that reactor, to keep my people from working on it. Nobody'll ever find out just what happened, but they were in a hurry; they probably shoved things in any old way. Somehow, that big subcritical nugget must have got back in, and the breeding-cans, which were pretty ripe by that time, must have been shoved in too close to it and to one another. You know how fast those D-G's work. It just took this long to build up CM for a bomb-type reaction. You remember what I was saying before the lights went out? Well, it happened. Some moron—some untested and undetected moron—made the wrong kind of a mistake.''

"Too bad about Crandall. He was a good kid, only he didn't stop to think often enough," Cronnin said. "Well, I guess the strike's off, now; that's one thing.''

"But all those people, out there!" Womanlike, Doris Rives was thinking particularly rather than generally and of humans rather than abstractions. "It must have killed everybody for miles around.''

Sid Keating, Melroy thought. And Joe Ricci, and Ben Puryear, and Steve Chalmers, and all the workmen whom he had brought here from Pittsburgh, to their death. Then he stopped thinking about them. It didn't do any good to think of men who'd been killed; he'd learned that years ago, as a kid second lieutenant in Korea. The people to think about were the millions in Greater New York, and up the Hudson Valley to Albany, and as far south as Trenton, caught without light in the darkness, without heat in the dead of winter, without power in subways and skyscrapers and on railroads and interurban lines.

He turned to the woman beside him.

"Doris, before you could get your Board of Psychiatry and

Neurology diploma, you had to qualify as a regular M.D., didn't you?'' he asked.

''Why, yes—''

''Then you'd better report to the nearest hospital. Any doctor at all is going to be desperately needed, for the next day or so. Me, I still have a reserve major's commission in the Army Corps of Engineers. They're probably calling up reserve officers, with any radios that are still working. Until I hear differently, I'm ordering myself on active duty as of now.'' He looked around. ''Anybody know where the nearest Army headquarters is?''

''There's a recruiting station down on the thirty-something floor,'' Quillen said. ''It's probably closed, now, though.''

''Ground Defense Command; Midtown City,'' Leighton said. ''They have a medical section of their own; they'll be glad to get Dr. Rives, too.''

Melroy helped her on with her coat and handed her her handbag, then shrugged into his own overcoat and belted it about him, the weight of the flashlight and the automatic sagging the pockets. He'd need both, the gun as much as the light—New York had more than its share of vicious criminals, to whom this power-failure would be a perfect devilsend. Handing Doris the light, he let her take his left arm. Together, they left the room and went down the hallway to the stairs and the long walk to the darkened street below, into a city that had suddenly been cut off from its very life-energy. A city that had put all its eggs in one basket, and left the basket in the path of any blundering foot.

BEST-SELLING
Science Fiction
and
Fantasy